Reviewers

The DEAD *in* THEIR VAULTED ARCHES

#1 *Library Journal* pick
#6 *New York Times* bestseller
#3 Indie bestseller
#3 NPR bestseller
#10 *Publishers Weekly* bestseller

"Bradley's award-winning Flavia de Luce series . . . has enchanted readers with the **outrageous** sleuthing career of its precocious leading lady. . . . This latest adventure contains all the winning elements of the previous books while skillfully establishing a new and intriguing story line to explore in future novels. . . . Fans will be more than pleased."

—*Library Journal* (starred review)

"Bradley's latest Flavia de Luce novel reaches a new level of perfection. . . . These are **astounding, magical** books not to be missed."

—*RT Book Reviews* (Top Pick)

"It's **hard to resist** either the genre's pre-eminent preteen sleuth or the hushed revelations about her family."

—*Kirkus Reviews*

"Excellent . . . Flavia retains her droll wit. . . . The solution to the murder is typically neat, and the conclusion sets up future books nicely."

—*Publishers Weekly* (starred review)

"There is period detail, as well as deft portraiture of the entire de Luce family and friends, in this character-driven series. . . . *The Dead in Their Vaulted Arches* moves the series in an **exciting** new direction. Flavia will surely remain as brilliant and stubbornly contrary as ever."

—*Library Journal*

"Young chemist and aspiring detective Flavia de Luce [uses] her knowledge of poisons, and her indefatigable spirit, to solve a dastardly crime in the English countryside while learning new clues about her mother's disappearance."

—National Public Radio

SPEAKING FROM AMONG *the* BONES

"The precocious and irrepressible Flavia **continues to delight**. Portraying an eleven-year-old as a plausible sleuth and expert in poisons is no mean feat, but Bradley makes it look easy."

—*Publishers Weekly* (starred review)

"Bradley's Flavia cozies, set in the English countryside, have been **a hit** from the start, and this fifth in the series continues to charm and entertain."

—*Booklist*

"An excellent reminder that crime fiction can **sparkle with wit, crackle with spirit and verge on the surreal** . . . Flavia, once more, entertains and delights as she exposes the inner workings of her investigative mind to the reader."

—*National Post* (Canada)

I AM HALF-SICK *of* SHADOWS

"**Every Flavia de Luce novel is a reason to celebrate,** but Christmas with Flavia is a holiday wish come true for her fans."

—*USA Today* (four stars)

"This is a classic country house mystery in the tradition of Agatha Christie, and Poirot himself would approve of Flavia's skills in snooping and deduction. Flavia is everything a reader wants in a detective—she's smart, logical, intrepid and curious. . . . This is a **refreshingly engaging** read."

—*RT Book Reviews*

"This is **a delightful read through and through**. We find in Flavia an incorrigible and wholly lovable detective; from her chemical experiments in her sanctum sanctorum to her outrage at the idiocy of the adult world, she is unequaled. Charming as a stand-alone novel and a guaranteed smash with series followers."

—*Library Journal* (starred review)

"Bradley masterfully weaves a ghoulish Yuletide tale. . . . The story breathes characters full of charisma, colour and nuance. . . . Bradley gives **a thrilling ride.**"

—*The Globe and Mail*

A **RED HERRING** *Without* **MUSTARD**

"Bradley's third book about tween sleuth Flavia de Luce will make readers forget Nancy Drew."

—*People*

"Outstanding . . . In this **marvelous blend of whimsy and mystery,** Flavia manages to operate successfully in the adult world of crimes and passions while dodging the childhood pitfalls set by her sisters."

—*Publishers Weekly* (starred review)

"Oh, to be eleven again and pal around with irresistible wunderkind Flavia de Luce. . . . A splendid romp through 1950s England led by the world's smartest and most incorrigible preteen."

—*Kirkus Reviews* (starred review)

"Think preteen Nancy Drew, only savvier and a lot richer, and you have Flavia de Luce. . . . Don't be fooled by Flavia's age or the 1950s setting: *A Red Herring* isn't a dainty tea-and-crumpets sort of mystery. It's shot through with real grit."

—*Entertainment Weekly*

"Whether battling with her odious sisters or verbally sparring with the long-suffering Inspector Hewitt, our cheeky heroine is **a delight**. Full of pithy dialog and colorful characters, this series would appeal strongly to fans of Dorothy Sayers, Gladys Mitchell, and Leo Bruce as well as readers who like clever humor mixed in with their mysteries."

—*Library Journal* (starred review)

"[Flavia] remains irresistibly **appealing** as a little girl lost."

—*The New York Times Book Review*

"**Delightful** . . . The book's forthright and eerily mature narrator is a treasure."

—*The Seattle Times*

"Bradley's characters, wonderful dialogue and plot twists are a most winning combination."

—*USA Today*

The WEED *That* STRINGS *the* HANGMAN'S BAG

"Flavia is incisive, cutting and hilarious . . . **one of the most remarkable creations in recent literature.**"

—*USA Today*

"Bradley takes everything you expect and subverts it, delivering **a smart, irreverent, unsappy mystery.**"

—*Entertainment Weekly*

"The real delight here is her droll voice and the eccentric cast. . . . **Utterly beguiling.**"

—*People* (four stars)

"**Endlessly entertaining** . . . The author deftly evokes the period, but Flavia's sparkling narration is the mystery's chief delight. Comic and irreverent, this entry is sure to build further momentum for the series."

—*Publishers Weekly* (starred review)

The SWEETNESS *at the* BOTTOM *of the* PIE

THE MOST AWARD-WINNING BOOK OF ANY YEAR!

WINNER:
Macavity Award for Best First Mystery Novel
Barry Award for Best First Novel
Agatha Award for Best First Novel
Dilys Award
Arthur Ellis Award for Best Novel
Spotted Owl Award for Best Novel
CWA Debut Dagger Award

"**Impressive** as a sleuth and enchanting as a mad scientist . . . Flavia is most endearing as a little girl who has learned how to amuse herself in a big lonely house."

—Marilyn Stasio, *The New York Times Book Review*

"Sophisticated, series-launching . . . It's **a rare pleasure** to follow Flavia as she investigates her limited but boundless-feeling world."

—*Entertainment Weekly* (A–)

"**A delightful new sleuth.** A combination of Eloise and Sherlock Holmes . . . fearless, cheeky, wildly precocious."

—*The Boston Globe*

BY ALAN BRADLEY

The Sweetness at the Bottom of the Pie

The Weed That Strings the Hangman's Bag

A Red Herring Without Mustard

I Am Half-Sick of Shadows

Speaking from Among the Bones

The Dead in Their Vaulted Arches

The DEAD *in* THEIR VAULTED ARCHES

...

The DEAD *in* THEIR VAULTED ARCHES

A Flavia de Luce Novel

ALAN BRADLEY

BANTAM BOOKS
NEW YORK

The Dead in Their Vaulted Arches is a work of fiction. Names, characters, places, and incidents either are the product of the author's imagination or are used fictitiously. Any resemblance to actual persons, living or dead, events, or locales is entirely coincidental.

A Bantam Books International Edition

Published by Bantam Books, an imprint of Random House, a division of Random House LLC, a Penguin Random House Company, New York.

BANTAM BOOKS and the HOUSE colophon are registered trademarks of Random House LLC.

A hardcover edition has been published in the United States by Bantam Books, an imprint of Random House, a division of Random House LLC.

This book contains an excerpt from the forthcoming book *As Chimney Sweepers Come to Dust* by Alan Bradley. This excerpt has been set for this edition only and may not reflect the final content of the forthcoming edition.

ISBN 978-0-553-84128-2
eBook ISBN 978-0-345-53969-4

Cover design: Joe Montgomery
Cover images: Suksakon Soponpatumruk / Depositphotos (keyhole and ladder); Sirylok / Yay Images (tree branches)

Printed in the United States of America

www.bantamdell.com

9 8 7 6 5 4 3 2 1

Beloved Amadeus

The Marble Tombs that rise on high,
Whose Dead in vaulted Arches lye,
Whose Pillars swell with sculptur'd Stones,
Arms, Angels, Epitaphs and Bones,
These (all the poor Remains of State)
Adorn the Rich, or praise the Great;
Who while on Earth in Fame they live,
Are senseless of the Fame they give.

Thomas Parnell,
A *Night-Piece on Death* (1721)

The DEAD *in* THEIR VAULTED ARCHES

•••

PROLOGUE

"Your mother has been found."

Nearly a week after he had made it, Father's shocking announcement was still ringing in my ears.

Harriet! Harriet found! Who could believe it?

Harriet, who had been lost in a mountaineering accident when I was barely a year old; Harriet, whom I can't remember seeing, ever, with my own eyes.

My reaction?

Numbness, I'm afraid.

Sheer stupid silent numbness.

Not joy—not relief—not even gratitude to those who had found her more than ten years after her disappearance in the Himalayas.

No, I felt only a cold numbness: a cold, shameful sort of numbness that made me need desperately to be alone.

·ONE·

To BEGIN WITH, IT was a perfect English morning: one of those dazzling days in early April when a new sun makes it seem suddenly like full-blown summer.

Sunshine broke through the fat white dumplings of the clouds, sending shadows chasing one another playfully across the green fields and up into the gently rolling hills. Somewhere in the woods on the other side of the railway line, a nightingale was singing.

"It's like a colored plate from Wordsworth," my sister Daphne said, almost to herself. "Far too picturesque."

Ophelia, my oldest sister, was a still, pale, silent shadow, lost in her own thoughts.

At the appointed time, which happened to be ten o'clock, we were all of us gathered more or less together on the little railway platform at Buckshaw Halt. I think it was the first time in my life I had ever seen Daffy without a book in her hand.

Father, who stood a bit apart from us, kept glancing every few minutes at his wristwatch and looking along the track, eyes squinting, watching for smoke in the distance.

Directly behind him stood Dogger. How odd it was to see these two men—gentleman and servant—who had been through such ghastly times together, standing dressed in their Sunday best at an abandoned country railway station.

Although Buckshaw Halt had once been used to bring both goods and guests to the great house, and although the rails remained, the station proper, with its weathered bricks, had been boarded up for donkey's years.

In the past few days, though, it had been hurriedly made ready for Harriet's homecoming: swept out and tidied up, its broken windowpanes replaced, the tiny flower bed weeded and planted with a small riot of flowers.

Father had been asked to go up to London and ride with her back to Buckshaw, but he had insisted on being at the little station at Buckshaw Halt to meet the train. It was, after all, he had explained to the vicar, the place and manner in which he had first met her all those many years ago when both of them were young.

As we waited, I noticed that Father's boots had been polished to a high-gloss perfection, from which I deduced that Dogger was currently in a much improved state. There were times when Dogger screamed and whimpered in the night, huddled in the corner of his tiny bedroom, visited by the ghosts of far-off prisons, tormented by the devils of the past. At all other times he was as competent as any human is capable of being, and I sent up thanks that this morning was one of them.

Never had we needed him more.

Here and there on the platform, small, tight knots of villagers, keeping a respectful distance, talked quietly to one another, preserving our privacy. More than a few of them stood huddled closely round Mrs. Mullet, our cook, and her husband, Alf, as if doing so made them, by some magic, part of the immediate household.

As ten o'clock approached, everyone, as if at an arranged signal, fell suddenly quiet, and an unearthly hush settled upon the countryside. It was as though a bell jar had been lowered upon the land and all the world was holding its breath. Even the nightingale in the woods had abruptly ceased its song.

The very air on the station platform was now electric, as it often becomes when a train is approaching but not yet in sight.

People shifted uneasily from foot to foot, and the faint wind of our collective breathing made a soft sigh on the gentle English air.

And then, finally, after what seemed like an eternal stillness, we saw in the distance the smoke from the engine.

Nearer and nearer it came, bringing Harriet—bringing my mother—home.

The breath seemed sucked from my lungs as the gleaming engine panted into the station and squealed to a stop at the edge of the platform.

It was not a long train: not more than an engine and half a dozen carriages, and it sat resting for a few moments in the importance of its own swirling steam. There was an odd little lull.

Then a guard stepped down from the rear carriage and blew three sharp blasts on a whistle.

Doors opened, and the platform was suddenly swarming with men in uniform: military men with a dazzling array of full medals and clipped mustaches.

They formed up quickly into two columns and stood stiffly at attention.

A tall, tanned man I took to be their leader, his chest a wall of decorations and colored ribbons, marched smartly to where Father stood and brought his arm up in a sharp salute that left his hand vibrating like a tuning fork.

Although he seemed in a daze, Father managed a nod.

From the remaining carriages poured a horde of men in black suits and bowler hats carrying walking sticks and furled umbrellas. Among them were a handful of women in severe suits, hats, and gloves; a few, even, were in uniform. One of these, a fit but forbidding woman in RAF colors, looked such a Tartar and had so many stripes on her sleeve that she might have been an Air Vice-Marshal. This little station at Buckshaw Halt, I thought, in all of its long history, had never before been so packed with such an assortment of humanity.

To my surprise, one of the suited women turned out to be Father's sister, Aunt Felicity. She hugged Feely, hugged Daffy, hugged me, and then without a word took up her station beside Father.

At an order, the two columns marched smartly towards the head of the train, as the large door in the luggage van slid open.

It was difficult, in the bright daylight, to make out anything in the dim depths of the van's interior. All I could see at first was what seemed to be a dozen white gloves dancing suspended in the darkness.

And then gently, almost tenderly, a wooden box was handed out to the double column of waiting men, who shouldered it and stood motionless for a moment, like wooden soldiers staring straight ahead into the sunshine.

I couldn't take my eyes off the thing.

It was a coffin which, once clear of the shadows of the luggage van, gleamed cruelly in the harsh sunlight.

In it was Harriet. *Harriet.*

My mother.

·TWO·

WHAT DID I THINK? How did I feel?

I wish I knew.

Sadness, perhaps, that our hopes were dashed forever? Relief that Harriet had come home at last?

It should have been dull black, her coffin. It should have had frosty silver fittings, with covered urns and cherubs with downcast eyes.

But it did not. It was of rich oak, polished to such an obscene brilliance that it hurt my eyes. I found that I could not look at the thing.

Oddly enough, the scene which popped into my mind was that one at the end of Mrs. Nesbit's novel *The Railway Children*, in which Bobbie, on the station platform, flings herself into the arms of her wrongfully imprisoned daddy.

But there was to be no such tender ending for me, or, for that matter, for Father or Feely or Daffy, either. No, there was to be no such happy conclusion.

I glanced quickly at Father, as if he might give me a clue, but he, too, stood frozen in his own private glacier, beyond all grief and beyond all expression, as the coffin was draped with a Union Jack.

Alf Mullet snapped a sharp salute and held it for a very long time.

Daffy gave my ribs a dig with her elbow and pointed with the faintest inclination of her chin.

At the south end of the platform, a rather stout old gentleman in a dark suit was standing apart from the others. I recognized him instantly.

As the bearers moved slowly away from the train, bent under their sad burden, he removed his black hat in respect and lowered it to his side.

It was Winston Churchill.

Whatever could have brought the former Prime Minister to Bishop's Lacey?

He stood there alone, watching in the deadly hush as my mother was carried to the open doors of a motor hearse, which had appeared in uncanny silence as if from nowhere.

Churchill watched as the coffin, preceded by an officer with a drawn sword, was borne gently past Father, past Feely, past Daffy, and past me, then placed himself shoulder to shoulder with Father.

"She was England, damn it," he growled.

As if awakening from a dream, Father's eyes lifted, came to rest, and focused on Churchill's face.

After a very long time, he said, "She was more than that, Prime Minister."

Churchill nodded and seized Father's elbow. "We can ill afford to lose a de Luce, Haviland," he said quietly.

What did he mean by that?

For a moment, they stood there together in the old sunshine, these two seemingly defeated men, brothers in something far beyond me: something I could not even begin to imagine.

Then, having shaken hands with Father, with Feely, with Daffy, and even with Aunt Felicity, Mr. Churchill came over to where I was standing, a little apart from the others.

"And have you, also, acquired a taste for pheasant sandwiches, young lady?"

Those words! Those exact words!

I had heard them before! No—not *heard* them—*seen* them!

The roots of my hair were suddenly standing on tiptoe.

Churchill's blue eyes were piercing, as if he were staring into my soul.

What did he mean? What on earth was he suggesting? What was he expecting me to say?

I'm afraid I blushed. It was all I could manage.

Mr. Churchill stared intently into my face, taking my hand and giving it a gentle squeeze with his remarkably long fingers.

"Yes," he said at last, almost as if to himself, "yes, I do believe you have."

And with that, he turned and walked away from me along the platform, acknowledging, with solemn nods to the left and to the right, the recognition of the villagers as he slowly made his way through them to his waiting car.

Although he had been out of office for ages, there was still a remarkable air of greatness about this plump little man with his bulldog face and the startling stare of his great blue eyes.

Daffy was already whispering in my ear. "What did he say?" she asked.

"He said that he was sorry," I lied. I didn't know why, but I knew that it was the thing to do. "Just that he was sorry."

Daffy gave me that squinty evil look of hers.

How could it be, I wondered, that with our mother lying dead under our very noses, two sisters could be almost at each other's throats over a simple fib? It seemed ridiculous, but it was happening. I can only suppose that that's the way life is.

And death.

What I *did* know for certain was that I needed to get home, that I needed to be locked in the silence of my own room.

Father was busy shaking hands with all the people who wanted to give him their condolences. The very air was alive with the reptilian hissing of their *S*s and the little animal squeals of their *Y*s.

"Sorry, Colonel de Luce . . . sorry . . . sorry," they were telling him, over and over again, each in his or her own turn. It's a wonder Father didn't go mad on the spot.

Could no one think of anything original to say?

Daffy once told me that there are approximately half a million words in the English language. With so many to choose from, you'd think that just one person, at least, could find something more original than that stupid word "sorry."

That's what I was thinking when a tall man in a coat too

long and much too heavy for such a lovely day detached himself from the crowd on the platform and made directly for me.

"Miss de Luce?" he asked, in a surprisingly gentle voice.

I was not accustomed to being addressed as "Miss de Luce." It was a name usually reserved for Daffy or Feely—or for Aunt Felicity.

"I am Flavia de Luce," I said. "And you are?"

It was a response Dogger had taught me to give automatically when spoken to by strangers. I glanced over and saw Dogger hovering solicitously at Father's side.

"A friend," the man said. "Just a friend—of the family. I need to talk to you."

"I'm sorry," I said, taking a step backwards. "I'm—"

"Please. It's *vitally* important."

Vitally? Anyone who used the word "vitally" in everyday conversation could hardly be a villain.

"Well . . ." I said, wavering.

"Tell your father that the Gamekeeper is in jeopardy. He'll understand. I must speak to him. Tell him that the Nide is under—"

The man's eyes widened suddenly in puzzlement—or was it horror?—as he looked over my shoulder. What—or whom—had he seen?

"Come along, Flavia. You're keeping everyone waiting."

It was Feely. My sister gave the stranger a tight, polite smile as she put a hand on my shoulder and gave it an unnecessarily hard tug.

"Wait," I said, ducking to one side and breaking away from her grip. "I'll be there in a minute."

Dogger was already holding open the door of Harriet's

old Rolls-Royce Phantom II, which he had parked as close to the platform as he possibly could. Father was halfway to the car, shuffling alarmingly, his head bowed.

It was not until that moment, I think, that I realized what a crushing blow this whole business must be to him.

He had lost Harriet, not once, but twice.

"Flavia!"

It was Feely again, her eyes bugging with cold blue impatience. "Why," she hissed, "must you always insist on being such a—"

A shriek from the engine's whistle blotted out her last few words, but I was easily able to lip-read their shocking shape.

The train began to move, slowly at first. We had been told during our briefing by the undertakers that, as we departed the station, the train would be taken to a disused railway yard somewhere north of East Finching to be turned round for its return run up to London. It was a breach of undertaking etiquette, as well as being "uncommon bad luck," according to Mr. Sowerby, of Sowerby & Sons, to run a funeral train backwards.

By now, Feely was dragging me—literally—towards the waiting Rolls.

I tried to break free, but it was no use. Her fingers dug deeply into the muscle of my upper arm, and I was dragged stumbling along, gasping in her wake.

A sudden shout broke from among the stragglers at the station. I thought at first it was Feely's cruel treatment of me that had caused the outcry, but I saw now that people were running towards the edge of the platform.

The guard's whistle was blowing frantically, someone was

screaming, and the engine banged to an abrupt halt with clouds of steam billowing out from beneath its driving wheels. I struggled free of Feely's grasp and elbowed my way back along the carriages, squeezing past the possible Air Vice-Marshal, who seemed rooted to the spot.

The villagers stood transfixed, many hands clapped to many mouths.

"Someone pushed him," said a woman's voice from somewhere behind me in the crowd.

At my feet, as if reaching for my shoes, a human hand stuck stiffly out, with awful stillness, from beneath the wheels of the last carriage. I knelt down for a closer look. The newly filthy fingers were wide open, reaching for help that would never arrive. On the wrist, which was almost indecently naked, tiny golden hairs stirred gently in the moving air beneath the train.

My nostrils filled with the smell of hot, oily steam, and with something else: a sharp coppery odor which, once experienced, is never forgotten. I recognized it at once.

It was the smell of blood.

Shoved up nearly to the dead elbow was the still-buttoned cuff of a coat too long and much too heavy for such a lovely day.

·THREE·

THE ROLLS CREPT ALONG the lane at a snail's pace behind the hearse.

Even though Buckshaw Halt was little more than a mile from the house, I knew already that this sad journey was going to take simply ages.

The analytical part of my brain wanted to make sense of what I had just witnessed on the railway platform: the violent death of a stranger beneath the wheels of the train.

But a wilder, more primitive, more reptilian force would not allow it, throwing up excuses that seemed reasonable enough at the time.

These precious hours belong to Harriet, it was telling me. *You must not steal them from her. You owe it to the memory of your mother.*

Harriet . . . think only of Harriet, Flavia. It is her due.

I let myself sink back into the comforting leather of the seat and allowed my mind to fly back to that day last week, in my laboratory. . . .

Their drowned faces are not so white and fishy as you might expect. Floating barely beneath the surface in the blood-red light, they are, in fact, rather the color of rotted roses.

She still smiles in spite of all that has happened. He wears a shockingly boyish expression upon his face.

Beneath them, coiled like tangled tentacles of seaweed, black ribbons dangle down into the liquid depths.

I touch the surface—write their initials in the water with my forefinger:

HDL

So closely are this man and this woman tied together, that the same three letters stand for them both: Harriet de Luce and Haviland de Luce.

My mother and my father.

It was odd, really, how I had happened upon these images.

The attics at Buckshaw are a vast aerial underworld, containing all the clutter, the castoffs, the debris, the dumpings, the sad dusty residue of all those who have lived and breathed in this house for centuries past.

Piled on top of the moldering prayer chair, for instance, upon which the terrible-tempered Georgina de Luce had once perched piously in her powdered periwig to hear the whispered confessions of her terrified children, was the crumpled wreckage of the home-built glider in which her ill-fated grandson, Leopold, had launched himself from the parapets of the east wing scant seconds before coming to grief on the steel-hard frozen ground of the Visto, bringing to an abrupt end that particular branch of the family. If you looked carefully, you could still see the stains of Leopold's oxidized blood on the glider's frail linen-covered wings.

In another corner, stacked in a stiff spinal curve, a pile of china chamber pots still gave off their faint but unmistakable pong in the tired, stuffy air.

Tables, chairs, and chimneypieces were squeezed in cheek by jowl with ormolu clocks, glazed Greek vases of startling orange and black, unwanted umbrella stands, and the sad-eyed head of an indifferently stuffed gazelle.

It was to this shadowy graveyard of unwanted bric-a-brac that I had fled instinctively last week after Father's shocking announcement.

To the attics I had flown, and there, to keep from thinking, I had crumpled into a corner, reciting mindlessly one of those shreds of childhood nonsense which we fall back on in times of great stress when we can't think what else to do:

"A was an archer who shot at a frog;

"B was a butcher who had a black dog.

"C was a crier—"

I *wasn't* going to bloody well cry! No, I bloody well wasn't!

Instead of archers and criers, I would distract my mind by rehearsing the poisons:

"A is for arsenic hid in a spud,

"B is for bromate that buggers the blood . . ."

I was up to "C is for cyanide" when a slight movement caught my eye: a sudden scurrying that vanished swiftly behind a crested French armoire.

Was it a mouse? Perhaps a rat?

I shouldn't be at all surprised. The attics of Buckshaw are, as I have said, an abandoned dumping ground where a rat would be as much at home as I was.

I got slowly to my feet and peeked carefully behind the armoire, but whatever it had been was gone.

I opened one of the dark doors of the monstrosity, and there they were: the smart black carrying cases—two of them—shoved into the far corners of the armoire, almost as if someone hadn't wanted them to be found.

I reached in and dragged the matching containers out of the shadows and into the half-light of the attic.

They were covered in pebbled leather with shiny nickel-plated snaps, each case with its own key, which hung, fortunately, from the carrying handles by a bit of ordinary butcher's string.

I popped open the first box and swung back the lid.

I knew at once by its metallic crackle finish, and the way in which its mechanical octopus arms were folded into their fitted plush compartments, that the machine I was looking at was a ciné projector.

Mr. Mitchell, proprietor of Bishop's Lacey's photographic studio, owned a similar device with which he occasionally exhibited the same few tired old films at St. Tancred's parish hall.

His machine was larger, of course, and was equipped with a loudspeaker for the sound.

Once, during a particularly dreary repeat showing of *The Paper Wasp and Its Vespiaries*, I had whiled away the time by inventing riddles, one of which I thought rather clever:

"Why is the House of Commons like a ciné sound projector?"

"Because they both have a Speaker!*"*

I could hardly wait to tell it at the breakfast table.

But that had been in happier times.

I fingered the snap and opened the second box.

This one contained a matching device, smaller, with a clockwork crank on its side and several lenses mounted in a rotating turret on its snout.

A ciné camera.

I lifted the thing to my face and peered through the viewfinder, moving the camera slowly from right to left as if I were filming.

"Buckshaw," I intoned in a newsreel voice. "Ancestral home of the family de Luce since time immemorial . . . a house divided . . . a house apart."

I put the camera down rather abruptly—and rather roughly, I'm afraid. I did not feel like going on with this.

It was then that I noticed for the first time the little gauge on its body. The indicator needle was calibrated from zero to fifty feet, and it stood nearly—but not quite—at the end of its range.

There was still film in the camera—even after all these years.

And if I were any judge, about forty-five feet of it had been exposed.

Exposed but never developed!

My heart lunged suddenly into my throat, trying to escape.

I nearly choked on it.

If my suspicions were correct, this film, this camera, might well contain hidden images of my dead mother, Harriet.

Within the hour, having made my preparations, I was in my chemical laboratory in Buckshaw's abandoned east wing. The lab had been constructed and outfitted towards the end of the Victorian era by the father of Harriet's uncle Tarquin de Luce, for a son whose spectacular collapse at Oxford was still, even after more than half a century, only whispered about among those dreaming spires.

It was here in this sunny room at the top of the house that Uncle Tar had lived, worked, and eventually died, his research into the first-order decomposition of nitrogen pentoxide having led, or so it had been hinted, to the destruction in Japan, six years ago, of Hiroshima and Nagasaki.

I had happened upon this kingdom of abandoned and glorious glassware some years ago during a rainy-day exploration of Buckshaw and promptly claimed it as my own. By poring over his notebooks and duplicating many of the experiments in my late uncle's remarkable library, I had managed to make of myself a more than competent chemist.

My specialty was not, though, the pentoxide of nitrogen, but rather the more traditional poisons.

I pulled the ciné camera from under my jumper where I had stuffed it just in case, in my descent from the attics, I had been intercepted by one of my sisters. Feely had turned eighteen in January and would be, for just a short while longer, seven years older than me. Daffy, with whom I shared a birthday, would soon be fourteen, while I was now almost twelve.

In spite of being sisters, we were none of us what you would call great friends. We were still working out new ways to torture one another.

In the small photographic darkroom at the far end of the laboratory, I reached for a brown glass bottle on the shelf. METOL, it said on the label in Uncle Tar's unmistakable spidery handwriting.

Metol, of course, was nothing more than a fancy name for plain old monomethyl-p-aminophenol sulfate.

I had skimmed through the dark-stained pages of a photo reference manual and found that what needed to be done with the film was actually quite straightforward.

First step was the developer.

I groaned as I pulled the stopper from the bottle and decanted a sample into a beaker. Twenty years on the shelf had taken its toll. The metol had oxidized and become an acrid brown sludge, the color of last night's coffee grounds.

My groan turned slowly to a grin.

"Do we have any coffee?" I asked, strolling into the kitchen with an air of pretended boredom.

"Coffee?" Mrs. Mullet asked. "What you want with coffee? Coffee's no good for girls. Gives you the colly-wobbles, like."

"I thought that if someone came to call, it would be nice to offer them a cup."

You'd think I'd asked for champagne.

"And 'oo was you expectin', miss?"

"Dieter," I lied.

Dieter Schrantz was the German ex–prisoner of war from Culverhouse Farm who had recently become engaged to Feely.

"Never mind," I told Mrs. M. "If he comes, he'll have to settle for tea. Do we have any biscuits?"

"In the pantry," she said. "That nice tin with Windsor Castle on the lid."

I gave her an idiotic grin and popped into the pantry. At the back of a high shelf, just as I had remembered, was a bottle of Maxwell House ground coffee. In spite of the rationing, it had been brought as a gift from the nearby American air base at Leathcote by Carl Pendracka, another of Feely's admirers who, in spite of Father's belief that Carl was of the bloodline of King Arthur, had been unhorsed in the recent matrimonial sweepstakes.

Offering up a silent prayer of thanks for the general bagginess of old-fashioned clothing, I shoved the coffee under one side of my sweater, stuffed a large wire kitchen whisk under the other, clamped a couple of Empire biscuits between my teeth, and made my escape.

"Thanks, Mrs. M," I mumbled around the mouthful of biscuits, keeping my hunched back to her.

Safely back upstairs in my laboratory, I emptied the coffee into a cone-shaped paper filter, placed it in a glass funnel, and, lighting a Bunsen burner, waited for the distilled water in the teakettle to come to the boil.

Chemically speaking, I remembered, the developing of film was simply a matter of reducing its silver halide crystals through deoxidization to the basic element, silver. If metol would do the job, I reasoned, so would caffeine. And so, for that matter, would vanilla extract, although I knew that if I absconded with Mrs. Mullet's vanilla extract, she'd have my guts for garters. The hoarded coffee was a much safer bet.

When the water had boiled for two minutes, I measured out three cups and poured it over the coffee. It smelled almost good enough to drink.

I stirred the brown liquid to break up the bubbles and foam, and when it had cooled sufficiently, stirred in seven teaspoons of sodium carbonate: good old, jolly old washing soda.

The initially welcoming coffee aroma was now changing—the stench increasing by the second. To be perfectly honest, it now smelt as if a coffeehouse in the slums of Hell had been struck by lightning. I was happy to be able to leave the room, even if only for a few minutes.

One more quick trip to the attics to retrieve the enamel bedpan I had spotted among the de Luce family relics, and I was nearly ready to proceed.

That being done, I gathered up my equipment and locked myself into the darkroom.

I switched on the safelight. There was a brief red flash—a tiny *pop*.

Oh no! The blasted bulb had blown out.

I opened the door and set out in search of a new one.

There were times when we grumbled about the fact that Father had ordered Dogger to replace most of the bulbs at Buckshaw with ten-watt substitutes in order to save on electricity. The only one of us who didn't seem to mind was Feely, who needed only a dim and feeble light to write in her diary and to examine her spotty hide in the looking glass.

"Low wattage wins wars," she said, even though the War had been over for six years. "And besides, it's so much more romantic."

So I had no difficulty deciding which bulb to pinch.

Before you could count to eighty-seven—I know that for a fact, because I counted in my head—I was back in the laboratory with the bulb from Feely's bedside lamp as well as the bottle of "Where's the Fire?" nail varnish with which she had recently taken to uglifying her fingers.

To my mind, if Nature had wanted us to have bright red fingertips, She would have caused us to be born with our blood on the outside.

I painted the bulb with the varnish, blew wolfish huffs and puffs of air onto it until it was dry, then gave it a second coat, making sure that the surface of the glass was completely covered with the ruby lacquer.

With the critical job I was about to undertake, I couldn't afford the slightest leakage of white light.

Again I latched myself into the darkroom. I clicked on the switch and was rewarded with a dim red glow.

Perfect!

I gave the crank on the side of the camera a bit of a windup and pushed the button. There was a clattering whir as the film inside jerked into motion. After no more than about ten seconds, the end of the ribbon went through and flapped lazily on the spool.

I undid the snap, opened the side of the camera, and removed the full reel.

Now came the tricky part.

I wound the film, one slow turn at a time, off the reel and onto the wire whisk, securing it at each end with a paper clip.

I had already half filled the bedpan with my coffee "developer," and into this I dipped the whisk, turning it ever so slowly . . . slowly . . . like a chicken on a spit.

The thermometer in the coffee bath was spot on at 68 degrees Fahrenheit.

The twelve minutes recommended by the photo manual went by like flowing sludge. As I waited with one eye on the clock, I remembered that in the early days of photography, film had been developed with gallic acid, $C_7H_6O_5$, which was obtained in small percentage from oak apples, those tumors that grew on the twigs and branches of the gall, or dyer's oak, wherever they had been punctured by the gallfly in laying its eggs.

Oddly enough, those same galls, dissolved in water, had also once been used as an antidote to strychnine poisoning.

How pleasant it was to reflect that without the female gallfly, we might never have had either photography or a convenient means of saving one's rich uncle Neddy from the hands of a would-be killer.

But would this film I had found in the camera have retained its latent images? Interesting, wasn't it, that one word—"latent"—was used to describe the invisible, undeveloped forms and shapes on photographic film as well as yet-invisible fingerprints?

Would the film show anything at all? Or rather just the wet, gray, disappointing fog that might well have resulted from too many baking summers and freezing winters in the attic?

I watched fascinated as, at my very fingertips, hundreds of tiny negative images began to form, fading into existence as if from nowhere—as if by magic.

Each frame of the film was too small to guess at its content. Only when the film was fully processed would its secrets—if any—be revealed.

Twelve minutes had now passed, and still the images did not yet seem to be fully developed. The coffee developer was obviously slower-acting than metol. I would keep up my twirling of the whisk until the images seemed as dark as a normal negative.

Another twelve minutes went by and I was beginning to flag.

When it comes to chemistry, impatience is not a virtue. Half an hour is far too long to engage in any activity, even one that's enjoyable.

By the time the images seemed satisfactory, I was ready to scream.

But I wasn't finished yet. Far from it. This was merely the first step.

Now came the first wash: five minutes under running water.

Waiting was agony. I could hardly resist the urge to load the partly processed film into the projector and hang the consequences.

And then the bleach: I had already mixed a quarter teaspoon of potassium permanganate into a quart of water and added to it a second solution of sulfuric acid in a little less water.

Another five minutes to wait as I slowly rotated the ribbon of film in the liquid.

Another wash as I counted slowly to sixty to make a minute.

Now the clearing solution: five teaspoons of potassium metabisulfite dissolved in a quart of water.

It was now safe to switch on the room lights.

The opaque silver halide—the part of the film that would eventually become black—was now a creamy yellow in color, like images daubed onto a ribbon of transparent glass with Mrs. Mullet's abominable custard.

By reflected light these images appeared to be negative, but when I held them up in front of the white light, they looked suddenly positive.

I could already make out what seemed to be a distant view of Buckshaw: a yellow, aged Buckshaw like a dwelling from a dream.

Now for the reversal.

I held the whisk up at arm's length until it was about eighteen inches from the white room light, then rotated it slowly as I counted to sixty, this time using a variation on a method I had learned while studying artificial respiration in Girl Guides before being sacked (unjustly) by that organization.

"One cy-an-ide, two cy-an-ide, three cy-an-ide," and so on.

The minute flew by with surprising speed.

At the end of that time, I removed the film from the whisk, turned it over, and similarly exposed the other side.

Time for the coffee again: what the manual referred to as the second developer. The yellow objects in each frame would now become black.

Six more minutes of dunking and dipping, turning the whisk to be certain that all parts of the film were equally immersed in the reeking liquid.

The fourth wash—even though it took only sixty seconds—seemed an eternity. My hands and arms were becoming stiff from the constant rotation, and my hands smelled as if they had been—well, never mind.

No need for a fixer: The bleach and clearing solutions would have already removed the reduced silver from the first developer, and whatever silver halide remained had been reduced to elemental silver by the second developer and was now forming the black parts of the image.

Easy as Cottleston pie.

I let the film rest for a few minutes in a tray of water to which I had added alum for hardening purposes, in order to make it scratch-resistant.

After a time, I pulled up a length of the film and peered at it through a magnifying glass.

My heart skipped a beat.

The images were heartbreakingly plain: In frame after frame, Harriet and Father were seated on a picnic blanket in front of the Folly on the island in Buckshaw's ornamental lake.

I turned off the room light and let the film sink into the water, leaving the dim red safelight as the only illumination, not because it was necessary, but because it seemed somehow more respectful.

As I have said, I traced their initials in the water:

HDL

Harriet and Haviland de Luce. I was not able, at least for now, to look at their faces in anything other than light the color of blood.

It was too much like spying on them.

Finally, reverently, almost reluctantly, I removed the film from the water and wiped it clean with a bath sponge. I carried it out into the laboratory and hung it up to dry, draping it in great drooping festoons from the framed table of the elements on the west wall to the signed photograph of Winston Churchill on the east.

In my bedroom, waiting for the film to dry, I dug out from the pile under my bed the disc I wanted: Rachmaninoff's *Eighteenth Variation on a Theme by Paganini*, the best piece of music I could think of to accompany the recalling of a great love story.

I wound up my gramophone and dropped the needle into the spinning shellac groove. As the melody began, I seated myself, knees drawn up under my chin, in one of the window seats overlooking the Visto, the long-overgrown lawn upon which Harriet had once tied down her de Havilland Gipsy Moth, *Blithe Spirit*.

I fancied I could hear the clatter of her engine as Harriet lifted off among the swirling morning mists, rising up above the chimney pots of Buckshaw, up above the ornamental lake with its Georgian Folly, and vanishing into a future from which she would not return.

It had been more than ten years since Harriet had disappeared, killed, we were told, in a climbing accident in Tibet: ten long, hard years, nearly half of which Father had spent in a Japanese prisoner-of-war camp. He had made his way home at last, only to find himself wifeless, penniless, and in grave danger of losing Buckshaw.

The estate had belonged to Harriet, who had inherited it from Uncle Tar, but because she had died without leaving a will, "the Forces of Darkness" (as Father had once referred to the gray men of His Majesty's Board of Inland Revenue Department) had been hounding him as if, rather than a returning war hero, he were an escapee from Broadmoor.

And now Buckshaw was crumbling. Ten years of neglect, sadness, and shortage of funds had taken its toll. The family silver had been sent up to London for auction, budgets had been trimmed and belts tightened. But it was no use, and at Easter, our home had finally been put up for sale.

Father had, for ages, been warning us that we might have to leave Buckshaw at a moment's notice.

And then, just days ago, having received a mysterious

telephone message, he had at last summoned the three of us—Feely, Daffy, and me—to the drawing room.

He had looked slowly from one of us to the other before breaking the news.

"Your mother," he said at last, "has been found."

More than that: She was coming home.

·FOUR·

I REALIZED THAT, EVER since Father's shocking announcement, I had been shutting myself off from reality: shoving the facts into some kit-bag corner of my mind and pulling tight the drawstring, in much the same way as you would try to trap a tiger in a sack.

Although it is shameful to admit, I knew that I had been trying to hang on to the past, attempting to awaken every morning to my old world: a world in which Harriet was still comfortably missing, a world in which, at least, I knew where I stood.

I was grasping at every chance to avoid change in the same way a drowning man tries to grab at his own rope of bubbles.

Not that I didn't want Harriet home: I did. Of course I did.

But what would it do to my life?

The finding of the film had been a godsend. Viewing it, I thought, might provide a new window into the past: a window that would help me see more clearly into the future.

This was one of those troublesome thoughts with which I had recently begun to be plagued: new, raw, and still not entirely to be trusted. It was like thinking, sometimes, with someone else's brain. It had something to do with being almost twelve, and I wasn't sure I approved of it entirely.

I darkened my bedroom by covering the windows with quilts, fastening them to the frames with drawing pins round the edges. Buckshaw's shabby and threadbare draperies were not nearly enough to keep out the sunlight.

In the laboratory, I had given the film a sharp flick with my fingernail. A hard, satisfying *tick* indicated that the same sunlight had dried it completely. I had wound it back onto its spool and brought it to my bedroom.

I threaded the film into the projector, which I had set up on my washstand, and pointed the projector into the fireplace. The walls of my bedroom were covered with such vile Victorian wallpaper—red clots on bilious blue—that there was no blank surface upon which to project the developed ciné film.

Fortunately, Mr. Mitchell, who was an expert in such things, had once told me, during a Film Night at the parish hall, that a white projection screen is not really required.

"Everyone supposes it is," he had told me, "but only because they've never seen a black one."

He went on to explain that a projector will provide

those shades which are missing from a screen: that in fact, while watching the latest Ealing comedy in the cinema, those parts of the screen which appeared to our eyes to be black were actually white.

"Aye, white—but unilluminated," he'd said.

Well, that made sense, and it seemed logical to me that the vast flat brickwork at the back of the fireplace, blackened by eons of soot, would provide the perfect surface.

And I was right!

As I switched on the projector and twisted the lens to bring it into sharp focus, the image on the fireplace bricks was formed of luxurious, velvety blacks.

Here was a view of Buckshaw, as seen from the Mulford Gates, moving now along the avenue of arched chestnuts towards the house. Next, a closer view: Harriet's Rolls-Royce Phantom II, parked on the sweep of gravel near the front door.

Then came a shot of Harriet seated in the cockpit of *Blithe Spirit*. I recognized several of the statues in the background as those which now, more than a decade later, lay strewn in ruins among the overgrown hedges of the Visto. Harriet grinned at the camera and, seizing the sides of the cockpit in both hands, boosted herself up and swung her feet out onto the aircraft's lower wing.

Harriet! My mother. Moving and breathing—as if she were still alive! And even more beautiful than I could have imagined. She seemed to glow from within, illuminating the world and all that was in it with the radiance of her smile.

With her short, tousled bobbed hair, she reminded me

of one of those celebrated female aviators in the old newsreels, but without the sense of doom that overhung so many of them.

She waved, and the camera moved away to focus upon two little girls who waved madly back, holding their hands up as if to shield their eyes from the sun.

Feely and Daffy—aged about seven and two respectively.

As Harriet lowered herself carefully down from the wing, I saw for the first time her protruding belly. Although the bump was partially hidden by her flying gear, it was easy enough to see that she was pregnant.

That bump in her bloomers was me!

How peculiar it was to be present in the scene, and yet not present, like the assistant in a conjuring show.

What was I feeling? Embarrassment? Pride? Happiness?

It was none of these things. It was the bittersweet fact that while Feely and Daffy were sharing that long-ago sunshine with Harriet, I was not.

Now a close-up of Father approaching as if ambling out from the house. He glances up shyly and fiddles with something in his jacket pocket, then smiles at the camera. This scene was apparently filmed by Harriet.

A quick change of scene, and as, in the background, Feely and Daffy dabble like ducks at the edge of the ornamental lake, Father and Harriet, filmed by someone else, picnic on a blanket in front of the Folly. This was the scene I had examined in the laboratory.

She smiles at him, and he at her. He turns away to remove something from a wicker hamper, and in that instant, she becomes dead serious, turns to the camera, and mouths a couple of words, miming them in an exaggerated manner, as if giving instructions to someone through a windowpane.

I was caught off guard. What had Harriet said?

Normally, I'm a first-rate lip-reader. It is a skill I taught myself, first by sitting at the breakfast and dinner tables with my fingers stuffed into my ears, and later using the same technique at the cinema. I had sat at Bishop's Lacey's single bus stop with wads of cotton in both ears ("Dr. Darby says it's a very bad infection, Mrs. Bellfield"), eavesdropping on early-morning shoppers as they headed for the market in Malden Fenwick.

Unless I was greatly mistaken, the words on Harriet's lips had been "pheasant sandwiches."

Pheasant sandwiches?

I stopped the projector, pushed the reverse lever, and backed the film up, then viewed the scene again. The Folly and the blanket. Harriet and Father.

She speaks the words again.

"Pheasant sandwiches."

She articulates the words so clearly I can almost hear the sound of her voice.

But to whom had she been speaking? Since she and Father were clearly in front of the camera, who had been behind it?

What unseen third party had been present at that long-ago picnic?

My options of finding out seemed limited. Feely and Daffy—at least Daffy, for certain—had been too young to remember.

And I could hardly ask Father without admitting to finding and developing the forgotten film.

I was on my own.

As usual.

"Feely," I said, stopping her dead in the middle of the Andante cantabile from Beethoven's Piano Sonata No. 8, the *Pathétique*.

Any interruption when she was playing made Feely furious, which gave me the upper hand automatically as long as I remained perfectly calm, cool, and collected.

"What?" she demanded, jumping to her feet and slamming down the lid on the keyboard, which made a lovely sound: a kind of harmonic mooing that went on echoing through the piano strings for a surprisingly long time, like the Aeolian harps whose strings, Daffy had told me, were played by the wind.

"Nothing," I said, forming my face into its slightly-hurt-but-bearing-up-in-spite-of-it look. "It's just that I thought you might like a cup of tea."

"All right," Feely demanded. "What are you up to?"

She knew me as well as the magic mirror knew the wicked queen.

"I'm not up to anything," I replied. "I was merely making an effort to be nice."

I had her off balance. I could see it in her eyes.

"Yes, all right, then," she said suddenly, seizing the opportunity. "I think I *should* rather fancy a cup of tea."

Ha! She thought she'd won, and the game had barely even begun.

* * *

"Her Majesty is demanding a cup of tea," I told Mrs. Mullet. "If you'll be so good as to make one, I'll take it in to her myself."

"Of course," said Mrs. Mullet. "You shall 'ave it in two shakes of a dead lamb's tail."

Mrs. M always said "in two shakes of a dead lamb's tail" when she was peeved but didn't want to show it.

"'A dead lamb's tail' is a way of saucin' 'em off without gettin' yourself into 'ot water. It means 'kiss my chump' without actually sayin' so," she had once confided, but had now, obviously, forgotten she'd told me.

Feely was by this time back into the Beethoven sonata. I put the teacup silently on the table and sat down in a bolt upright, attentive position with my knees together, my hands folded daintily in my lap, modeling my posture on Cynthia Richardson, the vicar's wife.

I even pursed my lips a little prunishly.

When Feely had finished, I let a respectful silence hang in the air while I counted to eleven, partly because it was my age (although not for much longer) and partly because eleven seconds seemed to me a perfect balance between awe and insolence.

"Feely, I was thinking . . ." I said.

"How novel," she interrupted. "I hope nothing was damaged."

I ignored her.

"Have you ever thought of playing for the cinema? Like *Brief Encounter*, or the Warsaw Concerto in *Dangerous Moonlight?*"

"Perhaps," she said rather dreamily, forgetting her recent sarcasm. "Perhaps one day I shall be asked."

Feely's only professional film performance had been as a pair of disembodied hands in a never-to-be-completed Phyllis Wyvern film, of which only a few scenes had been shot at Buckshaw before its star came to what I believe is called rather a sticky end.

I knew how disappointed Feely had been.

"I remember how beautiful your hands were in the film. It was remarkable, considering that you'd never before so much as seen a ciné camera."

I waited for her to contradict me but she didn't.

"Some people are fortunate enough to have had ciné films taken of them when they were children. They say that it builds much greater confidence for later on. Eileen Joyce said so on the BBC."

This was a brazen lie. Eileen Joyce had said no such thing, but I knew that since she was Feely's musical idol, the mere mention of the famous pianist's name would add credibility to my twisting of the truth.

"Too bad there were no ciné films taken of you when you were a child," I said. "It might have given you a leg up."

Feely, lost in thought, gazed out the drawing room window and across the ornamental lake.

Was she thinking of that long ago day when she was seven? I couldn't leave it to chance.

"Odd, isn't it," I prompted, "that Harriet didn't own a ciné camera? I should have thought that someone like her would have—"

"Oh, but she did!" Feely exclaimed. "Before you were born. But when you came along she put it away—for obvious reasons."

Ordinarily I'd have made some rude comeback, but necessity, as someone once remarked—or should have remarked—is the mother of keeping your lip zipped.

"Obvious reasons?" I asked. I was willing to suffer any indignity to keep this conversation alive.

"She didn't want to risk breaking it."

I laughed too loudly, hating myself. "I'll bet she wasted lots of film on you, though," I said.

"Miles of it," Feely said. "Simply miles, and miles, and miles."

"Where is it, then? I've never seen it."

Feely shrugged. "Who knows? Why are you so suddenly interested?"

"Curiosity," I said. "I believe you, though. It sounds so like Harriet to have wasted all that film on others. I wonder if anyone ever thought to take any films of her?"

I could hardly put it any more plainly than that.

"Not that I remember," Feely said, and gave herself back to Beethoven.

I stood behind her, peering over her shoulder at the music, an invasion of her personal boundaries which I know perfectly well gives her the creeps.

Nevertheless, she ignored me and kept on playing.

"What does *Tempo rubato* mean?" I asked, pointing at her penciled words in the margin.

"Stolen time," Feely said without missing a note.

Stolen time!

Her words hit me in the stomach like a sledgehammer!

Wasn't that what I was doing by developing a film that was taken before I was born? Stealing time from the past of others and trying to make it my own?

For some stupid reason my eyes were suddenly full of warm water, dangerously close to brimming over.

I stood for a while behind my sister, letting the *Pathétique* wash over me.

After a time, I reached out and put my hand on her shoulder.

We both of us pretended it wasn't happening.

But both of us knew that it was.

Because Harriet was coming home.

·FIVE·

NOW, STILL CRADLED IN the comforting upholstery of the Rolls-Royce, I roused myself from my memories. We had not yet reached Buckshaw. Outside the car's windows, the narrow lane was lined on both sides with spectators who had strung themselves out along the weedy verge to watch Harriet's homecoming. So many of the dear village faces, I thought, starched into stiffness by the death of one of their own.

It was a scene most of them would remember for the rest of their lives.

Tully Stoker; his daughter, Mary; and Ned Cropper, the potboy of the Thirteen Drakes, all of whom had been perched on a stile as we approached, jumped smartly to the ground and moved closer. Tully removed his cap, his eyes following the hearse.

Ned craned his neck, trying to get a look at Feely in the

backseat of the Rolls, where she rode behind me in silence with Father, Daffy, and Aunt Felicity.

I was sitting beside Dogger, who was at the wheel, and I could see Feely's face clearly in the mirror. She was staring straight ahead.

No one spoke.

Now we were creeping past the Misses Puddock, Lavinia and Aurelia, the joint proprietresses of the St. Nicholas Tea Room in Bishop's Lacey. Both of them were dressed in a kind of ancient bombazine which had once been black but was now a shade of curdled brown; both clutched matching Victorian evening bags which were weirdly out of place in a country lane. I couldn't help wondering what was inside them. Miss Aurelia gave us a cheery wave as we hove alongside, but her sister seized her hand and shoved it down roughly.

Dieter stood a little way back from the verge, almost in the ditch, with his employer, Gordon Ingleby of Culverhouse Farm. Although Father had invited Dieter to join us on this sad occasion, he had politely declined. As a former German prisoner of war, his presence might be resented, he had said, and even though he wanted desperately to be at Feely's side, he felt it best to keep a respectful distance—at least for now.

There had been a row about this at Buckshaw, with much slamming of doors, raising of voices, reddening of faces, and, on the part of a certain person not to be named, tears, followed by the brutal kicking of a wastebasket and a flinging of oneself facedown upon one's bed.

Now, as we drove slowly past, Feely didn't give Dieter so much as a glance through the glass.

Ahead of us in the narrow lane, Harriet's hearse glinted unnervingly in the dappled sunlight, seeming to shift out of this world and into another and back again as its polished paint reflected darkened versions of the moving fields, the trees overhead, the hedgerows, and the sky.

The sky.

Heaven.

Heaven was where Harriet was, at least according to Denwyn Richardson, the vicar.

"I think that I am quite correct in assuring you, Flavia, that she is sipping tea with her ancestors even as we speak," he had told me.

I knew he was doing his best to comfort me, but a part of me knew, all too well and from personal experience, that Harriet's ancestors—and mine, come to think of it—were moldering away in crumbling coffins in the crypt of St. Tancred's and quite unlikely to be sipping tea or anything else, unless it was the seepage from the church's rotting rainspouts.

He was a dear man, the vicar, but dreadfully naïve, and I sometimes thought that there were certain aspects of life and death which eluded him completely.

Chemistry teaches us all that can be known about corruption, and I realized with a shock that I had learned more at the altar of the Bunsen burner than at all the altars of the competition combined.

Except about the soul, of course. The only vessel in which the soul could be studied was the living human body, which made it as difficult as trying to study the soul of a Mexican jumping bean.

We could learn nothing about the soul from a corpse, I

had decided, after several firsthand encounters with cadavers.

Which brought me back to the man under the wheels of the train. Who was he? What was he doing on the platform at Buckshaw Halt? Had he come down from London on Harriet's funeral train with the other dignitaries? Presumably he had, since I hadn't seen him there before the train pulled into the station.

What had he meant about the Nide being under? And who on earth was the Gamekeeper?

I didn't dare ask. It was neither the time nor the place.

The stony silence inside the Rolls told me that each of us remained lost in our own thoughts.

To each of the mourners outside in the lane, I would be no more than a pale face glimpsed for a moment behind the glass. I wished I could smile at each of them, but I knew I must not, since a grinning mug would spoil their memories of this sad occasion.

We were all of us mourners overtaken by the moment: It was not ours to shape. We must give ourselves over to being the Grieving Family, upon whom others must be permitted to shower sympathy.

All of this I knew without ever having been told. It had somehow been born in my blood.

Perhaps this was what Aunt Felicity had meant when she had told me that day upon the island in the ornamental lake that it had been left to me to carry the torch: to carry on the glorious name de Luce. "*Wherever it may lead you,*" she had added.

Her words still rang in my head: "*You must never be deflected by unpleasantness. I want you to remember that. Al-*

though it may not be apparent to others, your duty will become as clear to you as if it were a white line painted down the middle of the road. You must follow it, Flavia."

"Even when it leads to murder?" I had asked.

"Even when it leads to murder."

Could it be that the slightly dotty old woman sitting in rigid silence behind me in the Rolls had actually spoken those words?

I knew that I needed now, more than ever, to get her alone.

But first there was the arrival at Buckshaw to be got through. It was the part of the day I had been dreading more than anything.

We had been briefed on the scheduled events:

At ten A.M., Harriet's coffin would arrive at Buckshaw Halt, which it had now done. It would be transported by hearse to the front door of Buckshaw, from which point it would be carried inside and placed on trestles in Harriet's boudoir, which was upstairs at the extreme south end of the west wing.

This seemed at first a peculiar choice of rooms for a lying-in-state. The enormous foyer with its dark wood paneling, black-and-white checkered floor tiles, and double rising staircases would have provided a much grander setting than Harriet's private apartments, which Father had preserved as a shrine to her memory.

Except for the looking glass on the dresser, and the cheval glass in the corner, each of which had been covered just yesterday with a black pall, everything in the boudoir, from Harriet's Fabergé combs and brushes (one of which still had several strands of her hair caught up in its bristles) and

Lalique scent bottles to her absurdly practical carpet slippers standing ready beside her great princess-and-the-pea four-poster bed, was precisely as she had left it on that last day.

Only afterwards had it occurred to me not only that Father wanted Harriet to be returned to her private sanctuary, but that the room where she was to lie in state was connected to his own by a private door.

Now Dogger was turning the car in at the Mulford Gates, whose mossy stone griffins stared down impassively upon the procession. I thought, just for a moment as we swept past, that the drops of green water which still oozed from the smutty corners of their eyes after last night's rain were actually tears.

Out of respect, the "For Sale" sign had been uprooted and put discreetly out of sight until after the funeral.

Up the long avenue we went, under the canopy of chestnuts.

"Arrive Buckshaw 1030 hours," it had said on the schedule Father posted in the drawing room, and it was so.

Even as we stepped from the Rolls, the clock in the tower of St. Tancred's, a mile to the north across the fields, struck the half hour.

Dogger opened the car's doors for us, one at a time, and we formed a respectful double line on both sides of the front entrance. There we stood, looking everywhere but straight ahead as Harriet's coffin was hauled on chromium rollers from the hearse by six black-suited bearers—all of them strangers—and carried into the house.

I had never seen Father look more haggard. A wayward bit of breeze ruffled the front of his hair, causing it to stand on end, like a man frightened out of his wits. I wanted to fly to his side and comb it down with my fingers, but of course I didn't.

I fell in behind the coffin, as I thought was only right: As youngest of the family, I would be a sort of flower girl—first in the procession.

But Father stopped me with a hand on my shoulder. Although his sad blue eyes looked directly into mine, he said not a word.

And yet I understood. As if he had handed me a fat procedures manual, I knew that we were meant to linger a bit longer out of doors. Father didn't want us to see Harriet's coffin being manhandled up the stairs.

It's things like this that really shake me: sudden terrifying glimpses into the world of being an adult, and they are sometimes things that I am not sure I really want to know.

There we stood, like stone chessmen: Father, the checkmated king, graceful, but fatally wounded in defeat; Aunt Felicity, the ancient queen, her black hat askew, humming some tuneless tune to herself; Feely and Daffy, the rooks, the two remote towers at the distant corners of our castle world.

And me: Flavia de Luce.

Pawn.

Well, not quite, actually—although that was how I felt at the time.

Since Harriet's body had been found in a Himalayan glacier, our lives at Buckshaw seemed to have fallen under the control of some unseen force. We were told the when, the where, and the how of everything, but never the why.

Somewhere, in some far-off vastness, arrangements were being made, plans being laid, all of which seemed to trickle down to us as if they were the freshly melted decrees of some unknown ice god.

"Do this, do that—be here, be there," they commanded, and we obeyed.

Blindly, it seemed.

That was what I was thinking when my acute hearing picked up a clattering noise coming from the direction of the gates. I turned just in time to see a most unusual vehicle appearing from among the chestnuts and the hedges and coming to a halt on the gravel forecourt.

The thing was mint green and boxy, like the caged lift from a Welsh coal mine. It had an open frame upon which a canvas roof could be strapped in case of rain, and a winch mounted on its nose. I recognized it at once as a Land Rover: We had seen a similar model not all that long ago in a safari film at the cinema.

Seated at the wheel was a middle-aged woman in a black short-sleeved dress. She braked and yanked the Liberty scarf off her head as if it were the starting cord for an outboard motor, letting her long red hair tumble to her shoulders in the process.

She stepped down from the Land Rover as if she owned the world and looked about at her surroundings with what was either partial amusement or total contempt.

"Undine, come," she said, extending a hand in the manner of God on the ceiling of the Sistine Chapel. There was an alarming flutter in the depths of the Land Rover, and a most peculiar child shot up her head.

She bore no resemblance to the woman, whom I took to be her mother. She had a pasty moon face, pale blue eyes, black-rimmed spectacles of the National Health variety, and the haunting, ageless look of one of those bruised-looking baby birds that has fallen helpless and unfinished from the nest.

Some primal fear stirred inside of me.

They crunched across the gravel and stopped in front of Father.

"Lena?" Father said.

"Sorry we're late," the woman answered. "The Cornish roads were—well, you know what Cornish roads can be, and the ones in—good heavens! Could this be little Flavia?"

I said nothing. If the answer was "yes," she wasn't going to hear it from me.

"She's awfully like her mother, isn't she?" the supposed Lena asked, still talking to Father and not looking at me at all, as if I wasn't there.

"And you are?" I asked, just as I had asked the stranger at the station. It may have been rude, but on such an occasion as today, one was entitled to a certain brittleness.

"Your cousins, dear—Lena and Undine, of the Cornwall de Luces. Surely you've heard of us?"

"I'm afraid not," I said.

And all the while, Feely and Daffy were standing open-mouthed. Aunt Felicity had already turned abruptly away and vanished into the black maw of the open door.

"Shall we go inside?" Lena said, and it was not a question. "Come along, Undine, it's chilly here. We're likely to catch our deaths of cold."

It was chilly all right, but not the way *she* meant. How could you be chilly on such an unseasonably sunny day?

Undine stuck out her tongue as she marched past me and into the house.

In the foyer, Father spoke quietly to Dogger, who went quickly about removing the intruders' luggage from the Land Rover and hauling it to an upstairs room.

With that seen to, Father turned and began to trudge heavily up the stairs himself, as if his shoes were filled with lead.

Bongggggggg!

A sudden deafening explosion of noise filled the foyer. Father stopped in his tracks and I spun round. Undine was hacking away at the Chinese dinner gong with Father's prize malacca walking stick, which she had pulled from the umbrella stand inside the front door.

Bongggggggg! Bongggggggg! Bongggggggg! Bongggggggg! Bongggggggg!

The mother seemed oblivious. Cousin Lena—if indeed that's who the woman was—stood staring appreciatively, with her head thrown back, at the paneling and the paintings as if she were the Prodigal Daughter being welcomed home, peeling off her black gloves almost obscenely as she mentally totted up the value of the artwork.

Now the child was running up and down the staircase—

upon which Father had stopped in disbelief—clattering the cane along the uprights of the banister as if they were a picket fence.

Drrrrrrrrrr! Drrrrrrrrrr! Drrrrrrrrrr!

Feely and Daffy were, for the first time in living memory, speechless.

Feely was the first to make a move: She drifted off towards the drawing room. Daffy opened her mouth, then shut it and made for the library at full speed.

"Flavia, dear," Lena said, "why don't you show Undine round the house. She's quite keen on paintings and so forth, aren't you, Undie?"

I felt what tasted like black vomit rising in my throat.

"Yes, Ibu," Undine said, slashing at the air with the cane as if she were cutting her way through the jungle.

I kept my distance.

"Perhaps Miss Undine would like to view the sharks," Dogger suggested. He had reappeared suddenly and silently on the staircase.

There were no sharks at Buckshaw, I was quite sure of that, but part of me was hoping desperately that Dogger had rounded up a few. Perhaps he had secretly stocked the ornamental lake.

·SIX·

THE GREAT BLACK SHARK came boiling up from the surface, hung motionless for a moment, its massive jaws gnashing at the air, then fell writhing back into the choppy waters.

Undine shrieked. "Again!" she shouted. "Again! Again! Again!"

"Very well, but this one must be the last," Dogger said, manipulating his bare hands in front of the shaded desk lamp, and the black shadow shark rose up once more on the wall, snapped fiendishly at the air, and splashed back into the billows of waving fingers.

Dogger rolled down his sleeves, rebuttoned the cuffs, and switched off the lamp.

He removed the blankets he had hung over the kitchen windows, and we blinked in the sudden light.

When Dogger had gone, Undine said, "Does he always make sharks?"

"No," I said. "I've seen him form elephants and crocodiles. His crocodile is quite terrifying, actually."

"Huh!" Undine said. "I'm not scared of crocodiles."

I couldn't resist. "I'll bet you've never seen one," I said. "Not in real life, anyway."

"I have, too!"

Little did she know that when it came to the bluffing game, she was up against a master. *I'll teach her a trick or two*, I thought.

"Where, precisely?" I asked. She probably didn't even know the meaning of the word "precisely."

"In a mangrove swamp at Sembawang. It was a saltwater crocodile—they're the world's largest living reptile."

"Sembawang?" I must have sounded like the village idiot.

"Singapore," she said. She pronounced it Sing-a-PORE, with the accent on the last syllable. "Have you never been to Singapore?"

Since I had not, I wondered how I could best quickly change the subject.

"Why do you call your mother Ibu?" I asked.

"It's Malay," she answered. "It means 'mother' in Malay."

"Is Singapore in Malay?"

"No! Malay is a language, you silly goose. Singapore is a geographical location."

This discussion was not going at all as I had hoped. Time for another diversion.

"Undine," I said. "What a peculiar name."

Perhaps "peculiar" was a little harsh, but she had, after all, struck the first blow by calling me a silly goose.

"Not so peculiar as it might have been," she replied.

"My father wanted to call me Sepia, but my mother prevailed."

That was the way she spoke: "prevailed."

What a curious little creature she was!

At one moment, she was a baby bawling for more amusement, and the next, she was talking like some boring old stick from the Explorers Club.

Ageless, I thought. Yes, that was the word that best described Undine: *ageless*.

Still, I wasn't quite sure whether to believe her about the Singapore saltwater crocodile. I'd check her up later.

"I'm sorry about your mother," she said suddenly, out of the silence. "Ibu has spoken of her often."

"In *Malay*?" I asked, meaning to cut.

"In Malay and in English," she said. "In Singapore, we spoke both languages interchangeably."

Interchangeably? Don't make me hurl my gastric acids!

"Have I caused you great distress?" she asked.

"Distress?"

"Ibu said I was not to mention your mother's name at Buckshaw. She said it would cause great distress."

"*Ibu* speaks often of my mother, you say?"

I was still being more than a trifle snotty, but Undine didn't seem to notice.

"Yes, quite often," she said. "She cared for her a great deal."

I have to admit I was touched.

"She wept," Undine said, "when they took your mother's body from the train."

Quite suddenly my mind was reeling.

"From the train?" I asked, disbelieving her. "You weren't at the station."

"Yes, we were," Undine said. "Ibu said it was the least we could do. We were late. We parked off to one side, but we were still able to observe everything."

"I'm suddenly tired, Undine," I told her. "Find your own way upstairs. I'm going for a bit of a lie-down."

I stretched out on my bed, facedown, unable to keep awake, unable to sleep, and guilt was the culprit.

How could I have sat so calmly in the kitchen watching a carefree shadow-show when all the while my mother was lying dead upstairs?

Dead and lost: frozen in a glacier for a decade until some moronic mountaineer, posing for a snapshot, had stepped backwards into a crevasse, where a rescue party eventually found his—and her—icy remains.

How did I feel? Guilty as sin!

Why wasn't I blubbering and shrieking and ripping out my hair? Why wasn't I prowling the battlements of Buckshaw, howling into the wind?

Even Cousin Lena had been able to weep at the station. Why then had I stood there on the platform like a piece of rotted timber, more attentive to the death of a stranger than to that of my own mother?

Why had I needed to be reprimanded by a voice from the swamps of my mind?

How could my grief have failed me so miserably?

Perhaps Feely and Daffy had been right all along: Perhaps I really *was* a changeling. Perhaps Harriet really *had* plucked me from an orphanage—which would mean, of course, that I had no more real physical connection with her than does a monkey with the moon.

Never in my life had I wanted more desperately to be a de Luce, yet never had I felt less as if I actually were one. My family and I seemed to stand at opposite ends of the universe. I was as much a mystery to them as they were to me, and yet, in spite of it, we needed one another.

I rolled over, faceup, and stared at the ceiling. The great loose bags of water-damaged paper that hung like moldy barrage balloons above my head made me feel as if I were under attack from the very house itself.

I covered my head with a pillow. But it was no use.

In just a few hours, the people of the village would begin arriving at Buckshaw for Harriet's lying-in-state. Dogger would usher them in small groups up the west staircase to her boudoir, where they would stand gazing at their own reflections in the awful polish of that hideous coffin, whose contents were too horrible to be imagined.

I leapt from my bed and, picking up the ciné projector, carried it into my laboratory darkroom.

Again I threaded the film into the machine and switched it on. The picture was smaller but brighter than it had been in my bedroom fireplace, and, oddly enough, I was able to pick out more detail.

Here is Harriet, scrambling once more from the cockpit of *Blithe Spirit* with yours truly still invisible but present nevertheless beneath her flying togs. Feely and Daffy wave and shield their eyes.

Was it from the sun, as I had supposed?

Or had Harriet, in real life, been too radiant to look at?

Whatever the case, by developing this forgotten film, I had, with the magic of chemistry, restored my mother to life.

Deep inside me, something awoke, rolled over—and then went back to sleep.

Now Father strolls towards the camera, unaware that he is trapped in another world: the world of the past.

Daffy and Feely dabble at the edge of the ornamental lake, unaware that they are being filmed. The camera turns away, moving towards the blanket upon which Father and Harriet are picnicking.

But wait!

What was that shadow on the grass? I hadn't spotted it before.

I stopped the projector and threw it into reverse.

Yes! I was right—there *was* a dark blot on the grass: the shadow of the camera operator, whoever that may have been.

I let the film run on a bit: As Father turns away to remove something from the hamper, Harriet turns to the camera and mouths those words again.

Along with her, I speak them aloud, attempting to match my lips with hers, getting the feel of her words in my own mouth:

"Pheasant sandwiches," she says on the flickering image.

"Pheasant sandwiches," I say.

Again I back up the film for another glimpse of that

fleeting shadow on the grass. To whom had Harriet mouthed those mysterious words?

I watched it all again wondering if there was a way to freeze the picture.

"Pheasant—" Harriet said, and there was the most awful clatter and grinding.

The projector had jammed!

On the wall, the image had frozen mid-word. Before my very eyes, Harriet's face began to turn brown—to darken—to shrivel—to bubble—

The film had caught fire! A little column of dark, acrid smoke arose from somewhere inside the projector.

If the film was cellulose nitrate, as I knew some films to be, I was in trouble.

Even if it didn't explode—as was quite likely—the burning stuff could still fill the room almost instantly with a noxious mixture of hydrogen, carbon monoxide, carbon dioxide, methane, and various unpleasant forms of the nitrogen oxides, to say nothing of cyanide.

This little darkroom would, in an instant, become a perfect chamber of death. Buckshaw itself might then, in minutes, be reduced to ashes.

I tore a laboratory apron from its hook on the wall and flung it over the machine.

Cellulose nitrate doesn't require outside oxygen to burn: It contains its own.

Nothing—not even fire extinguishers or water—can extinguish a cellulose nitrate blaze.

Usually, when it comes to chemicals, I have my wits about me, but I must confess that in this case, I panicked.

I dashed out of the darkroom, slammed the door behind me, and threw my back against it to keep it shut. A cloud of smoke escaped with me.

I was standing like that—like a creature that had just dragged itself up out of the pit—when a voice from the smoke asked "Close call?"

It was Dogger.

All I could do was nod.

"I beg your pardon for intruding," he said, fanning his hands at the air and opening a window, "but Colonel de Luce wishes the family to congregate in the drawing room in a quarter of an hour."

"Thank you, Dogger. I shall be along directly."

Dogger didn't move. His nostrils dilated as he very slightly raised his chin.

"Acetate?" he asked, not even bothering to take a full-fledged sniff.

"I believe it is," I said. "If it had been cellulose nitrate we'd be in rather a sticky spot."

"Indeed," Dogger agreed. "May I be of assistance?"

I paused for only a fraction of a second before blurting out, "Can ciné film be patched?"

"It can indeed," Dogger replied. "It is referred to in the trade, I believe, as 'splicing.' A few drops of acetone should do the trick."

I reviewed the reaction in my mind.

"Of course!" I said. "A chemical bonding of the celluloid."

"Just so," Dogger said.

"I should have thought of that," I admitted. "Wherever did you learn it?"

A cloud drifted across Dogger's face, and for a few unsettling moments, I felt as if I were suddenly in the presence of an entirely different person.

A complete stranger.

"I—don't know," he said at last, slowly. "These fragments appear suddenly sometimes at the tips of my fingers—or on my tongue—as if—"

"Yes?"

"As if—"

I held my breath.

"Almost as if they were memories."

And with those words the stranger had vanished. Dogger was suddenly back.

"May I be of assistance?" he asked again, as if nothing had happened.

Now here was a pretty pickle! Much as I wanted Dogger's help, some dark and ancient part of me clung stubbornly to keeping the spool of film a secret.

It was all so beastly complicated! On the one hand, part of me wanted to be patted on the head and told "Good girl, Flavia!" while at the same time, another part wanted to hoard this new and unexpected glimpse of Harriet: to keep the film strictly to myself, like a dog with a fresh-flung soup bone.

But then, I thought, Dogger had never actually met Harriet in person: He had not come to Buckshaw until after the War. In an odd way, Harriet was no more to him than a shadow left behind by the deceased wife of his employer—in much the same way, I realized with an unpleasant pang, as she was to me.

Except, of course, that she was also my mother.

What it came down to, then, was this: How much did I trust Dogger?

Could I swear him to secrecy?

A minute later we were in the darkroom. Dogger had switched on the exhaust fan (which I hadn't known existed) and was examining the sticky residue in the guts of the projector. The smoke and the fumes had dissipated and with them, the fear of an explosion.

"No great harm done, I think," he told me. "Not more than a few frames burnt. Do you have scissors?"

"No," I said. I had recently ruined a perfectly good pair of scissors by using them to cut a piece of zinc in a failed experiment intended to retrieve fingerprints from a downspout by an acid etching process of my own invention.

"Anything else sharp?" Dogger asked.

Somewhat shamefaced, I pulled from a drawer Father's prized Thiers-Issard hollow-ground straight razor: one I had borrowed in the past, which had come in so handy that I was thinking of asking for one of my own next Christmas.

"Ah," Dogger said. "So *that's* where it got to."

"I took care to keep it in its case," I pointed out. "Accidents, and so forth."

"Very wise," Dogger said. He did not mention returning the thing to Father, as many people would have done. That's another of the things I love about Dogger: He's not a snitch.

"To begin with, we cut out the damaged section," Dogger explained, "then scrape the emulsion off the film at the two fresh ends."

"You sound as if you've done this before," I remarked casually, keeping a close eye on him.

"I have, Miss Flavia. Showing ciné films of an instructional nature to hordes of uninterested men was once a not insubstantial part of my responsibility."

"Meaning?" I asked.

Dogger's memory was always a puzzle. There were times when he could see his own past only, as Saint Paul puts it, "through a glass darkly," and yet at other times as if through a highly polished window.

I have often thought how maddening it must be for him: like trying to view the moon with a telescope through tattered clouds on a windy night.

"Meaning," Dogger said, "that we shall have this film repaired hubble-de-shuff. Ah! Here we are—most satisfactory."

He held out a length of the repaired film for my inspection, flexing it and giving the new join a good hard snap. It seemed as good as new.

"You're a wizard, Dogger!" I told him, and he did not contradict me.

"Shall we give it a try?" he asked.

"Why not?" I said. My fears had vanished with the smoke.

Having scraped the melted muck out of the projector—I suggested using Father's razor again, but Dogger wouldn't hear of it—we reloaded the film, switched off the lights, and watched closely as the flickering black-and-white images brought Harriet back to life.

Here she was again, hauling herself once more from the

cockpit of *Blithe Spirit*, Father strolling self-consciously towards the camera.

"Hullo!" I said suddenly. "Who's that?"

"Your father," he said. "It's just that he's younger."

"No—behind him. In the window."

"I didn't see anyone," Dogger said. "Let's back things up."

He reversed the projector. He seemed more familiar with the controls than I had been.

"Just there—look," I insisted. "In the window."

It happened so quickly. No wonder he had missed it.

As Father approached the camera, there was a mere shifting of the light in an upstairs window—and then it was gone.

"A man—in shirtsleeves. Tie and braces. Papers in his hand."

"You've a sharper eye than I have, Miss Flavia," he said. "It was too quick for me. We shall have another look."

With infinitely patient fingers he reversed the film again. "Yes," he said. "I see him now. Quite distinct: shirtsleeves, tie, braces, papers in his hand—hair parted in the middle."

"I think you're right," I said. "Let's take another squint."

Dogger smiled and ran the scene again.

Was I seeing what I was seeing? Or was my imagination playing up on me?

But it wasn't the man in the film that interested me so much as his location.

"How odd," I said with a private shiver. "Whoever he is, he's in this very room."

And it was true. Mr. Tie-and-Braces—it was quite easy to make him out clearly once you'd got used to it—had been shuffling papers at the window of my chemical laboratory: a room which had been abandoned and locked up in 1928 after Uncle Tarquin had been found by his housekeeper, stone cold at his desk, gazing sightlessly through his microscope.

Judging by the ages of Feely and Daffy, and by the fact that I had not yet made my appearance in the world, the film had been made in about 1939: not long before I was born, and about a year before Harriet's disappearance.

More than ten years after Uncle Tar's death.

No one should have been in that room.

So who was the man at the window?

Had Father known he was there? Had Harriet? Surely they must have done.

"What do you make of it, Dogger?"

One of the things I love about myself is my ability to remain open to suggestion.

"American, I should say. Military, by the shirt. An NCO. Probably a corporal. Tall—six foot three, or perhaps four."

I must have gaped in awe.

"Elementary, as Sherlock Holmes might have said," Dogger explained. "Only an American NCO would have the blade of his tie tucked into his shirt in such a way—between the second and third button—and his height can be judged easily against the top of that sash rail, which I judge to be six feet above the floor."

He pointed at the very window which had appeared in the film.

"The question remains," he went on, "as to what an American clerk was doing at Buckshaw in 1939."

"My thoughts precisely," I said.

"We'd best be getting along," Dogger said suddenly. "They shall be awaiting us."

I'd completely forgotten about Father and Harriet.

·SEVEN·

I MADE AN APOLOGETIC entrance to the drawing room. I needn't have bothered. No one paid me the slightest bit of attention.

Father, as usual, was standing at the window, lost in his own thoughts. At the railway station, he had worn a suit of darkest blue with a black band on one arm, as if clinging desperately to the hope that even the slightest tinge of color might bring Harriet home alive. But now he had given up and was dressed in black. His white face hanging above his mourning attire was awful.

Feely and Daffy, too, wore black dresses I had never seen before. I shuddered at the thought of what ancient wardrobes must have been plundered to turn out something decent, something proper.

Why hadn't Father dressed me *in black?* I wondered. Why had he let me be seen at Buckshaw Halt in a white summer dress which, come to think of it, must have stuck out like a firework in the night sky?

Like a fizzler at a funeral, I thought, but quickly forced it out of my mind.

The problem with bereavement, I had already decided, was learning when to put on and when to take off the various masks that one was required to wear: with anyone who wasn't a de Luce, profound and inconsolable grief, complete with limp hands and downcast eyes; with family, a distant coolness which, to tell the truth, was not all that different from our everyday life. Only when one was alone in one's own room could one pull faces at oneself in one's looking glass, hauling the corners of one's eyes down with first and fourth fingers spread, lolling one's tongue out and crossing one's eyes horribly just to assure oneself that one was still alive.

I can't believe I just wrote that, but it describes precisely how I felt.

We might as well face it: Death is a bore. It is even harder on the survivors than on the deceased, who at least don't have to worry about when to sit and when to stand, or when to permit a pale smile and when to glance tragically away.

A pale smile came into my mind because that was what Lena had given me as she looked up from the newspaper through which she had been leafing at far too fast a clip to be actually reading.

She took a last suck on her cigarette and crushed it without mercy in the ashtray before lighting another with a long match from the hearth.

In the corner, Undine was idly tearing off strips of the wallpaper.

"Undine, dear," her mother said. "Stop doing that and run upstairs for my cigarettes. You shall find them in one of our portmanteaus."

Father seemed at last to realize that we were all present, but even at that, he did not turn away from the window as he began to speak in a dull voice: "The lying-in-state shall commence at 1400 hours," he said. "I've drawn up a rota. We shall each of us take turns standing vigil in six-hour watches in order of age, which means that I shall begin and Flavia shall finish. Kneeling benches have been laid on and Mrs. Mullet has seen to the candles."

I thought I heard him swallow.

"From now until the funeral tomorrow, your mother is not to be left alone—not even for a moment. Do I make myself perfectly clear?"

"Yes, Father," Daffy said.

And there fell one of those de Lucean silences during which you could hear the ancient stones of Buckshaw shedding their dust.

"Are there any questions?"

"No, Father," we said in unison, and I was surprised to hear my own voice leading all the rest.

Feely and Daffy took his words as a signal of dismissal and left the room as quickly as respect allowed. Lena drifted idly off in their wake.

We stood there not moving, Father and I. I hardly dared breathe. What I should have done, of course—what my heart was demanding me to do—was to run at him and throw my arms around him.

But I did not, of course. I had at least the decency to spare him that embarrassment.

After a time, perhaps because of my silence, he thought I had gone.

When he turned away from the window, I saw that his eyes were brimming.

Naturally, I couldn't let him know that I had seen his tears. Pretending I hadn't noticed, I walked from the room with my fingertips pressed together, as if in procession.

I needed to be alone.

Suddenly, and for the first time in my life, I felt as if I were one of those prisoners in Daffy's French novels who finds herself shackled hand and foot at the bottom of an old well in a dungeon with the water rising.

The only thing for it was to go to my laboratory and do something constructive with strychnine. There had been that business of the poisoned beehive written up in the *News of the World* not all that long ago, and I had hoped to add to scientific knowledge—to say nothing of the art of criminal investigation—with a number of my own insights into the possibilities of poisoning at the breakfast table.

I climbed the stairs, fishing the key from my pocket as I went. When working with deadly potions I had found it best to keep the door tightly locked.

I twisted the doorknob and stepped inside.

Esmeralda, my Buff Orpington hen, lay stretched out

stiffly on the floor in a beam of sunlight, her neck and both legs fully extended, one wing unfurled as if she had been reaching for help. Sweep marks in the dust showed all too clearly her recent frantic floundering.

"Esmeralda!"

I dashed to her side.

Her only visible eye was staring at me blankly.

"Esmeralda!"

The eye blinked.

Esmeralda got dreamily to her feet and gave herself a good shaking, like a fat feather duster.

I cradled her in my arms, buried my face in the softness of her breast, and burst into tears.

"You goose!" I said into her feathers. "You silly goose! You frightened me half to death."

Esmeralda pecked at my mouth, as she sometimes did when I put millet seeds between my lips for her to discover.

"How did you manage to get in here?" I asked, even though I thought I already knew the answer.

Dogger must have brought her up to my laboratory, as he did when she was being a nuisance in the greenhouse. And now that Dogger came to mind, I remembered he once told me that some chickens were given to treating themselves to dust baths during which they behaved as if hypnotized. And the floor was certainly dusty.

The truth of the matter is, I wanted to throw myself down on the floorboards and have a jolly good wallow in the dirt myself. I was sick of this constant being on show that Harriet's sudden reappearance had brought us: this going about in utter silence; this being dressed forever in our best; this perpetual watching of our words; this being always on our best behavior; these round-the-clock reminders of returning to dust.

It was probably time to think about giving the place a good housecleaning.

But not just yet. My sudden tendency to tears had shaken me.

"What am I going to do, Esmeralda?" I asked.

Esmeralda fixed me with her yellow eye: an eye as warm and mellow as the sun, and yet, at the same time, as old and cold as the mountains.

And in that instant, I knew.

Harriet.

Harriet was in the house and I needed to go to her.

She had something to tell me.

·EIGHT·

I SLIPPED SILENTLY OUT of my laboratory, locked the door, and made my way towards the seldom-used north hall which paralleled the front of the house. Even though Dogger had installed Lena and Undine in one or another of these cavernous crypts, there was little chance of running into them if I kept my wits about me.

Father had told us that he would be first to stand watch. And yet he was, as far as I knew, still in the drawing room, entranced by his grief. There would be little enough time, but perhaps if I hurried . . .

At the south end of the west wing, I put my ear to the door of Harriet's boudoir. I could hear nothing but the breathing of the house.

I tried the door and found it unlocked.

I stepped inside.

The room was hung in black velvet. The stuff was everywhere: on the walls, across the windows; even Harriet's bed and dresser were swathed in the dismal material.

In the center of the room, on draped trestles—a catafalque, Father had called it—was Harriet's coffin. The Union Jack had been replaced with a black pall bearing the de Luce coat of arms: per bend sinister sable and argent, two lucies haurient counterchanged. The crest, the moon in her detriment, and the motto "Dare Lucem."

"The moon in her detriment" was a moon eclipsed, and the "lucies," of course, were silver and black luces, or pikes, a double pun on the name de Luce. "Haurient" meant simply that the pikes were standing on their fishy tails.

And the motto, another pun on our family name: *Dare Lucem*—to give light.

Precisely what I was attempting to do.

At the head and foot of the catafalque, tall candles flickered with a weird glow in iron sconces, making the darkness dance with scarcely visible demons.

An almost perceptible mist hung round the candle flames, and in the awful silence I detected a faint odor upon the air.

I couldn't hold back a shudder.

Harriet was here—inside this box!

Harriet, the mother I had never known, the mother I had never seen.

I took three steps forward, reached out, and touched the gleaming wood.

How oddly and unexpectedly cold it was! How surprisingly damp.

Of course! Why hadn't I thought of it before?

In order to preserve it for the long trip home, Harriet's body would most likely have been packed in the solid form of carbon dioxide, or "card ice" as it is called. The stuff had first been described by the French scientist Charles Thilorier in 1834 after he had discovered it almost by accident. By mixing crystallized CO_2 with ether, he had been able to achieve the remarkably cold temperature of minus 100 degrees on the centigrade scale.

So inside this wooden shell there would have to be a sealed metal container—zinc, perhaps.

No wonder the bearers at the railway station had moved so slowly under their burden. A metal casing filled with card ice, plus the oaken coffin, plus Harriet would strain the shoulders of even the strongest men.

I sniffed at the oak.

Yes, no doubt about it. Carbon dioxide. Its faint, pungent, pleasantly acid smell gave it away.

How difficult would it be, I wondered, *to*—

Suddenly I heard the sound of footsteps in the hall. Father's boots! I was sure of it!

I whipped round behind the catafalque and ducked out of sight, hardly daring to breathe.

The door opened and Father came into the room and the door closed again.

There was a long moment of silence.

And then there came the most heartbreaking sound I have ever heard as great shuddering sobs began slowly to break off from my father like floes from an iceberg.

I jammed my forefingers into my ears and screwed them down. There are certain sounds which are meant never to be heard by children—even though I am no longer really a child—and the chiefest of these is the sound of a parent crying.

It was agony.

I crouched there behind the catafalque, above my head my frozen mother, a few feet away my convulsively crying father.

There was nothing to do but wait.

After a very long time, the muffled sounds seemed to have lessened, and I removed my fingers from my ears. Father was still weeping, but very quietly now.

He sucked in a convulsive, broken breath.

"Harriet," he said at last in a hoarse whisper. "Harriet, my heart, forgive me. It was I."

"It was I"?

Whatever could he mean by that? Father was obviously out of his mind with grief.

But before I could think about it, I heard him turn and leave the room.

It would soon be two o'clock, and the villagers would begin arriving at Buckshaw to pay their respects to Harriet's remains. Father would not want to be seen with moist eyes and had obviously gone next door to his own room to regain his composure. I knew that when the mourners arrived, they would find him showing only the stony face of that cold-fish colonel in whose shell he lived.

Stiff upper lip, and all that.

There were times I could kill him.

I waited long enough to count to twenty-three, then

crept to the door, listened, and tiptoed like a wraith into the corridor.

Moments later, I was soberly descending the staircase into the foyer.

Miss Deportment of 1951.

As I reached the bottom step, the doorbell rang.

For a moment, I thought of ignoring it. It was, after all, Dogger's duty to greet visitors, not mine.

"*What a shabby thought, Flavia,*" an unwelcome voice said inside my head. "*Dogger has enough on his plate without having to run to the door for every passing stranger.*"

My feet walked me across the foyer. I wiped my mouth with the back of my hand in case of overlooked jam or drool, straightened my clothing, adjusted my pigtails, and opened the door.

If I live to be a hundred I shall never forget the sight that met my eyes.

On the doorstep stood the Misses Puddock, Lavinia and Aurelia, the latter holding a bouquet of papery silver-white flowers.

"We've come, dear," Miss Lavinia said simply, clutching her string bag tightly in front of her chest. Miss Aurelia nodded happily and waved her free hand vaguely behind her.

I followed the direction of her gesture.

I could scarcely believe what I saw: Behind Miss Aurelia, a long column of mourners snaked down the steps, out across the gravel sweep, across the lawn to the drive, along the avenue of chestnuts, and into the distance, all the way to the Mulford Gates and beyond.

Rich people, poor people, friends and strangers, men, women, and children, all with their eyes on the front door of Buckshaw and every last one of them dressed in black.

Aside from in cinema films, I had never seen so great a horde of people gathered together in one place.

"We've come, dear," Miss Aurelia reminded me, poking my shoulder with a sharp finger. Miss Lavinia twisted her string bag, and I knew at once that she had come prepared: that she had brought sheet music suitable for the occasion in the hope that she and her sister would be called upon to perform some appropriate dirge.

I have to admit I was thrown into a tizzy. For the first time in my life, I didn't know what to do.

How was I to deal with all these people? Was I to greet them one by one? Usher them, one or two at a time, in an orderly fashion into the house and herd them up the stairs to the chamber of mourning?

What was I to say to them?

I needn't have worried. My elbow was suddenly seized in an iron grip and a voice hissed into my ear: "Get lost."

It was Feely.

In spite of the dark circles under her eyes, which, I noticed, had been artfully retouched, not to hide but to enhance them, she was the image of bereaved beauty. She simply *glowed* with grief.

"Oh, Miss Lavinia," she said in a weak, exhausted voice, "Miss Aurelia. How awfully good of you to come."

She stuck out a pale hand and touched each of them in turn on the forearm.

As she turned her head Flavia-wards, she gave me *such* a glare!

Feely had the knack of being able to screw one side of her face into a witchlike horror while keeping the other as sweet and demure as any maiden from Tennyson. It was, perhaps, the one thing I envied her.

"We brought these, dear," Miss Aurelia said, thrusting the flowers at Feely. "They're *immortelle*. Xeranthemum. They're said to represent, you know, the Resurrection and the Life. They're from our greenhouse."

Feely took the flowers and sandwiched herself between the sisters as if for support, and was already moving with them into the foyer, leaving me alone on the doorstep to face what Daffy would call the madding crowd.

I was taking a deep breath, determined to do my best, when a voice at my ear said, "I'll look after this, Miss Flavia."

It was Dogger. And, as always, in the nick of time.

With a grateful and yet bereaved smile, since we were still on public display, I turned and floated wistfully into the house. In the foyer, I took to my heels and was up the east staircase like a rocket.

"*The resurrection and the life*," Miss Aurelia had said.

There it was again! From the Apostle's Creed: " . . . *the resurrection of the body and the life everlasting*."

I recalled instantly my own thought: "*I have restored my mother to life through the magic of chemistry*."

After developing the ciné film upon which Harriet's images appeared, those words had rung out in my mind like Christmas bells. Something else, too, had chimed: the sound of the inner shiver which indicated that something unknown was being stored up for a later time.

Now it came shooting with full awareness back into my brain.

I would bring my mother back to life! And this time, it would not be just a dopey dream, but an actual scientific accomplishment.

There was so much to do—and so precious little time.

·NINE·

FATHER HAD DECREED THAT we, the immediate family, would take turns standing watch over Harriet. He himself would take the first shift of six hours, he had decided, from two until eight o'clock. Feely, as next oldest, would serve from eight till two in the morning, followed by Daffy until eight A.M., at which time I was to take over until two in the afternoon. Aunt Felicity had at first been written off on grounds of age.

"Nonsense, Haviland!" she had told him. "I'm as capable as you are. More, when you come right down to it. You must not deny me my vigil."

And so the rota had been rearranged. We each would be assigned a watch of 4.8 hours, which came out neatly, as Daffy pointed out, at 4 hours and 48 minutes per person.

Aunt Felicity would stand watch from 2:00 this afternoon until 6:48 in the evening; Father from 6:48 until

11:36; Feely from 11:36 until 4:24; Daffy from 4:24 until 9:12 in the morning; and me from then until 2:00 tomorrow afternoon, the time of the funeral.

It was a typical de Luce solution: logical beyond question, and yet, at the same time, mad as a March hare.

There was just one problem: In order to carry out the work I intended to do, my watch needed to be in the latest hours of the night and the earliest hours of the morning.

In short, I needed to switch shifts with Feely.

Feely, however, was busy soaking up sympathy from the Misses Puddock and I didn't want to deprive her of that. I'd tackle her later about swapping shifts.

Meanwhile, I needed to prepare for what might well prove to be the greatest chemical experiment of my life. There wasn't an instant to lose.

Upstairs in my laboratory I riffled through my notebook. I knew I had written down the details somewhere.

Ah, yes—here it was: *Hilda Silfverling, a Fantasy*, by Lydia Maria Child. Daffy had once entertained us with it at the breakfast table: the tale of a poor, unfortunate woman in Sweden who was about to have her head chopped off after being falsely accused of infanticide.

I had never forgotten the learned chemist of Stockholm in the story, "*whose thoughts were all gas, and his hours marked only by combinations and explosions*."

To be perfectly honest, it was the only part of the tale that had really interested me. This scientist, whose name was never given so that I could look him up in *Scientific*

Lives, had discovered a process of artificial cold by which he could suspend animation in living creatures. Even more importantly, he had discovered a way to restore the subject, Hilda Silfverling in this case, to life whenever he wished.

"Is that really possible?" I had asked.

"It's fiction," Daffy had said.

"I know. But couldn't it be based on truth?"

"All writers would have you believe that their stories are based on truth, but the word 'fiction' is formed from a word meaning 'to contrive.' You, in particular, ought to relate to that."

I bit my tongue, hoping she would continue, and she did.

"Take Jack London, for instance," she said. My sister loved to show off.

"What about him?"

"Well, he wrote what amounted to essentially the same story. 'A *Thousand Deaths*,' it was called. About a man whose occupation was allowing himself to be killed in as many different ways as you can imagine, then brought back to life by his father, who was something of a mad scientist."

"Like Dr. Frankenstein!" I said excitedly.

"Exactly. Except that this fool let himself be poisoned, electrocuted, drowned, strangled, and suffocated. Among other things," she added.

Now this was my kind of reading!

"Where can I find a copy?"

"Oh, in the library, somewhere," Daffy had sniffed, waving me away with an impatient hand.

It had taken quite a while, but in the end, I had found it almost by accident in a rather grubby penny book.

And what a disappointment! Rather than giving any specific details about his many deaths and resurrections, the author allowed his character to ramble on vaguely about magnetic fields, polarized light, nonluminous fields, electrolysis, molecular attraction, and a hypothetical force called apergy, which was claimed to be the opposite of gravity.

What a load of bloody codswallop!

I could have come up with a better theory of resurrection from the dead with both hands tied behind my back at the bottom of a pond in a potato sack.

In fact, I did, even though I couldn't take full credit for it myself.

I had been passing the time of day with Dogger in the greenhouse, trying to think of ways to ask him about his imprisonment with Father in a Japanese prisoner-of-war camp, but without actually seeming to.

"Dogger," I had asked with a burst of sudden inspiration, "do you know anything about jiujitsu?"

He pulled a root-bound plant from its pot and prodded it tenderly with his trowel. The root ball looked like a Martian's brain.

"Perhaps," he said at last, "a little."

I tried to breathe through my ears so as not to break his fragile train of thought.

"Long ago, before I—"

"Yes?"

"As a student—" Dogger said, picking at the roots with his fingers as if he were unraveling the strands of the

Gordian knot, "as a student, I had occasion to study for a time the Kano system of jiujitsu. It was popular in my day."

"Yes?" I couldn't think of anything else to say.

"I was much interested in the art of kuatsu, that branch of the subject which deals with the lethal blows, but much more important, the healing and restoration of life to those who may have suffered them."

My eyes must have widened. "Restoration of life?"

"Just so," Dogger said.

"You're pulling my leg!"

"Not at all," Dogger said, giving the plant a gentle shake to dislodge the old soil. "Professor Kano's methods were used for a time, I believe, in certain special instances by the Royal Life Saving Society, in cases of drowning."

"They restored drowning victims to life? Dead people?"

"I believe so," Dogger said. "Of course I never actually witnessed it myself, but I was nevertheless taught the sharp blow which was needed to restore life to the dead."

"Show me!" I said.

Dogger stood up and turned round. "Stick your finger into my spine."

I gave him a halfhearted prod.

"Higher," he said. "A little higher yet. Yes, that's it. The second lumbar vertebrum. A sharp blow there with the second knuckle will do the trick."

"Shall I try it?" I asked eagerly. "Get ready!"

"No," Dogger said, turning round to face me. "In the first place, I'm not dead, and in the second, the fatal blows are never actually delivered except in cases of dire emergency. In practice, it is sufficient to announce them."

"Biff!" I said, delivering a powerful punch with a projecting knuckle, but pulling it at the last possible instant. "Consider it delivered!"

"Thank you," Dogger said. "Very good of you, I'm sure."

"Phew!" I said. "Imagine that: the resurrection of the dead by a poke in the back. There's no mention of that in the Bible, but perhaps Jesus wasn't aware of it."

"Perhaps." Dogger smiled.

"It seems crazy, doesn't it? Completely crazy, when you come right down to it, I mean."

"Perhaps," Dogger said again, "and perhaps not. It is quite widely known that in the primitive societies, and perhaps no less in our own, the healers are quite often neurotics or psychotics."

"Meaning?"

"That they suffer from certain nervous disorders—that they may even be deranged."

"Do you believe that?"

The greenhouse was so still that I fancied I could hear the plants growing.

"Sometimes I must, Miss Flavia," Dogger said at last. "I have no other choice."

Those, then, had been the two instances that had set my mind on restoring Harriet to life. Although the very thought of such a thing might be repellent to some, I found it nevertheless exciting. Exhilarating, even!

In the first place, I had no fear of corpses: none whatsoever. The past year had brought me face-to-face with a half dozen of the deceased, and I must admit that I had found them all, each in his or her own way, far more interesting than their living counterparts.

Then, too, there was Father. How deliriously happy he would be to have his beloved restored to him! In all the years I could remember, I had never seen Father smile—I mean *really* smile and show his teeth.

With Harriet home and alive and happy among us on the drawing room hearth, Father would be a different person. He would laugh, make jokes, hug us, ruffle our hair, play games with us, and, yes, perhaps even kiss us.

It would be like living in an earthly paradise: a modern-day land of Cockaigne, such as is seen in those paintings by Pieter Brueghel that Feely is so fond of; a land of milk and honey in which there was no rationing, no bitterly cold rooms, and no decay.

Buckshaw would be new again, and we all of us would live together happily ever after until the cows came home.

All I needed now was to work out a few of the chemical details.

·TEN·

When I turned the key in the lock of my laboratory and stepped inside, I found Esmeralda perching contentedly on a nearby test-tube rack and Undine boiling an egg over a Bunsen burner.

"What are you doing in here?" I demanded. "How dare you! How did you get in?"

The place was becoming as peopled as Paddington Station.

"I came across the roofs," she said cheerily, "and down that little staircase." She pointed.

"Bugger!" I'm afraid I said, making a mental note to install a deadbolt.

"I needed to talk to you," she said, before I could say something worse.

"Talk to me? Why ever would you want to do that?"

"Ibu said I was never to go to bed angry with anyone."

"Well, what difference does that make? Besides, it isn't bedtime yet."

"No," Undine agreed, "it isn't. But Ibu sent me for my nap, and a nap counts as bed, doesn't it?"

"I suppose it does," I said grudgingly. "But what has that to do with me?"

"I'm cheesed off with you." She pouted, planting her fists on her hips. "I have a bone to pick with you and I can't possibly nap until we've had a jolly good chin-wag about it."

"Chin-wag?"

"A powwow. A council of war."

"And *what*," I asked, making my voice drip with sarcasm, "have I done to deserve your displeasure?"

"You treat me like a child."

"Well, you *are* a child."

"Of course I am, but that's hardly reason enough to treat me like one, do you see what I mean?"

"Yes, I think I do," I admitted.

How Daffy is going to love talking to this curious, nitpicking little creature! I thought.

"What, in particular, have I done?" I was almost afraid to ask.

"You underestimate me," she said.

I nearly chucked my kippers. "Underestimate you?"

"Yes, you set me at naught."

"I beg your pardon?" I laughed. "Do you even know what that means?"

"Set me at naught. It means you disbelieved me. You disbelieved me about the saltwater crocodile and you disbelieved me again when I told you that Ibu and I were at the railway station this morning."

"I did not!"

"Come off it, Flavia—admit it."

"Well," I said, "perhaps just a little . . ."

"See?" Undine crowed. "I told you so! I knew it!"

A sudden clever thought popped into my mind. Daffy had more than once accused me of possessing a certain low cunning, and she was right.

"When did you arrive at the station? Before or after the train?"

"Before—but only just. Ibu said, 'Here it comes now' as she was parking at the end of the platform."

"Which end?" I asked, almost too casually.

"The far end. I don't know my directions very well, but the end farthest from Buckshaw."

"The south end," I said. "The direction from which the train arrived."

Undine nodded. "Near the luggage trolley."

Now I knew she was telling the truth. Although there had been no luggage trolleys on the platform at Buckshaw Halt for years, someone had managed to rustle one up from somewhere for the occasion of Harriet's sad return. Part of my mind had noticed it being piled high with the luggage of those strangers, whoever they may be, who had brought her body home.

"Let's play a game," I suggested brightly.

"Oh," Undine said. "Yes, let's. I adore games."

"Do you know how to play Kim's Game?"

"Of *course*," she scoffed. "Ibu used to read to me from *Kim* at bedtime in Sembawang. She said it was a good fairy tale, even if Kipling *was* a goddamn Tory, and a jingoist to boot. He visited Sembawang, you know."

"Jingoist?" She had caught me by surprise. It was likely that even Daffy didn't know the meaning of the word.

"Yes, you know: like in the song."

And she began to sing in a curiously sweet and innocent voice:

"We don't want to fight but by jingo if we do,

"We've got the ships, we've got the men, we've got the money, too!

"Old England and Saint George!" she shrieked suddenly. *"One, two, three, four, five, six, seven, eight, nine, ten, eleven, twelve!*

"That's the way the song ends," she explained. "It's all I can remember."

I'll admit it: I was out of my depth. I needed to get this conversation back under control.

"Kim's Game," I reminded her.

"Kim's Game!" she cried, clapping her hands together with delight. "Twelve assorted objects are placed on a tray and covered with a silk scarf. We'll have Dogger do it! Then he whisks away the scarf and we have sixty seconds to study the items. The scarf is replaced and we each write down the names of as many as we can. Whoever remembers the most wins. That will be me."

There was no need for her to explain it to me. We had been made to play the wretched game to distraction on rainy evenings in Girl Guides—that is, until the night I had managed to smuggle a toad and a quite decent-sized adder under the silk.

As I have said before, elsewhere, that organization is not

noted for its sense of humor, and I had found myself on that occasion being made to sit in the corner once again wearing Miss Delaney's handmade but highly irregular "Crown of Thorns," which may have been amusing to some but not to me.

"Exactly," I said to Undine. "But just to keep things interesting, let's play the game a different way this time."

Undine clapped her hands happily again.

"Let's pretend that the railway platform is the tray and that all the people on it are the objects we have to remember."

"That's not fair!" Undine protested. "I don't know any of the people—except you and your family . . . and Mr. Churchill, of course. Ibu pointed you out."

"You had quite a good view of us, then?"

My Daimler mind was firing on all twelve cylinders.

"Top hole!" she said. "Like a box at the pantomime."

Something twisted inside me. It didn't seem right that the arrival of my mother's body at Buckshaw had been viewed by anyone, let alone this little twerp, as some kind of cheap music-hall entertainment.

"All right, then," I said, holding myself in check. "I'll begin. There was Aunt Felicity. She counts for one."

"And the men in uniforms who lifted your mother from the train. That's six—I'm winning!"

This was insane, I thought, but the game needed to go on.

"Father, Feely, Daffy, and me," I said. "And Dogger, of course. Six all."

"Not fair! I already counted the lot of you. Eleven to me!"

"Mrs. Mullet," I said, "and her husband, Alf."

"The vicar!" Undine shouted. "I knew him by his collar! Twelve ho!"

I counted on my fingers: "The woman with Aunt Felicity . . . the officer who saluted Father . . .

"The engine driver on the footplate," I added with sudden inspiration, "the conductor, and the two guards on the van. That's nine, plus Sheila and Flossie Foster and Clarence Mundy, the taxicab driver."

Although I thought I had spotted Sheila and Flossie at the edge of the platform, I had picked Clarence's name out of thin air. Undine would never know the difference.

"Tied at twelve," I told her. "I'm finished. Last chance."

Undine gnawed at her knuckles, her brow furrowed. "That man in the long coat!" she said, her face lighting up.

My heart stopped.

"What man in the long coat?" I managed, my voice trembling a little. "You're making him up."

"The one who was talking to Ibu!" she shouted. "I win!"

Her face was a little, round glowing orb, red with excited accomplishment.

I even smiled a little myself.

I watched as Undine's happy smile slowly froze—and then solidified. She was staring over my shoulder—like the stranger at the station—as if she had spotted a specter.

The hair at the back of my neck was already bristling with strange electricity as I turned slowly round.

Lena was standing in the doorway and I swear her eyes were glowing like red coals in the darkness of the hall. How long she had been there, and how much she had overheard, I couldn't begin to guess.

"Go to your room, Undine," she said in a voice that was like a cold wind blowing through frozen grass.

Without a word, Undine brushed past me and vanished.

"You mustn't encourage her," Lena said when the little girl was gone. She spoke in that same odd voice, as if she were a ventriloquist's dummy being operated by a cobra. "She's far too excitable. Living too much in one's imagination may be detrimental to one's health."

She smiled at me and lit a cigarette. When it was drawing to her satisfaction, she blew a trumpet of smoke from a protruding lower lip towards the ceiling.

"Do you understand?"

"Detrimental to one's health," I repeated.

"Exxxs-zactly!" Lena said, and let out another cannonade of smoke.

I made a swift calculation of the risk involved and then blurted out: "Who was he? The man in the long coat, I mean?"

Lena touched her cigarette to her lips in a picturesque fashion. "I don't know what you're talking about."

"The man on the railway platform. The one Undine saw you talking to."

Lena walked over to one of the laboratory's casement windows, placed her palms on the sill, and stood looking down upon the Visto for what seemed like an eternity.

Was she remembering happier days? Those days when Harriet took off and landed in *Blithe Spirit* on that grassy expanse?

"How well did you know my mother?" I asked. She had not even answered my first question and here I was already pelting her with another. I was almost, but not quite, aghast at my own boldness.

"Not as well as I should have liked," she said. "We de Luces, as you know, are a peculiar lot."

I smiled at her as if I knew what she was talking about.

"'Cousin Excelsior,' we used to call her in Cornwall. Harriet flew further, farther, and faster than any human being has a right to do. I suppose in some quarters that was resented."

"In yours?"

I couldn't believe my mouth!

"No, not in mine." Lena turned away from the window. "I cared for her a great deal."

Cared for her a great deal? Those were the precise words Undine had used to express her mother's feelings towards Harriet.

"In fact," Lena went on, "we were quite chummy, your mother and I—at least when we ran into each other outside of a family setting."

I sat there in utter stillness hoping the vacuum created by my silence would attract more words about my mother. I had learned by close observation of Inspector Hewitt's questioning techniques that silence is a question mark that cannot be ignored.

"I'm going to confide in you," Lena said at last.

Hallelujah! My trap had worked!

"But you must promise me that what I say goes no further than this room."

"I promise," I said, meaning it at the time.

"Undine is a most unusual child," she said.

I nodded sagely.

"Hers has not been an easy life. She lost her father in tragic circumstances when she was no more than a baby—much like yourself."

For a moment I took this to be an insult, but then I saw what she meant—that both Undine and I had lost a parent while still in the cradle.

I nodded again, this time sadly.

"Undine is rather a highly strung child, I'm afraid. She requires a very particular kind of handling."

Lena stopped and stared at me as if she were allowing time for some crucial meaning to penetrate my brain.

Although I knew instantly what she was getting at, I decided to receive her barely coded message by letting my face melt into a slack, village idiot expression. I stopped short, though, of letting my tongue loll out of the corner of my mouth.

One of the marks of a truly great mind, I had discovered, is the ability to feign stupidity on demand.

She ignored me and looked slowly round the room as if she had never noticed it before—as if she were awakening gradually from a dream.

"This was your uncle Tarquin's laboratory, was it not?"

I nodded, barely capable.

There was another restless silence, and she went again to the casement window—the same window, I realized with a small ripple of gooseflesh, at which the military stranger had appeared in the ciné film.

What remarkable things windows are when you stop to think about it: silica, potash, soda, and lime combining in thin sheets to form a solid you can see through.

Even now, I realized—at this very instant—Lena was looking out at the world through the same crystal lattice as the stranger had so many years ago, the same crystal lattice through which the ciné camera had looked in at the stranger.

A window, I realized, can exist almost unchanged itself while looking out upon the ever-changing ages. A miracle of chemistry right here under our very noses!

Window glass, technically, is a liquid. A slow-flowing liquid, but a liquid nonetheless. Drawn by gravity, it can take hundreds—or even thousands!—of years to flow the same quarter inch that water can travel in a thousandth of a second.

My friend Adam Sowerby, the flora-archaeologist, had not long ago remarked that a simple flower seed was our one true time machine. I made a mental note to set him straight: Next time I saw him, I would insist he add plain ordinary window glass to his somewhat hasty theory.

"I've decided to enlist your assistance, Flavia," Lena said with sudden determination, turning away from the window and breaking in upon my thoughts.

Her face was half in shadow and half in light, like one of those black-and-white Venetian carnival masks you sometimes see in the illustrated papers.

I made plummy lips and gave her the barest nod of submission.

"Undine, you see," she began, choosing each word as carefully as if she were choosing diamonds, "Undine, you see—Good Lord!"

Something shot past the window outside, blocking the sunlight and, for an instant, plunging the room into semidarkness.

"Good Lord," Lena said again, her hand to her breast, "what in the name of—"

I was already at the window, pushing past her to get my nose against the glass.

"It's *Blithe Spirit*!" I shouted. "Harriet's plane! It's come home!"

And indeed it had. As I watched, the de Havilland Gipsy Moth touched down as lightly as a feather in the scrubby grass of the Visto and came to a jaunty stop among the foxgloves and the odd bits of shattered statuary that projected here and there from the weeds.

With its engine revving, it turned and teetered, its control surfaces waggling and flapping saucily as if to say "There! Wasn't that something?"

Needless to say, I was out of the room like a brick from a ballista, down the east staircase, out the front door—where the long queue of waiting mourners watched in silent astonishment as I flew past them—galloping across the overgrown ruins of the tennis courts and onto the weedy wasteland of the Visto.

I was alongside *Blithe Spirit* even before her propeller clattered to a halt, and a tall man—an excessively tall man—began to unfold himself from the cockpit.

There was more of him than it seemed possible for such a frail craft to have contained, but he kept coming and coming until at the end of one of his impossibly long legs a foot appeared, a foot which lifted itself neatly out over the cowling and planted itself on the root of one of the wings.

He shoved up the goggles covering his eyes, then unsnapped his flying helmet and lifted it to reveal the most golden head of hair that had ever existed on the planet since Apollo flew about in his personal cloud during the Trojan War.

Suddenly, and for just an instant, my heart seemed to have filled with air, and just as suddenly, it deflated and the feeling passed.

I raked my toe in the dust. What was happening to me?

"Miss de Luce, I expect?" he asked, extending a hand. "I'm Tristram Tallis."

His voice was clipped and yet mellow: frank, man-to-man.

I didn't dare touch him. Even the simple act of shaking hands with a god could turn one into a thornbush, and I knew that for a fact.

"Yes," I managed. "Flavia. How did you know?"

"Your mother," he said gently. "You are her very image."

Suddenly, and without an instant's warning, hot globs of water had sprung from my eyes and were streaming down my cheeks. I had, for days, intentionally been trying to keep my brain so busy with details, so full of this and that, that there was no farthest nook or cranny left to think about the fact that my mother was dead.

And now, in a single unguarded instant, a word from a stranger had reduced me to a sodden pulp.

Fortunately, Mr. Tallis was enough of a gentleman to pretend he hadn't noticed. "I say, pity about Oxford, isn't it?"

"Oxford?" He had caught me completely off guard.

"The University Boat Race. Easter weekend. At Henley. Oxford sank. Hadn't you heard?"

Of course I'd heard, and so had everyone else in England—in the whole world, for that matter. By now it had likely been shown in cinema newsreels from London to Bombay.

But that had been several days ago. Only an Englishman of a certain type could still have the incident running foremost in his brain.

Or was he joking?

I peered carefully at his face, but he gave away nothing.

I couldn't stop the smile from creeping up my cheeks.

"I *had* heard, as a matter of fact," I said. "Bugger Cambridge."

I'll admit I was taking a chance. I had no idea, rather than the slightest hint in his accent, to which of our great universities he might belong. But since he had said "pity about Oxford," I was going to take a chance that he was not being sarcastic.

His ready smile told me that I had judged correctly.

"RAW-ther!" he said, laying it on a bit thick.

The crisis had passed. We had managed a delicate moment quite nicely, the two of us, in the most civilized way of all: deflection.

Father would be proud of me—I know *I* was.

I laid an affectionate hand on *Blithe Spirit*'s taut fabric, which gave off in the warm sunlight a slight but comforting reek of nitrocellulose lacquer. How perfect, in a way, I thought, that an aircraft's skin should be painted with explosive guncotton in its liquid form.

I sniffed my fingers surreptitiously, and in that instant added to my store of memories a smell that would from now and forever, until the end of time, never fail to remind me of Harriet.

I glanced up—guiltily, for some odd reason—at the laboratory windows to see if Lena was watching, but the old glass, like the clouded eyes of some village ancient, showed no more than the reflected sky.

·ELEVEN·

"BEAUTY, ISN'T SHE?"

Tristram Tallis brushed away an imaginary particle of dust from one of *Blithe Spirit*'s wings. "I bought her from your mother just before the War. We've had some grand times together, the old girl and I."

And he suddenly went the color of pickled beetroot. "*Blithe Spirit* and I, I mean. Not your mother."

I looked at him blankly.

"I must make a clean breast of it, though: I renamed her years ago. *She's* now a *he*: *Typhon*."

It seemed a sacrilege but I didn't say so.

"I trust you've spent many pleasant hours flying her—him."

"Not so many as I'd like. *Typhon*—"

He saw the pained look on my face.

"All right, then, *Blithe Spirit*, if you like, has been hangared for years."

"So you haven't done much flying."

"I shouldn't say that," he said quietly. "No, I shouldn't say that at all. I've had my innings."

"You were in the RAF!" I said as the light came on in my brain.

"Biggin Hill." He nodded modestly. "Mostly Spitfires."

Crikes! Here I was condescending to one of the young men Mr. Churchill had called "The Few": one of those youthful warriors who had climbed high into the sky above England's green and pleasant land to take on the German Luftwaffe.

I had seen their photos in the back issues of *Picture Post* that littered the library of Buckshaw like drifts of fallen autumn leaves: those boyish pilots who, in their life vests and sheepskin flying boots, draped themselves in canvas deck chairs in the grass, awaiting the grated voice from the Tannoy system to call them to action.

I couldn't wait to introduce Tristram Tallis to Dieter! And to Feely!

"When I heard about your mother," he said, "I knew I needed to bring *Blithe Spirit* back to Buckshaw. I—I mean—dash it all! I'm not very good at this sort of thing."

But I understood him perfectly.

"My mother would have been grateful," I told him. "And she'd have wanted me to thank you."

"Look, this is deuced awkward," he said. "I don't know what your family will think of me barging in at a time like this—" He waved his hand vaguely towards where the long queue of villagers shuffled slowly and mournfully towards the house. "Dash it all! I mean, landing on your lawn as if Buckshaw were the bally old airfield at Croydon. I mean—"

"Think nothing of it, Mr. Tallis," I told him, desperately trying to cover up the fact that I was floundering badly. When it came to the social graces, I was in far over my head.

How would Feely handle this? I wondered. I tried to put myself for a moment into my sister's shoes.

"Perhaps you'd care to come in and freshen up," I said, touching his wrist lightly and flashing him my most charming smile. "I expect flying gives you the most awful craving for a cup of tea."

It was exactly the right thing to say. A broad schoolboy grin split his face, and a moment later he was leading the way, with alarmingly long strides, towards the kitchen door.

"You seem to have been here before," I called to him, struggling to keep up.

I had meant it as a joke, but almost instantly, I realized what I had said. In a hidden room of my mind, a clinker fell in the bars of an iron grate and the fire blazed up.

That tall figure in the ciné film at the window of the laboratory. "Six foot three, or perhaps four," Dogger had said.

Tristram Tallis stopped so abruptly in his tracks that I almost collided with his posterior.

He turned round. Too slowly . . . ?

He pinned me with his hooded flyer's eyes.

"Of course I've been here before," he said. "The day your mother handed over *Blithe Spirit*."

"Were you wearing an American corporal's uniform?" I wanted to ask, but I did not. *"Were you poring over papers at the window of Uncle Tar's laboratory?"*

"Oh, yes—of course," I said. "I'd forgotten. How foolish of me."

The shadow passed, and a moment later we were strolling side by side along the red brick wall of the kitchen garden as if we were old pals.

I thought—but only for a moment—of taking his hand, but rejected the idea at once.

It would have been excessive.

"I hope you don't mind using the kitchen entrance," I said, thinking of the long queue of mourners at the front of the house.

"It wouldn't be the first time." He grinned, holding the door open for me in an elaborate manner.

"Mr. Tristram!" Mrs. Mullet shrieked when she saw his face. "Or should I call you Squadron Leader now?"

She came rushing towards us, extending a soapy hand, withdrawing it before he could grasp it, and collapsing into a sort of comic curtsy that left her stuck on one knee.

Tristram hoisted her gallantly to her feet. "Is the kettle on, Mrs. M? I've come for a cup of that wizard tea of yours."

"Just go right through to the drawing room," she said, suddenly formal. "If you'll be so good as to show Mr. Tristram in, Miss Flavia, I shall be in with the tea directly."

"I'd prefer to stay here with you in the control tower," he said. "Rather like old times."

Mrs. Mullet was now blushing like billy-ho, rushing round the kitchen, darting into the pantry, and clasping her hands whenever she looked at him.

"I've come at a sad time," he said, pulling out a chair at the kitchen table and folding himself into it.

"That's right. Sit yourself down. I shall fetch you a bit of my Arval bread. I made it special, like, for Miss 'Arriet—for 'er funeral, I mean, bless 'er soul."

She mopped at her eyes with her apron.

Meanwhile, my mind was flying circles above the conversation. "*Squadron Leader,*" Mrs. Mullet had said. And hadn't Tristram himself claimed to have been with one of the Biggin Hill fighter squadrons during the Battle of Britain?

How on earth, then, could he possibly have been at Buckshaw before the War dressed in the uniform of an American corporal?

Well, of course, there had been that laughable film *A Yank in the R.A.F.*, which we had been made to sit through as part of the parish hall cinema series, in which Tyrone Power and Betty Grable hopped across the pond to help save us from a fate worse than death.

But Tristram Tallis was no Yank. I was sure of it.

"I'll leave you two to catch up," I said, with what I hoped was a considerate smile. "I have a few things to do."

Up the east staircase I flew, two steps at a time.

First things first. The very thought of Lena being left alone in my laboratory was enough to give me the crowjinks. I should have shown her out politely before making my mad dash to the Visto, but there hadn't been time to think.

I needn't have worried, though. The laboratory door was closed, and the room itself was empty of everyone but

Esmeralda, who still sat dreamily perched on the test-tube rack, much as I had left her.

I checked the various traps I always leave set for unwary intruders: single hairs gummed across cupboards, ends of paper sheets jammed haphazardly in drawer openings (on the assumption that no snoop would ever be able to resist straightening them), and, behind each of the inner doors, a thimble filled to the brim with a solution of insoluble ferrocyanide of iron, or Prussian blue, which, once spilled, could not be washed away if seven maids with seven mops swept it for half a year.

My bedroom, too, was untouched, and I grudgingly awarded Lena a couple of mental marks for honesty.

Now, at last, having set the stage, I was ready to undertake the next and most difficult act: the tackling of Feely.

I had not forgotten my plan to resurrect Harriet: Oh no!—far from it. I had been banishing the idea from the forefront of my mind simply to keep from shrieking out with delight.

The very thought of how ecstatic Father would be was enough to make me hug myself inwardly.

As I crossed the foyer, the strains of the Adagio cantabile from Beethoven's *Pathétique* came drifting along the hall from the drawing room in the west wing. Each note hung for an instant in the air like a cold, crystalline drop of water melting from the end of an icicle. I had once referred to this sonata as "the old *Pathetic*" in Feely's hearing, and had been rewarded with a near miss by a flung metronome.

This particular bit of Beethoven is, I think, the saddest piece of music ever written since the beginning of time, and I knew that Feely was playing it because she was devastated. It was meant for Harriet's ears alone—or for her soul—or for whatever might remain of her in this house.

Even listening to it from as far away as the foyer made my eyes damp.

"Feely," I said at the drawing room door, "that's beautiful."

Feely ignored me and played on, her eyes fixed firmly on something in another universe.

"The sonata *Pathétique*, isn't it?" I asked, taking great care to pronounce it as if I had been born on the Left Bank and baptized in Notre-Dame.

I could do such things when I wanted to.

Feely slammed down the lid and the piano let out an injured roar of strings, which went echoing on and on for an impressive amount of time.

"You just can't resist, can you?" she shouted, waving her arms in the air as if she was still at the keyboard. "You do it every time!"

"What?" I asked. I don't mind having my knuckles rapped when I'm guilty, but I hate it when I've done nothing.

"You know perfectly well," Feely snarled. "And don't give me that gaping simpleton look of yours. Close your mouth."

I hadn't the faintest idea what she was talking about.

"You're just being tetchy," I told her. "We agreed that I could point out to you when you were being tetchy without having my head bitten off. Well, you're being tetchy."

"I am *not* being tetchy!" she shouted.

"If you're not being tetchy," I said, "then your brain is most likely being devoured by threadworms."

Threadworms were one of my latest enthusiasms. I had recognized at once their criminal possibilities when Daffy had brought them up one morning at the breakfast table. Not brought them up in the sense of vomiting, of course, but mentioned that she had been reading about them in some novel or another where they were being bred by a mad scientist with nefarious intentions who reminded her of me.

I had seized at once on the possibilities: a colony of threadworms raised in a glass tank in the laboratory, where they were allowed to crawl through soil saturated with cyanide. Was cyanide poisonous to the threadworm? Would they themselves survive while spreading the deadly poison through the brain of their victim with those bristles—*setae*, Daffy said they were called—which they possess instead of feet?

Feely was gathering a head of steam to erupt when I stopped her dead in her tracks.

"Actually, I've come to apologize," I told her.

"For what?"

"For being inconsiderate. I know how difficult all of this has been on you. I worry about you, Feely—I really do."

"Oh, horsewater!" she said.

In certain circumstances, my sister Feely had a remarkable way with words.

"Well, I do worry," I went on. "I know you're not getting enough sleep. Look at yourself in the mirror."

If there was one thing Feely did not need to be told, it

was to look at herself in the mirror. The looking glasses at Buckshaw—every last one of them—were flaking and peeling from Feely's constant examination of her own image: her eyes, her hair, her tongue, her complexion. . . .

Every last crater of her old phizog was cataloged as carefully as it would be by an astronomer mapping the moon.

Yes! It had worked. I could already see Feely craning her neck surreptitiously to have a squint at herself in the chimneypiece mirror. She had fallen for my clever ruse.

"You're pale," I said. "You've been like that since—" I bit off the next words and gnawed a little at my lower lip. "You always give too much of yourself to others, Feely. You never think of yourself."

I could see that I had her undivided attention.

"Miss Lavinia and Miss Aurelia, for instance," I went on. "I could have shown them upstairs to pay their respects. You didn't need to do that on top of everything else. You should be resting, damn it all!"

I surprised not only Feely, I surprised myself.

"Do you really think so?" she asked, drifting, as if absently, towards the chimneypiece and the hanging glass.

"Yes," I said. "I *do* think so. I also think you ought to let me take the late vigil with Harriet and let you get some sleep. You won't want to look haggard at the funeral, will you?"

This appeal to Feely's vanity was not exactly fair play, but all's fair in love and war and manipulating a stubborn sister.

Seeing that she was off guard, I decided to sit tight and see what happened. As I have mentioned before, it has been my experience that a prolonged silence has the same effect as a W.C. plunger when it comes to unclogging a stuck conversation.

And it worked. As I knew it would.

After a time, Feely drifted over to a sideboard and took out a piece of sheet music.

"Look what I found tucked into Tchaikovsky," she said, handing it over.

I knew that Feely never played Tchaikovsky if she could help it.

"Too many sequins," she had once told Flossie Foster, and Flossie had nodded knowingly.

Feely handed me a rather dog-eared piece of sheet music.

I took the music from her and read the cover. "Bitter Sweet, *an operetta in three acts by Noël Coward.*"

Feely flipped the fragile pages. "Look here—near the end."

Ta-ra-ra Boom-de-ay, I read.

"Harriet loved it. I think it was her favorite song. She used to sing it to Daffy and me when we were children."

"*She never sang it to me*," I wanted to say, but of course I didn't. I was just a baby when Harriet vanished in Tibet.

"It's an old music-hall song," Feely said, spreading the pages open on the piano's music holder.

She placed her hands on the keys and began to play, quietly, so as not to be overheard by the mourners.

"Ta-ra-ra BOOM-de-ay!" she sang. "Ta-ra-ra BOOM-de-ay.

"Do you know it?"

Actually I did, but I pretended I didn't. I shook my head. We had been forced to sing the thing in Girl Guides back in the days before I was cashiered.

It was not the most intelligent song I had ever heard.

"I sometimes wonder," Feely mused, "how well we really knew Harriet—if she was really the person we thought she was."

"I wouldn't know about that," I said sourly.

Feely repeated the first couple of bars on the piano—softly, almost wistfully in a minor key—then picked up the music and put it away.

"About the vigil—" I began.

But before I could say another word, Feely drifted back towards the looking glass.

"Agreed," she said, leaning in for a closer look at her cantankerous hide.

And that, incredibly, was that.

From 11:36 in the evening until 4:24 in the morning—four hours and forty-eight minutes, to be precise—I was to have Harriet entirely to myself.

·TWELVE·

AN ENDLESS QUEUE OF bodies snaked in through the open door and across the foyer, shuffling unaware across the black line which, in an earlier century, the warring brothers Antony and William de Luce had painted from front door to butler's pantry, dividing the house effectively into two distinct halves: a line which was never to be crossed.

Everyone wanted to catch my eye; everyone wanted to touch me, to clasp my hand or my arm and tell me how sorry they were that Harriet was dead.

There was a woman with a lantern jaw and her seven children, each with its own little lantern jaw. It was like looking at a display in the window of a chandler's shop. I could not remember ever seeing any of them before.

On the far side of the foyer was a skinny gentleman who looked like a startled broomstick. He, too, was a stranger.

"Dear Flavia," Bunny Spirling wheezed, taking my hand. He was one of Father's oldest friends, and as such, required some kind of personal response.

I gave him a glum smile, but it was not easy.

Although it seems shocking to say so, grief is a funny thing. On the one hand, you're numb, yet on the other, something inside is trying desperately to claw its way back to normal: to pull a funny face, to leap out like a jack-in-the-box, to say "Smile, damn you, smile!"

It is impossible for a young heart to remain gloomy for long, and I could already feel the muscles in my face growing tired from trying.

"The daffodils are so beautiful," I heard myself telling Bunny, and I saw the tears spring to his eyes as he thought about how brave I was.

Bunny was unaware that the toe of one of his polished black shoes was planted directly on the black painted line: the line that split the house—and our family—into two.

When you came right down to it, it was all about lines, wasn't it? This black line in the foyer, and the white one that Aunt Felicity had told me I must walk: "*Although it may not be apparent to others, your duty will become as clear to you as if it were a white line painted down the middle of the road. You must follow it, Flavia.*"

They were one and the same, this black line and that white line. Why hadn't I realized that before?

"*Even when it leads to murder.*"

An icy chill seized me as a horrible thought crept from my brain to my heart.

Had Harriet been murdered?

"It was decent of the government to lay on a special train to bring her down," Bunny was saying, his spread hands cradling his substantial stomach as if it were a football. "Damnably decent, but no less than what she deserved."

But I hardly heard his words. My mind was racing in overlapping circles like a motorcycle in the Wall of Death.

Harriet . . . the stranger under the wheels of the train . . . were their deaths connected? And if so, was their killer still at large? Could their killer be here at Buckshaw?

"You must excuse me, Mr. Spirling," I said. "I'm feeling rather . . ."

I did not need to finish.

"Take the girl to her room, Maude," Bunny said in a commanding voice.

A little woman appeared beside him as if she had materialized from thin air. She had been there all along, I realized, but so tiny was she, so still, so quiet, and so transparent that I had not noticed her.

I had seen Mrs. Spirling around the village, of course, and at church, but always in the shadow of the looming figure of her husband, Bunny, in whose shade she was nearly invisible.

"Come along, Flavia," she said in a voice far too deep for such a frail creature, and, taking my arm in an iron grip, she steered me towards the stairs.

I felt slightly ridiculous, being led along by someone who was shorter than myself.

Halfway up the first flight she stopped, turned to me, and said, "There's something I want you to know: something I feel I must say to you. Your mother was a remarkably strong woman. She was not as other people."

We continued upwards. At the landing she said, "How very difficult this must be for you."

I nodded.

As we climbed the second flight she said, "Harriet always told us that she would come back—that no matter what happened, she would return—that we mustn't worry. One always hopes, of course," she said, letting go of my arm, "but now—"

At the top of the stairs she took my hand. "We came to think of her as being immortal."

I could see that she was controlling the muscles of her face with only the greatest difficulty.

"I like to think that, too," I replied, feeling suddenly and inexplicably wiser, as if I had just returned from a voyage of discovery.

"I don't suppose you've had more than a couple of hours' sleep in the past week, have you?" she asked.

I shook my head stupidly.

"I thought not. The thing is to get you to bed. In you go."

We had arrived at the door of my bedroom.

"I'll have Bunny tell your father you're not to be disturbed. I'd ask Dogger to bring you up some hot milk to help you sleep, but he's busy with the hordes at the door. I shall bring it myself."

"No need, Mrs. Spirling," I said. "I'm so tired, I—"

I threw out a hand to brace myself against the door jamb.

"A few hours' sleep will work wonders. I'm sure of it," I told her, opening the door just enough to slip inside and peer back out at her.

"Thank you, Mrs. Spirling," I said with a frail grin. "You're a lifesaver."

I shut the door.

And counted to thirty-five.

I dropped to my knees and applied my eye to the keyhole.

She was gone.

I took a piece of stationery from the drawer of my bedside table and wrote on it with a pencil, in an intentionally weak and spidery scrawl: *Unwell. Ps. Do not disturb. Thnk you. Flavia.*

I dragged the *Ls* a bit so they looked as if I hadn't the strength to lift the pencil from the paper.

Checking that the coast was clear, I stepped out into the hall, stuck my note to the door with a bit of chewing gum purloined from the supposedly secret dragon's horde of the stuff at the back of Feely's U-wear drawer.

I locked the door and pocketed the key.

Moments later I was barricaded in my laboratory, ready to begin preparations for the most important chemical experiment of my life.

For nearly twenty years after the death of Tarquin de Luce, his notebooks had stood untouched: row upon row of sober black-clad soldiers. There was nothing I loved better than to browse in their pages, dipping into a volume at random, savoring each delicious chemical insight as if it were a treacle tart.

Needless to say, the word "poison" always caught my eye, as it did in a brief footnote in which Uncle Tar mentioned the work of Takaki Kanehiro, a Japanese naval surgeon whose work led to the discovery—by Eijkman, Hopkins, and others—that a solid diet of white rice produced in the body a nerve poison whose antidote, oddly enough, was the very husk which had been removed in preparing the rice for consumption!

It was a theory I had postulated myself after being subjected to a lifetime of Mrs. Mullet's rice puddings, of which the least said, the better.

This antidote, which was at first called *aneurin* because of what its absence did to the nerves, turned out to be thiamine, which was later given the designation vitamin B_1.

The existence of vitamins, or "vital amines," as he had called them, had been suggested by Kazimierz Funk: these somewhat mysterious organic compounds which are required by all living organisms but cannot be synthesized by the organism itself.

One of Uncle Tar's many correspondents, a Cambridge student named Albert Szent-Györgyi, had written to ask his advice regarding his recent discovery of what he was then calling *aneurin*.

Aneurin again! Vitamin B_1.

Uncle Tar had replied suggesting that Szent-Györgyi's aneurin might play an important role in the generation of the energy by which all oxygen-dependent organisms convert into carbon dioxide the acetate they derive from the fats, proteins, and carbohydrates of the diet.

Life, in short!

He also hinted that an injectable form of the vitamin called cocarboxylase hydrochloride was vital in restoring life to deceased laboratory rats that had been frozen.

I shall never forget the electric thrill that shot through me from head to toe upon reading these words.

The restoration of life! Precisely as promised in the Apostle's Creed!

And yet cocarboxylase hydrochloride was only part of the story.

There was also the matter of adenosine triphosphate, or ATP, which had been discovered in 1929 at Harvard University Medical School: too late for Uncle Tar, who had died suddenly of a heart attack the previous year, but not too late for me.

I had first read about the stuff in *Chemical Abstracts & Transactions*, a journal to which Uncle Tar had fortunately purchased a lifetime subscription and which, nearly a quarter century after his death, was still being delivered by the postman every month to Buckshaw as regular as clockwork.

The introduction of ATP into the bloodstream was thought to have much the same reanimating effect upon the spines of the dead as cocarboxylase hydrochloride did upon the heart and pancreas.

This, then, was how I would restore Harriet to the land of the living: a monumental injection of ATP combined with a similar dosage of cocarboxylase hydrochloride.

With these two chemicals already at work in her thawing body, I would then apply Professor Kano's knuckle blow to her second lumbar vertebrum.

It was a brilliant idea, and because it was scientific, it simply could not fail.

·THIRTEEN·

THE PROBLEM WAS THIS: Where was I to find the ingredients?

The vitamin B_1 could, of course, be extracted from yeast, but the process was time-consuming and smelly and could not, I decided, be conducted under the very noses of family, guests, and visitors without raising certain embarrassing questions.

The ATP, though, was going to be a horse of a different hue. Although discovered more than twenty years ago, it had only been successfully synthesized recently by one Alexander Todd at Cambridge, and was probably as scarce as hen's dentures.

I could not even begin to guess how to get my hands on the stuff. It seemed reasonable to assume that if anyone in the vicinity of Bishop's Lacey possessed a sample, it would be a doctor, a veterinarian, or a chemist's shop.

I suppose I could have telephoned Dr. Darby, or Cruickshanks, the village chemists, but the telephone at Buckshaw, having been the instrument by which Father had first learned of Harriet's disappearance more than ten years ago, was strictly off limits.

Now that the news of her death had reached his ear through that same somber black earpiece, it held even greater terrors for him, and accordingly for us all.

There was nothing for it but to cycle into Bishop's Lacey and make my inquiries in person. Actually, I decided, it was preferable that way: With the telephone, people can always ring off with the feeblest of excuses. In person, it could be much more difficult to shake off Flavia de Luce.

"Gladys," I whispered at the door of the greenhouse. "It's me, Flavia. Are you awake?"

Gladys was my BSA Keep-Fit bicycle. She had belonged originally to Harriet, who had named her *l'Hirondelle*, "the swallow"—I suppose because of the way she swooped and darted while racing down deliciously steep hills—but I had rechristened her Gladys because of her happy nature.

Gladys *was* awake. Of course she was. Like the Pinkerton Detective Agency, her motto was "We Never Sleep."

"Quick conference," I told her. "We shall have to sneak out the back way. Too many people in front."

There was nothing that excited Gladys more than sneaking out the back way. We had performed that maneuver together on many occasions, and I think she took a certain naughty delight in having the opportunity to do it again.

She gave a tiny squeak of pleasure and I hadn't the heart to reprimand her.

I wheeled Gladys south and then west, taking great care to keep clear of the views from Father's study window and the drawing room. For a while, it was touch and go, darting from tree to tree, then peering back round to be certain that no one was following us.

After a time, it became less risky, and I pushed Gladys, my hand gently on her leather saddle, bumpety-bump across the rough fields to a country lane which led north to the main road.

Now, with my feet pressing happily down on her pedals, we sped along with a *tickety-tick* whirring noise that startled small birds in the hedgerows and caused an old badger to waddle comically for cover.

At the junction, we skidded to a stop. It was time for a decision. To the west lay Hinley and the hospital. Was there a chance that the dispensary there would have a supply of the needed ATP? Would Feely's friend's sister, Flossie Foster, be on duty? Would I be able to talk her into organizing a raid on the dispensary?

It seemed unlikely. The odds were probably staggering.

But—to the east lay Bishop's Lacey, in which were located both the surgery of Dr. Darby *and* Cruickshanks the Chemists.

With scarcely a pause, I turned Gladys's head towards the east, and off we sped to whatever might await us.

* * *

The bell over the door tinkled noisily in its bracket as I entered the chemists' shop.

The front of the place was bright enough, with sunlight streaming in through the large red and blue apothecary jars in the window, but beyond that, deeper into the shop, the light died a horrible death. The back of the room was a place of shadows, with a small dark counter at whose wicket Miss Clay was whispering, as if it were a confessional, into the ear of Lancelot Cruickshank, the chemist.

I pretended I couldn't hear them, even though the razor-keen sense of hearing I had inherited from Harriet had already told me that their conversation had to do with rhubarb pills and sulfur.

I drifted about the shop, staring as if hypnotized by the numbing collection of colorful tins, boxes, and bottles that lined the shelves: powders, pills, potions, lotions, elixirs, salves, salts, syrups, lozenges, ointments, and electuaries—a cure for every occasion.

"I shall be with you directly," Mr. Cruickshank called out, and then resumed his bluebottle buzzing with the unfortunate Miss Clay.

As they spoke, first one and then the other, I became aware that there was a third voice—a quieter voice, like a silken ribbon—weaving its way in and out of the conversation from time to time.

Although I could not see the speaker, I knew that it could be no one but Annabella Cruickshank, Lancelot Cruickshank's sister: a qualified chemist in her own right, but seldom seen about the village. A silent partner, so to speak. Silent and practically invisible.

She was, Daffy had once told me in a lighter moment, "the powder behind the throne," which seemed to me might possibly be a capital joke, and even though I didn't get the point of it, I had laughed too loudly and too long.

Out of no more than idle curiosity, really, I drifted somewhat closer to the back of the shop, hoping to overhear some snippet of gossip that I could parlay at home into a grown-up conversation with my sisters.

The closer I came to the dispensing counter, the more subdued the buzz of conversation became until—quite abruptly—it ended with a "Shhh" and the whispered word "Harriet."

At first, I was rather touched that they should be talking about my mother, but then I realized that they were talking about *me*.

"Excuse me, Mr. Cruickshank," I said, "I'm in rather a hurry. I wonder if you could please let me have some thiamine?"

There was a silence, and then his voice said from the shadows, "For what purpose is it required?"

"I'm afraid our poultry—" I was speaking of Esmeralda here, but I thought it best to imply that large quantities of the stuff might be required. "I'm afraid our poultry might be in need of a vitamin B supplement in their feed."

"Oh, yes?" Mr. Cruickshank said. I could already tell that he was not going to be helpful.

"Yes," I told him, flapping my arms like injured wings. "Classic symptoms: convulsions, tremors, staring at the sky, and so forth. Classic."

Dogger had described to me, during one of our discussions about the Buff Orpington breed, of which Esmeralda was a member in good standing, the so-called "Stargazer syndrome" in which a thiamine deficiency could cause the birds' neck muscles to contract and go awry, leaving the poor chickens able only to look upwards, and frequently causing them to fall over onto their backs.

"I thought I might pick up a bottle of B_1 tablets," I rattled on. "Pulverize them—add them to the feed. Sparingly, of course."

Mr. Cruickshank said nothing.

"It seemed like a good idea," I added lamely.

"The supplements in this shop are intended for human consumption only," he snapped. "They are not approved for poultry. I could not possibly be responsible for unforeseen consequences—"

"Nor would I expect you to, Mr. Cruickshank," I interrupted.

I always make it a point, when pleading, to speak aloud the name of the person being addressed. It makes things seem so much more—well, suckily subservient.

"No," Mr. Cruickshank said.

"I beg your pardon?" I asked. I couldn't believe my ears. I was not used to being cut dead at the first stroke of a duel.

"No," he repeated. "No thiamine."

"But—"

"And now if you'll excuse us," he said, nodding towards Miss Clay, who seemed to have been struck dumb by our exchange, "I expect you'll be having more to attend to than—"

He left the word "chickens" unspoken.

So much for sympathy. Things had not gone at all as I expected.

As often happens when one's brain locks up, I stood staring blindly at the floorboards until the low hum of conversation resumed.

Then I trudged heavy-footed to the door, defeated.

Outside, blinking in the sudden bright sunshine, I seized Gladys's handlebars and turned towards home. Without the thiamine, there was little sense in carrying on.

I hadn't gone more than a few yards when a voice, almost at my elbow, said, "Hist! Flavia."

I nearly leaped out of my skin.

I whipped round and found myself face-to-face with a wizened little woman whose skin was the dappled white and brown of an Indian pony in the cinema westerns. She had appeared suddenly from a narrow passageway that ran alongside the chemists' shop.

Annabella Cruickshank! It simply had to be.

"Here," she said, squinting in the sunlight, taking my hand in her mottled fingers, and forcing my own fingers to close around a brown bottle. "Take this."

"Oh, but I couldn't," I protested. "That is, thank you—but I insist on paying for it."

"No. I'm not doing this for you," she said, looking as piercingly into my eyes as if she were studying my soul. "I'm doing it for your mother. Let's just say it's the repayment of an old debt."

And then, as abruptly as she had appeared, she was gone.

·FOURTEEN·

I STOOD IN THE High Street realizing that I was utterly alone. The villagers were, for the most part, at Buckshaw mourning Harriet, leaving Bishop's Lacey a ghost town.

I placed the bottle in Gladys's wicker basket, shoved off, and pedaled to the east. Dr. Darby's surgery was just beyond Cow Lane.

His battered bull-nosed Morris was nowhere in sight.

I raised the door knocker—a serpent coiled round a staff—but couldn't bring myself to let it fall. Dr. Darby's wife was an invalid who was said never to leave her first-floor bedroom.

I was standing there with the brass serpent in my hand when a voice came drifting down from an open upper window.

"Who is it? Is that you, Flavia?"

"Yes," I called up. "Yes, it's me, Mrs. Darby. How did you know I was here?"

"The doctor's rigged up a mirror for me. Pulleys and so forth. All very clever. He's handy like that."

I looked up and spotted the glint of a glass surface wig-wagging from side to side before coming to rest.

"Is Dr. Darby at home?"

"No, I'm afraid not, dear. Have you cut yourself again?"

She was referring to an incident involving broken glass which I had yet to live down in certain quarters.

"I'm fine, Mrs. Darby. I just wanted to ask the doctor a question."

"Anything I can help you with, dear? I'm always happy to lend an ear if it's something in the nature of a personal problem."

How ridiculous this is, I thought. I had no personal problems—at least not any that I wanted to bellow back and forth to a woman in an upper room in the High Street who was keeping an eye on me with a mechanical mirror.

"No, nothing like that, thank you. I'll see him another time."

"He's at the hospital in Hinley," she informed me. "Very sad outcome there, I'm afraid. He rang up not half an hour ago saying he'd be late for lunch but he'd be here nonetheless."

"Thanks, Mrs. Darby. You've been extremely helpful. I hope you're feeling better soon. I'll bring you some flowers when I come back. The lilacs are in bloom at Buckshaw."

"*Dear* girl," she called down. "Dear *girl!*"

As I rode off, I realized that Mrs. Darby hadn't mentioned Harriet. Not a word. How very odd. Perhaps she didn't know. Ought I have told her?

The High Street was still empty as I pedaled along, head down, totally absorbed in my own thoughts.

There seemed to be so many questions—so few answers.

I hadn't forgotten the man under the train's wheels—how could I? But I simply hadn't had time to think about him. My brain was a whirlpool, rotating like all fury around the still center that was Harriet.

I was almost at St. Tancred's when I was deafened by a sudden loud noise: an earsplitting mechanical cawing of a klaxon horn and a hideous scream of brakes.

I looked up just in time to see an oncoming Morris leave the road, scrape past a hair's breadth from my elbow, go skidding across the verge, and come to an ominous-sounding stop against the churchyard wall.

Steam arose from its radiator.

I was fixed to the spot: frozen and trembling at the same time.

Dr. Darby, looking more than ever like John Bull, sprang out of the car with remarkable agility for a man his age and size, and came sprinting to my side.

"Damn it all!" he said. "Are you all right?"

I looked round rather stupidly, as if to find the answer in the church tower or the treetops, then nodded slowly.

He fished in the pocket of his waistcoat and pulled out a crystal mint, which he popped into his mouth.

He did not shout at me. He did not even raise his voice.

"Um. Near thing, that," he observed, offering me a lint-covered mint, which I took with shaking fingers. I could scarcely find my mouth.

When I'm finished growing up, I thought, *I want to be like him.*

"Come sit with me on the lych-gate," he said. "We both of us need a bit of a breather."

A moment later, I was dangling my legs as if I hadn't a care in the world, and so, after a minute or two, was Dr. Darby.

"How are you getting on?" he asked.

I blinked several times. The sun was dazzling my eyes.

"I'm all right," I said at last. "Thank you," I added.

"What are you up to these days? Any interesting experiments?"

I could have hugged him. He was not going to try to pry open my heart.

It was an opportunity sent by the gods. I couldn't resist.

"I was hoping to do some work with adenosine triphosphate," I blurted, "but I don't know how to get my hands on the stuff."

There was a silence.

"Good lord," Dr. Darby said at last. "ATP?"

I nodded.

"You're not planning to inject it into some poor, unsuspecting creature, I hope?"

It was the kind of philosophical question which might have baffled Plato—and even Daffy.

Was Harriet poor? Was she unsuspecting?

Not in the sense that Dr. Darby meant those words, I was sure.

Was she a creature?

Well, that would depend upon which definition one chose to use. I had looked up the word in the *Oxford English Dictionary* not long ago while trying to work out if it would be sinful to destroy a fly in the name of Science.

"*All things bright and beautiful,*" we sang in church,
"*All creatures great and small.*
"*All things wise and wonderful*
"*The Lord God made them all.*"

The *O.E.D.* wasn't much help. On the one hand, it said that "creature" meant anything created, animate or inanimate, while another definition stated that it referred to a living creature or animate being, as opposed to "man."

The moral choice was left up to the individual.

"No," I said.

"Not that it's my place to check you up." Dr. Darby smiled.

We sat there in silence for a few minutes, surrounded by the moundy graves in the churchyard, kicking at the wall with our four heels.

"It is good to sit on a wall with a young woman on a sunny summer day," the doctor said. He could see by my grin that I couldn't agree more. He was flattering me but I didn't mind.

"It makes up in part for the less happy occasions."

I let the silence lengthen until he said: "We lost a girl today . . . about your age. At the hospital. Her name was Marguerite and she didn't deserve to die."

"I'm sorry," I told him.

"There are times when all we doctors with all our fabled skills are simply not enough. Death defeats us."

"You must be sad," I said.

"I am. Damned sad. She suffered from what we call an idiopathic neuropathy. Do you know what that means?"

"It means you don't know the cause," I said.

"We're working on it," Dr. Darby said, nodding wearily, "but it's early days yet. Early, that is, for the rest of us—but too late, I fear, for Marguerite."

"Was she beautiful?" I asked. It seemed desperately important to know.

Dr. Darby nodded.

I pictured the dying Marguerite with her golden hair spread out across a pillow, her face pale and damp, her black-circled eyes shut, her mind already in another world. I pictured her grieving parents.

"And there was nothing you could do?"

"We had been going to administer ATP as a last-ditch attempt, but—how very odd, you see, that you should have mentioned it."

"ATP? Adenosine triphosphate?"

"It's in my bag." He pointed towards the still-steaming Morris. "An old school chum managed to wangle a couple of trial doses. Not much need for it now, I'm afraid."

Was Dr. Darby telling me what I thought he was telling me? I scarcely dared breathe.

"If you wish to have it, it's yours," he said, sliding down from the wall and walking towards his car. "I'll have to get Bert Archer to tow old Bessie into dry dock."

"I'm sorry about your car," I said. "I should have watched where I—"

Dr. Darby held up a hand, its palm towards me. "The poet Cowper," he said, "who knew whereof he spoke, once wrote, 'God moves in a mysterious way, his wonders to perform.' We mere mortals must never question what we sometimes take to be the blind workings of Fate."

He lifted his black doctor's bag out of the Morris, reached into its square mouth, and extracted two stoppered glass vials. "That's why I have faith in you, Flavia," he said, and handed them over without another word.

I suppose I should have been filled with feelings of warm gratitude, but I was not. Rather, I was overcome, sitting on that sunny wall, with something like a chill.

How laughably easy it had been, when you stopped to think about it, to extract the thiamine and the ATP from Annabella Cruickshank and Dr. Darby. It was almost as if their actions were being guided by some greater power.

Could it be that the spirit of my deceased mother, wherever it might be, was reaching through the veils from another world to assure her own resurrection?

Were we all of us no more than puppets in Harriet's dead hands?

·FIFTEEN·

MY ANKLES GREW FEATHERS like Mercury, the wing-footed god, as Gladys and I flew home—long way round, of course: west towards Hinley, then south along the same country lane by which we had come, until we were due west of Buckshaw.

I was pushing Gladys through a gap in the hedgerow, heading for the last lap across the fields, when a familiar blue Vauxhall emerged from a grassy turnout and rolled at an ominously low speed towards me.

It was, of course, Inspector Hewitt.

"I thought we might catch you coming round this way," he said, rolling down the window. On the other side of the car, at the wheel, Detective Sergeant Woolmer ducked his head slightly and turned his face to give me one of his stolid police-issue looks.

"I hope you weren't lying in wait too long, Inspector," I replied lightly, but he was not amused.

The door opened, and he stepped out into the lane.

"Let's take a walk," he said.

We strolled along in silence for about fifty yards before the Inspector stopped and turned to me. "I'm very sorry about your mother, Flavia. I can't even begin to imagine how you must feel."

At least the man had the sense to admit it.

"Thank you," I said, meaning it.

"If there's anything Antigone and I can do, don't hesitate to ask."

"I'd like both of you to come to the funeral," I said suddenly without even thinking. I don't know what made me blurt it out. "It's tomorrow."

Antigone, the Inspector's wife, was, to me, the sun. I adored the woman. Just the thought of having her there to share Harriet's funeral made it seem a little less dreadful.

"We were planning to come anyway," the Inspector told me, "but thank you for the invitation."

The formalities were out of the way, the right words spoken. It was time to get down to the real reason for his visit.

"I expect you'll be wanting to question me about the man who was murdered on the railway platform."

"Murdered?" the Inspector repeated. He almost—but not quite—gasped the word.

"Someone said he was shoved. I don't know who."

"Shoved? Is that what they said?"

"Actually, they said 'pushed': 'Someone pushed him.' I didn't see who said it, and I didn't recognize the voice. I'm surprised no one's told you that."

"Yes, well. We still have many witnesses to interview. I'm sure that one or more of them will be able to substantiate your statement."

If I were in charge of the police investigation, I thought, *I'd be looking first for the person who said "Someone pushed him," rather than those who might merely have overheard it.*

But I said nothing. I didn't want to aggravate the Inspector.

"It has been stated that you were the first to reach the victim's side."

"I was not the first," I told him. "There were others there before me."

Inspector Hewitt pulled a notebook from his pocket and made a note with his Biro. "Begin with the moment the train braked suddenly."

Thank heavens! I thought. *He's sparing my feelings about Harriet.*

There was no need, then, to tell him the words the stranger had spoken to me: no need to tell him that the Gamekeeper—whoever he may be—was in grave danger.

"The train braked," I said. "Someone screamed. I thought I might be able to help. I ran to the edge of the platform—but it was too late. The man was dead."

"How do you know that?" the Inspector asked, fixing me with a keen eye.

"There can be no mistaking that perfect stillness," I told him. "It cannot be faked. The only things moving were the hairs on his arm."

"I see," Inspector Hewitt said, and made another note.

"They were golden," I added.

"Thank you, Flavia," he said. "You've been more than helpful."

Ordinarily, a compliment like that from Inspector Hewitt would have wreathed my head in a blaze of glory, but not this time.

Was he being what Daffy called "ironical"? She had once told me that the word meant the use of veiled sarcasm: the dagger under the silk.

"*The smiler with the knife!*" she had hissed in a horrible voice.

I gave the Inspector a sad smile, which seemed appropriate to the occasion, then turned and walked off along the lane. I picked up Gladys and resumed our way home across the fields.

When I was far enough away, and under the pretense of adjusting my pigtails, I sneaked a quick look back over my shoulder.

Inspector Hewitt was still standing precisely where I had left him.

Undine met me at the kitchen door.

"They've been looking for you everywhere," she announced. "They're furious—I can tell. Ibu wants to see you at once."

In ordinary circumstances, I would have responded to such a command by sending up a reply that would have given Undine's mother a perm that would be truly everlasting, but I restrained myself.

There was enough pressure in the house already without my adding more.

And so, like a perfect little lady, I turned and walked gracefully up the stairs.

I could hardly believe it.

Dogger had billeted the Cornwall de Luces in a bedroom above the north front: a musty room with moldy cream and green wallpaper which made the room look like a cavern hung with Roquefort cheese.

I knocked and entered before Lena could tell me to come in.

"Where have you been?" she demanded.

"Out," I said. I was not going to make this easy for her.

"Everyone has been looking for you," she said. "Your father collapsed at the foot of your mother's coffin. It was dreadful. Dreadful!"

"What?" I could scarcely believe it.

"He wasn't to stand watch until this evening," I said.

"The poor man has barely left her side since they brought her into the house this morning. Your aunt Felicity was with him. Her vigil ends at 6:48, and they want you to relieve her—to take your father's place."

"Thank you, Cousin Lena," I said. "I shall see to it."

I stepped outside and quietly closed the door, leaving her to the Roquefort.

Safely alone in the hall, I leaned against the wall and took a deep breath.

I wasn't worried about Father: Dogger would have put him to bed, and I had no doubt that everything in that department was under control.

Lena had made no mention of the doctor being called, so I was quite sure that it was a case of exhaustion, pure and simple.

Father had barely rested since the news had come of Harriet's death, and now that she had been brought home to Buckshaw, he would be sleeping even less.

What concerned me was this: With only a few hours to go before my watch began, there was little time to prepare. Kind Fate had tripled the time I would have with Harriet: Instead of 4 hours and 48 minutes, I would now have more than 14 hours—albeit in three sessions: Father's, Feely's, and mine (interrupted by Daffy's, of course)—to bring Harriet back from the dead.

There would be one chance—and one chance only—to convince the family of my worth. If I failed, I would remain forever an outcast.

There wasn't a second to waste.

Everything now depended upon Flavia de Luce.

·SIXTEEN·

Alone in my laboratory with the door firmly bolted, I began my final preparations.

Esmeralda looked on from her perch, completely disinterested.

The first step was to lay out a kit of the required tools: screwdriver, tin-snips, gloves, galvanized coal scuttle, and torch.

The first of these items was to open Harriet's coffin; the second to cut through the metal lining; the third and fourth to receive whatever might remain of the dry ice in which I was counting on her being packed; and the fifth to add more light to the scene than would be provided by the flickering candles alone.

Then there were the hypodermic needles: two sturdy and somewhat suspicious specimens from Uncle Tar's truly comprehensive collection of laboratory glassware.

I removed from my pocket and unwrapped from my handkerchief the two vials of adenosine triphosphate which Dr. Darby had so generously contributed to my scheme, followed by the bottle of thiamine which Annabella Cruickshank had handed over in open defiance of her brother, Lancelot.

If Undine or Lena had noticed the peculiar bulges in my jumper they had said nothing.

Next, in preparation for the act itself, I reviewed the relevant pages from Uncle Tar's notebooks: those concerning the reanimation of the dead.

The resurrection of Harriet de Luce.

I pulled up a tall stool and began reviewing the spidery, handwritten texts.

It was obvious to even the most casual reader that Uncle Tar had actually experimented upon rabbits. Page after page was filled with his hand-drawn charts and graphs showing times, dosages, and results of his attempted resurrections of twenty-four rabbits, who had been given the names Alpha, Beta, Gamma, Delta, and so on, all the way up to Omega.

All of them—save Epsilon, who Uncle Tar suspected might have had a dicky heart to begin with—had been successfully revived from a state of clinical death and had lived to be experimented upon another day.

My eyes were heavy, not helped by my uncle's minuscule handwriting, as they plowed over the pages. Once or twice I nodded—recovered with a start—yawned several deep yawns and—

I awoke completely disoriented. The side of my face lay flat upon the laboratory bench in a puddle of drool.

I shook my head groggily and rotated it upon my neck, trying to ease the dull headache that invariably comes with sleeping during the day.

I unlocked the door and hurried to my bedroom to have a look at the clock.

It was 6:44!

I had slept away whatever little remained of the afternoon and now had just four minutes to get to Harriet's boudoir and take up my post. I would have to sneak back later for my tools and supplies.

With the speed of a music-hall quick-change artist, I removed my rumpled clothing and threw on my best black jumper and a clean white blouse. Long black stockings and a pair of detestable black goody-two-shoes completed the getup.

Using my fingers as a comb, I gave my hair a lick and a promise and straightened my pigtails.

Too late for decent grooming, I rubbed the crusty sleep from my eyes, removed a smudge of dirt from my chin with a bit of spit, and made haste for the west wing.

"You're two and a half minutes late," Aunt Felicity said, glaring at her wristwatch.

"I was held up by the crowd outside," I said, which had a morsel of truth in it. The straggling line of silent mourners still stretched along the upper hall, down the stairs, across the foyer, out the door, and, for all I knew, all the way into the village.

I had asked the woman at the head of the queue—a stranger, I hasten to say—to wait a bit longer before entering: There was an urgent family matter that must be seen to before the public visitations resumed. She had stared unflinchingly at me with her offended duck eyes. To be honest, she gave me the fantods.

"Orp!" I had wanted to shout in the woman's face. It was easier than saying "orpiment," which was the layman's term for As_2S_3, or "arsenic trisulfide."

Before Aunt Felicity could reply, I changed the subject.

"I'm worried about Father," I said. "What happened to him? I thought he wasn't due to begin his vigil until now."

"He couldn't bear to stay away," Aunt Felicity said. She nodded towards Harriet's catafalque. "He came up the stairs with her and remained at her side until he crumpled. It's a jolly good thing I was here to go for help."

"Dogger?" I asked.

"Dogger," she said. And that seemed to be that—until she added: "Whom else would I send for?"

"Well, Dr. Darby. I should have thought—"

"Pfah!" Aunt Felicity almost spat. "Dogger has better qualifications than half the medical men in the kingdom."

"Dogger?"

"Oh, don't look so shocked, girl. And close your mouth—it's not at all becoming. I thought you might have worked it out long before this."

"Well, I've always known he has buckets of medical knowledge, but it seemed—"

"'Seemed' isn't worth tuppence. How many solicitors or publicans, jockeys or bishops, do you know who could set a broken femur or snick out a pair of infected tonsils?"

"None," I admitted.

"Precisely," Aunt Felicity said. "There it was all the time, wasn't it? As plain as the nose on your face."

She was taking such great delight in my ignorance that I thought for a moment she was going to crow.

But everything fell suddenly into place. How many times in the past had Dogger described to me the most exact clinical details of various medical conditions? I couldn't even begin to count the occasions. Why is it, I wondered, that the facts closest to our noses are so often the most overlooked?

I felt an absolute chump. Although I prided myself on being able to put two and two together, for most of my life, I had been adding them up to get three. It was humiliating!

"He was with Father in the prisoner-of-war camp, wasn't he? In Changi—in Singapore?"

This was a bit of family history I had wheedled out of Mrs. Mullet and her husband, Alf, in particles of gossip too small individually to draw attention to themselves.

"Dogger saved your father's life on more than one occasion," she said, her voice suddenly soft. "And for that, he paid the price."

The light of the flickering candles threw such shifting shadows upon Aunt Felicity's features that it seemed as if the hovering face of a stranger were telling the tale.

"Your father had been sentenced to death by the Japanese. His crime? Refusing to name those men under his command who had been involved in planning an escape. I'm not going to tell you what they did to him, Flavia: It would not be decent."

She paused to let me realize what she had just said. "In

spite of the primitive conditions, and using not much more than the utensils from a mess kit, Dogger somehow managed to keep your father from bleeding to death."

My throat was instantly hard and dry. I could not swallow.

"For his troubles, Dogger was sent to work on the Death Railway."

The Death Railway! The brutal road that had been hacked by prisoners of war for more than two hundred miles through forbidding hills and jungles from Thailand to Burma. I had looked with horror at the ghastly images in the old news magazines: the skeletal laborers, the haunted faces, the crude graves by the wayside. A hundred thousand dead. There was more—much more—some of it too sickening to read.

"For Dogger," Aunt Felicity went on, "that was only the beginning. He was sent to work on what came to be known as Hellfire Pass, a notorious section of the line upon which he and his fellow prisoners were forced to dig through sheer rock using little more than primitive tools and their own bare hands."

"How awful," I said, aware even as I spoke of how trivial my words must sound.

"Cholera broke out, as it often does under such appalling conditions. Dysentery followed by starvation, followed by—

"In spite of his own shocking physical condition, Dogger attempted to deal with the casualties."

She broke off suddenly. "I think it best at this point, Flavia, to bring down a curtain upon the scene. There are things too terrible to be described by mere words."

My brain understood what she was saying, even if I did not.

"Your father and Dogger did not meet again until the end of the War, when they were thrown together by chance at a hospital operated by the British Red Cross.

"They didn't recognize each other until a chaplain introduced them. The padre said later of their reunion that even God cried—"

"Please, Aunt Felicity," I said. "I don't want to hear any more."

"You're a wise child," she said. "I don't want to tell you any more."

We stood there for a few more minutes saying nothing. Then, without a word, Aunt Felicity turned and left the room, leaving me alone with Harriet.

·SEVENTEEN·

I LISTENED AT THE door to the low hum of voices outside.

Taking a deep breath and turning the knob, I stepped solemnly into the hall.

"Ladies and gentlemen," I said. "Friends . . . neighbors—"

I was trying desperately to think how Father would phrase it. "I know that you've been waiting patiently for a very long time, and I can't tell you how much the family appreciates it. But I'm afraid that we're going to have to close the house for the rest of this evening. There are, as you can imagine, many details which must be seen to before my mother's funeral, and I—"

An appeal to their imaginations seemed like an inspired touch, but still, there was a murmur of disappointment.

"It's all right, ducks," said the woman with the duck eyes, and I nearly burst into hysterical laughter at my private joke.

"We all know what you've been through"—she pronounced it "froo"—"We all know what you've been froo, so you don't have to tell us twice when to clear out."

"You're very kind," I said. "I'm glad you understand. We shall resume in the morning at a quarter past nine."

By that time, Daffy would be ending her shift, and I, for better or for worse, would have finished most of what I had come to do.

If, as I hoped, history had been made in the night, tomorrow's early mourners would arrive to find the tomb empty, so to speak.

It promised to be a most interesting day.

The woman with the duck eyes had actually begun to walk away, but now she turned and called back to me, almost desperately: "Miss Harriet babysat me and my sister once. Our mam was taken sudden with the appendix, and Miss Harriet, God bless her, made us brown sugar sangriches."

I gave her a sad smile: sad because I hated her—no, not hated—*envied* her for this sudden stabbing memory of Harriet, who had never made brown sugar sandwiches—or any other kind, for that matter—for me, at least that I could remember.

My announcement was relayed from person to person back along the line; people began to turn reluctantly away, and in a few minutes, the hall was empty.

As the last few stragglers made their way down the west staircase, I slipped quietly through the baize door, which opened into the northwest corner of the house, and by a roundabout trek, made my way to the east wing. Again, except for Lena and Undine, there was little danger of a personal encounter.

Within minutes I was on my way back from the laboratory, ticking off once more in my mind a list of the tools I had carefully laid out for myself: tin-snips, torch, gloves, screwdriver, and coal scuttle, to say nothing of the ATP and the thiamine, which, wrapped in handkerchiefs, were stuffed safely into my pocket to keep from breaking or rattling. In the coal scuttle was a brass alarm clock I had brought from my bedroom: a last-minute addition which might have doomed the entire operation had it been forgotten.

Back in Harriet's boudoir, I leaned thankfully against the door and heaved a sigh of relief. I hadn't been spotted.

The lock gave a satisfying *click* as I turned the key, which I then removed and dropped into my pocket.

This is it, I thought, glancing at the clock. *Time to show them what you're made of, Flavia.*

It was 7:22.

Time to remove the black pall with which Harriet's coffin had been draped.

But before beginning my actual work, I replaced and relit each one of the now guttering candles at the head and foot of the catafalque.

I would be needing all the light and all the heat they could generate.

Dare Lucem.

The coffin screws were the easy part. Since they were new and had not been moldering and rusting away in some damp old churchyard, they would be almost ridiculously simple to remove. In such a short time that it surprised even me, I had them loosened.

Now came the moment of truth.

"Saint Tancred, help me," I whispered. "Harriet, forgive me."

And with that, I lifted the lid.

It was as I had expected: Beneath the wooden lid was an inner coffin of zinc. Zinc for lightness, and although it was a somewhat harder metal than lead, still as easy as butter to cut through with the tin-snips.

Beneath the zinc, though, would be the face of my mother. What would she look like?

I began to prepare myself mentally. I forced myself to think like a scientist.

If her body was corrupt, I would go no further. There would be no point in it.

But if, on the other hand, she had been preserved miraculously in the ice of the glacier, I would begin immediately my efforts to restore her to life.

I worried a small hole in the zinc with the tip of the screwdriver and inserted one of the blades of the metal-cutting scissors.

Snip!

It was more difficult than I had thought.

Snip!

Already my thumb and forefinger were starting to feel bruised.

A slight gush of wind—or was it my imagination?—escaped from the coffin. I wrinkled my nose at the peculiar odor of soil, ice—and something else.

Had there been the faintest whiff of Harriet's scent, *Miratrix*?

Perhaps I was only willing it to be so.

Snip!

My fingers were already in pain, but I kept on cutting.

After what seemed an eternity, I had made a three-sided incision of no more than a foot each side. If my calculations were correct, I was working directly over Harriet's face and chest.

Careful, I thought. *Mustn't damage her*.

It was at that precise instant that I realized I had forgotten the blowtorch. If I needed to reseal the inner coffin, I would have to solder shut the cuts I had made in the zinc.

In order to do that, I would need not only the torch and a good supply of lead/tin solder, but also a sufficient quantity of flux. The first two were easy enough: Uncle Tar had kept the laboratory stocked well enough with tools to keep from ever having to bring in overly inquisitive tradesmen to repair his plumbing. The flux, though, was another matter. I had planned to concoct it myself by "killing" a solution of hydrochloric acid and water with bits of zinc dropped into it.

If I needed to do that now, it would require another trip to the lab and further delay.

Snip!

And then there was this: Although I had no fear of corpses, this one was obviously different. Would the act of coming face-to-face with my frozen mother result in some completely unforeseen shock to my system?

There was only one way to find out.

I inserted the screwdriver into the top edge of the cut and pried back the zinc with my fingers.

A wave of weakness washed over me. I nearly fainted.

There, just inches from my invading eyes, cradled in tendrils of curling gases, was the face of my mother, the long-lost Harriet.

Except for a slight darkening of the end of her nose, she looked exactly as she had in all the photos I had ever seen.

Fortunately, her eyes were closed.

She had a tiny smile on her lips—that was the first thing I noticed—and her skin was as pale as that of any fairy-tale ice princess.

It was like coming face-to-face with an image of my older self in a frosty mirror.

I was shaken with a shiver.

"Mother," I whispered. "It's me—Flavia."

She did not respond, of course, but it had been necessary to speak to her nonetheless.

Something slipped and fell down beside her neck: a bit of solidified carbon dioxide. I had been right. They had packed her in card ice for the long trip home.

Vapors were rising from the coffin, swirling briefly in the light of the flickering candles before cascading in slow drifts to the floor to form an ankle-deep mist.

I touched her face with my forefinger. She was cold.

How easy it is to say that, and yet so difficult to do.

I became aware that my emotions were writhing inside me like snakes in a pit.

Some part of me of which I was not in control made me bend over and kiss her lips.

They were hard and as dry as parchment.

"Get on with it, Flavia," I was telling myself. "You haven't a lot of time."

I needed to know at the outset if there was any warmth—any heartbeat. There wouldn't be, of course, but I had to be sure. Every experiment must start with some basic given.

Harriet was still dressed in the climbing gear in which she had been found, with an outer coat of tan-colored gabardine that was already beginning to thaw, or at least to soften a bit from the heat of the candles.

I unfastened a stiff button on her breast and worked a hand inside, feeling for her heart.

As always, I had that brief irrational fear that I've had before with corpses: the feeling that the dead person is going to leap up suddenly, shout "Boo!," and seize one's hand in a deadly grip of ice.

Nothing of the sort happened, of course.

What *did* happen was that, among what felt like layered wool and silk and cotton, my fingers came into contact with something more substantial than fabric.

I moved my hand as gently as possible. Whatever was tucked inside Harriet's clothing felt somewhat damp from the card ice, and brittle.

I seized it with the scissors of my first and second fingers and slowly worked it out and into the light: a large oilcloth wallet. It was as rigid as frozen fish skin.

I opened it with great care, but even so, several large flakes peeled off and fell away onto Harriet's breast.

Inside was a single sheet of grayish musty paper, water-stained and folded into four.

My hands trembled as I flattened it out and read the penciled words:

> This is the last will and testament of Harriet de Luce.
>
> I hereby give, devise, and bequeath to my—

Bang!

I nearly leaped out of my hide.

A thunderous knock at the door was followed by another and another and yet another: *Bang! Bang! Bang! Bang!*

My immediate thought was that the noise would waken Father, whose bedroom was next door to Harriet's boudoir. Or had Dogger, perhaps, given Father something to make him sleep?

"Who is it?" I called, my voice shaky in the sudden silence.

"It's Lena," came the hissed reply, muffled by the heavy paneling. "Unlock this door and let me in."

I was too shocked to reply. Here I was standing over an open coffin, nearly nose-to-nose with my mother's body, her last will and testament shaking in my hand—

It was like a fevered nightmare.

"Flavia!"

"Yes?" It was all I could think of.

"Open this door at once."

Sometimes a very great shock has the effect of slowing down time, and this is exactly what happened. Almost as if disembodied, I watched myself shove the will into the wallet, drop it into the coal scuttle, close the zinc flap of the inner coffin, grab and replace the wooden lid from where I had leaned it against the wall, drape it with the black pall, shove the coal scuttle under and behind one of the heavy velvet hangings, turn the key, and open the door, all in slow motion.

"What are you doing?" Lena demanded. "Why did you have this door locked?"

As if I hadn't heard, I sank to my knees on the carved prie-dieu that had been provided for those who might wish to offer their prayers for the repose of Harriet's soul. I hoped that it would look as if I had been there all along.

"What are you doing?" she repeated.

"Praying for my mother," I said, after a long-enough pause.

I crossed myself and got to my feet. "What is it, Lena?" I asked. "What's the matter?"

One way of getting an immediate upper hand in a pinch is, as I have mentioned, to make use of an adult's name.

"You frightened me," I added.

Another way is to squeeze in an accusation—even a veiled one—before the other person has a chance to say a word.

"I thought I smelled smoke," she said. "It seemed to be coming from here."

"It's the candles," I said immediately. "They're awfully hot—and there are so many of them. With these heavy hangings—" I waved my hand vaguely. "And with all the windows shut—"

"I suppose," she said, sounding somewhat skeptical, but having a good look round the room nevertheless.

From where we stood near the door, everything appeared to be in order, every detail as it had been before I began.

It was at that instant that my supersensitive hearing registered a new sound in the room.

Drip.

Drip.

It was agonizingly slow, but as evident to my ears as a series of cannon shots.

Surely Lena must be able to hear it.

"So everything is all right, then?" she asked.

I gave her a sad nod.

"Very well," she said, but she made no move to leave. Rather, she looked slowly round the room as if satisfying herself that no stranger's ears were listening, although there might have been armies of eavesdroppers lurking behind the vast black velvet hangings.

"You will recall that I told you I was going to confide in you, Flavia. That I was going to seek your assistance. We were interrupted when that dreadful man terrified us with his aeroplane."

"Tristram Tallis," I said.

"Yes."

Drip!

Drip!

I knew at once where the sound was coming from. The card ice was melting and drops of water were falling to the oaken floor of Harriet's boudoir.

"I told you, did I not, that Undine requires a very particular kind of handling."

"Yes," I said.

"A very *special* kind of handling."

The candles closest to her face guttered in the peculiar hissing of her voice. A reflection danced on the floor: the merest flash of light under the catafalque.

It was water! Harriet's coffin was leaking!

I needed to get Lena out of here as quickly as possible.

"Undine likes you," she said. "She thinks you're keen. That was her own word: keen. You're very good with her."

I smiled indulgently.

"We need to talk. Not here, but somewhere where we can speak frankly without fear of interruption. Do you know the Jack O'Lantern?"

I did indeed. It was a skull-like outcropping of rock to the east of Buckshaw that overlooked the Palings, that somewhat sinister grove at a bend in the river Efon, which marked the eastern boundary of our estate. Gladys and I had ridden there on many occasions, most recently to consult with Father's old headmaster, Dr. Isaac Kissing, who was a resident of Rook's End, a nearby private institution.

"Yes," I said. "I've heard of it."

"It's at the end of Pooker's Lane," she said. "Do you know where that is?"

I nodded.

"Excellent. We shall go there tomorrow afternoon at half-three. We shall have a lovely picnic."

"After the funeral?" I asked.

"After the funeral. I shall have Mrs. Mullet put up a hamper and we shall make a day of it."

"All right," I said, anxious to get rid of the woman. At that point, I think I would have agreed to anything.

I flung open the door to speed her departure.

"Dogger!" I said. "I'm sorry! I didn't know you were there."

We had almost collided in the doorway.

"It's all right, Miss Flavia," he said. "No harm done. Mrs. Mullet wanted me to tell you that she's bringing up some cold meats. She has somehow formed the opinion that you haven't eaten today."

Lovely. Just what I needed: a nice bit of brawn to tide me over my long night's work!

"Please thank her, Dogger, but I had something in the village this afternoon. I couldn't manage another bite."

I think it was the first time in my life I had ever lied to Dogger, and I think he knew it, too.

"Very well," he said, turning away.

"If you don't want them, then I shall eat them," Lena said. I'd almost forgotten she was there.

Dogger nodded but said nothing. He watched as she walked away towards the stairs and the kitchen.

Poor Mrs. Mullet, I thought. Usually, by this time of day, she was safely home at her own hearth with Alf. She must have stayed past her time to see to the funeral meats and so forth. *I must remember to take her aside later*, I thought, *and express my gratitude*.

There was so much to be grateful for, when you stopped to think of it, in spite of all our hardships.

Dogger, for instance. This was the first time I had been alone with him since Aunt Felicity had told me his story.

How could I ever begin to thank him? How could I ever begin to make it up for what he had endured?

What can one possibly say to a person who, in saving one's father's life, has been made to endure the tortures of the damned?

I wanted to hug him, but of course I couldn't. It simply wouldn't do.

We stood there together for a few moments. I was the first to speak.

"God bless you, Dogger," I said at last.

"God bless you, too, Miss Flavia," he said.

"I'm sorry, Dogger," I admitted. "I didn't actually have anything to eat. But I'm not hungry. Honestly."

"I understand," he said with rather a sad smile. "I shall leave you to your task."

Only after he was gone did I think about what he had said.

·EIGHTEEN·

THE EVENING WAS WEARING on and I had much to do. I turned the key in the lock, removed the pall from Harriet's coffin, and was preparing to lift the wooden lid when there was another knock at the door.

I'm afraid I let slip a word which was not entirely suitable to the occasion.

Well, I thought, at least I hadn't gone too far with my experiment. Better to be interrupted sooner than later.

I replaced the pall, turned the key, and opened the door.

There stood Father.

He looked dreadful—as pale as if Death itself were standing in the doorway.

I had thought he was in bed, sedated. Whatever could be so important as to cause him to arise? Or had he been awake all along?

Behind him, in the hall, were two of the men I had seen on the station platform. They were not wearing their bowler hats, nor were they carrying their umbrellas, but I recognized them at once.

"This is my daughter Flavia—" Father began, but before he could finish, one of the two had brushed past both of us and into the boudoir. The taller one remained outside in the hall. I could now see that he was carrying a black bag somewhat like Dr. Darby's, but considerably larger.

I realized with a shock that I had seen his face before—and not just at the station. He had been pictured in the illustrated papers arriving in a trench coat at an old stone mortuary at the time of the Swindon Suitcase Murders.

Now, here he was at Buckshaw: Sir Peregrine Darwin, the legendary Home Office pathologist, with his famous head of wild white hair and all. I could hardly believe it. What on earth could have brought him all the way down from London?

"My daughter Flavia," Father began again. "Flavia has been keeping—"

"Thank you, Colonel de Luce," Sir Peregrine said. "If we require further assistance, we shall send for you."

Send for him? Send for Father in his own house? Who do these people think they are?

So gently that I hardly noticed it, Father took my arm and drew me out into the hall. The pathologist followed his colleague into the boudoir and the green baize door swung shut behind them. The key turned with a determined click.

Father and I were alone in the hall.

I think he could see that I was working up a rage, but before I could say a word, he bent down, put his mouth close to my ear, and whispered: "*Home Office*."

As if those two words explained everything.

"But why?"

Father put a forefinger to his lips to shush me, then crooked it and wiggled it as a signal for me to follow him.

He opened the door of his bedroom and waved me inside.

It was the first time I had been in Father's room in a year, but it was precisely as I remembered it: as if, like the British Museum, nothing was ever touched from age to age, but only stared at.

The dark, heavy Gothic bed, the Queen Anne washstand—even the Stanley Gibbons stamp catalog on the table seemed to have been suspended in time.

Father waved me to a chair, and as I settled, he made his way across the room to a window.

Windows, I believe, were as essential to Father's talking as his tongue.

I waited for him to begin.

"We must do as they tell us," he said at last.

"But why?" I couldn't help myself.

And yet, in my heart of hearts, I knew the chilling answer all too well. Sir Peregrine could have been sent here for only one reason.

"The Home Office is in charge now," Father said. "They have flown your mother home from Tibet, laid on the special train to bring her down to Buckshaw, and tomorrow, they shall take her to St. Tancred's."

He did not add the words "after the autopsy," but he might as well have.

His voice broke a little, but he steeled himself and carried on. I could almost see a pointer in his hand as he briefed me on what was undoubtedly to him a military campaign. A tragic one, to be sure, but a military campaign nevertheless.

His face was white at the window as he said: "At 1400 hours, your mother's coffin, draped again in the Union Jack, will be brought down to the foyer, where it will rest for ten minutes to allow the household staff to pay their respects."

Household staff? Could he be referring to Dogger and Mrs. M? Other than the Various Governesses, or "VG" as we called them—who were best not spoken about—there hadn't been household staff in the real sense of the word since I was a baby.

"At 1415, the hearse, with the first of the floral tributes, will depart Buckshaw and arrive at St. Tancred's at 1422. The family will—"

Seeing that he was near to tears—or was it me?—I walked softly across the carpet and stood by his side at the window.

"It's all right, Father," I said. "I understand."

Even though I didn't.

At that moment, I wanted more than anything to tell him about my accidental discovery of Harriet's will. The fact that it was thought Harriet had died without leaving a will had been at the center of our poverty-stricken existence for as long as I could remember.

On several occasions, kind Fate had seemed to dangle a financial solution under our very noses, only to snatch it away again as ruthlessly as if we were engaged in a rough-and-tumble round of Hook the Hankie.

For instance, there had been the First Quarto of Shakespeare's *Romeo and Juliet* which had turned up in the library, but which Father had steadfastly refused to part with, although a certain Big Name on the London stage—oh, all right, it was Desmond Duncan—continued to contrive new ways to get his scheming hands on the precious little volume.

And then there had been the Heart of Lucifer, that priceless diamond which had once ornamented the crozier of Saint Tancred and which had been recovered at the village church just a week ago, during the occasion of the opening of his tomb.

After vanishing for a while as it worked its way through my alimentary canal, the stone had come to light at last, so to speak, and had recently been handed over to the bishop for further investigation by the Ecclesiastical Authorities, who, after consultation with the Garter King of Arms, Somerset House, and the Public Record Office were to make the final decision upon whether or not the five-hundred-year-old Saint Tancred de Luci had been one of our de Luce ancestors, and, hence, whether the stone was ours in law, common or otherwise.

"Don't hold your breath," the vicar had advised Father.

The discovery of Harriet's will, then, would be crucial. But even so, some strange new urge was keeping me silent.

Why couldn't I just blurt it out and be done with it?

The answer to that simple question was a complex one, and I wasn't sure I even understood it myself, although my reasoning went something like this: In the first place, I had no right to interrupt Father's mourning. Good news, it seems to me, has no place in the midst of tragedy, when it cannot be fully appreciated—when it is dampened and diluted by the atmosphere in which it is announced and robbed of its healing power.

"Catharsis cannot possibly come until the bitter end," Daffy had lectured us as she read aloud from Aristotle.

Then, too, there was the less than admirable fact that I wanted to keep the will's existence to myself for as long as possible. In some strange way, I needed to feed upon and relish the possession of information that nobody knew but me.

I'm not really proud of that, but it's true. There is a strange strength in secrets which can never be achieved by spilling one's guts.

With those thoughts in mind, I slipped my hand into Father's, and the two of us stood together in silence for what seemed like a comforting eternity.

As we stood there at the window, my father and I, I fell into what Daffy would have called a *reverie*, and everyone else *a brown study*.

Images floated dizzily into and out of my mind: Harriet in the ciné film soundlessly forming the words "pheasant sandwiches"; those very same words in the mouth of Mr. Churchill; the horrible gleam of Harriet's coffin before it was mercifully shrouded by the Union Jack; the tall man at the window of the laboratory; the man (was it the same man?)—or at least his arm—sticking grotesquely out of the steam beneath the wheels of the train; his last words—his message to Father: "The Gamekeeper is in jeopardy."

Had I done as he had asked? No, I hadn't. My only excuse was that the time hadn't been right. Whatever was I waiting for?

If I couldn't give him good news, I could at least give him bad.

It didn't make much sense, but there it was.

"Father," I blurted, "that man at the station—the one who fell under the train—he told me to tell you that the Gamekeeper is in jeopardy. He also said something about the Nide, but I'm afraid I missed it."

Father was galvanized. The muscles of his face twitched as if he were wired up to an array of chemical batteries in some fiendish laboratory experiment.

His eyes came slowly and jerkily around to focus on my face. "Man? Station? Train?"

Could he have been so distracted by grief, I wondered, *that he didn't see or hear the accident?*

Or was it murder? Hadn't someone said that the stranger was pushed?

"This man," Father asked, his face, if possible, even more gray than it had been. "What did he look like?"

"He was tall," I said. "Very tall. He was wearing a heavy coat."

"Thank you, Flavia," Father said, drawing himself up, pulling himself visibly together as if he were an aged warhorse hearing the bugle call to battle.

"And now if you will excuse me," he said, "I am freeing you from your vigil. You must go to bed now. We all of us have much to do tomorrow."

I was dismissed.

There was no point in asking Father the meaning of the message. I would have to work it out for myself.

And I knew exactly where to begin.

The library door was shut, as I knew it would be.

I gave three long scratches at the panel with what was left of my bitten fingernails, followed by a pause, then three short, and three long again: the signal for a brief truce that Daffy and I had privately agreed upon in happier days.

Even though we were not presently at war, it was best to go warily. If there was one thing that infuriated Daffy, it was being what she called "a barger."

A barger was one who burst suddenly into a room without so much as a "kiss-me-quick-and-mind-the-marmalade"; an invader of privacy; an insensitive clot; a thoughtless blockhead.

And I'll admit that at one time or another, I had been one or more of these, sometimes by accident and other times not.

"Come," Daffy called, just when I was about to give it up.

I opened the door with exaggerated care and stepped into the library. At first I couldn't see her. She was not draped across her usual armchair, nor was she sitting by the fireplace.

Bleak House had been returned to the bookcase, and *Paradise Lost* was now turned turtle on the table.

When I located my sister at last, I saw that she was standing at a window, staring out into the darkness.

I waited, to allow her the first word, but she said nothing.

"Father sent me to bed," I said. "He's let me off my vigil early. Some men from the Home Office have taken charge."

"They're everywhere," Daffy said. "Mrs. Mullet says they've booked every last cranny at the Thirteen Drakes."

"Better than sleeping at Buckshaw," I said, meaning it as a bit of a joke.

Daffy snorted. "We're already bursting at the seams with unwelcome bodies."

It seemed an odd thing to say, and for an instant, I was on the verge of asking if she included Harriet in that remark, but I restrained myself.

"What with Lena la-di-da de Luce and that brat of hers, plus your precious Mr. Tallis—"

"He's not mine," I protested. "I hardly know the man."

"And your precious Adam Sowerby—"

Adam Sowerby! I could scarcely believe my ears! I had met Adam, who claimed to be a flora-archaeologist and inquiry agent, during a recent murder investigation in which I had been able to point the police in the proper direction. Even after I had solved the case, and he had more or less declared us partners in investigation, Adam had refused to tell me whom he was working for.

"What's Adam Sowerby got to do with it?" I asked.

"He's here," Daffy replied. "Drove down from London. Arrived a couple of hours ago. Dogger's put him in one of the rooms in the Northwest Territories, with the rest of them."

The Northwest Territories was our playful name for that

vast and desolate expanse of unused bedrooms whose few remaining sticks of furniture were kept draped with dusty sheets, awaiting some distant and unlikely day when Buckshaw might be restored to its former fortunes—unlike the abandoned and decaying east wing in which, by choice, I worked and slept.

"No room at the inn, and so forth," Daffy said. "He and Father are old friends, remember? So I suppose that makes it all right for him to be a barger."

Her bitterness surprised me.

"Father probably needs old friends right now," I said.

"Father needs a good shaking!" she exclaimed, and as she turned abruptly away from the window, I could see the tears in her eyes.

I was suddenly as tired as if I had trudged barefoot across the Sahara desert. It had been a brutally long day.

My parched mind was shocked to hear my mouth uttering words I never thought would cross my lips: "Chin up, Daff. We'll come through all this. I promise."

·NINETEEN·

I SLEPT THE SLEEP of the damned, tossing and turning as if I were lying in a bed of smoldering coals.

Whenever I did manage to doze off, my mind was filled with tattered dreams: Dogger, standing atop a hill, his white hair and his gardener's apron flying and flapping in a wicked wind; Feely and Daffy as little children, watching a Punch and Judy show in which all the puppets—except the Hangman—had blank, formless faces; Harriet floating on an iceberg, paddling furiously with her hands to escape an Arctic tidal wave.

I jerked awake to find myself sitting bolt upright, a strangled cry in my throat. My mouth tasted as if a farmer had stored turnips in it while I slept.

I looked round in panic, for a moment not knowing where I was.

It was that hour of the very early morning when all the

world has begun to float to the surface of sleep, but has not yet really come awake. I cupped my hands behind my ears and listened for all I was worth. The house was in perfect stillness.

As I swung my feet out of the warm bed and onto the cold floorboards, my brain came instantly up to full throttle.

The will! Harriet's will!

I had shoved it into the coal scuttle and put it out of my mind.

I had to retrieve it—and there wasn't a moment to lose!

I was dressed in a flash and creeping as stealthily as a cat burglar towards the west wing. Dogger, who had difficulty sleeping, would soon be up and about. Not that I wanted to hide anything from him—no, far from it.

What I *did* want to do was to shield him from blame. There are a few instances in life where, in spite of everything, one has to swallow one's heart and go it alone, and this was one of them.

I had left the torch in Harriet's boudoir and would have to rely on the weird half-light that was coming in through the windows at the end of the hall. Sunrise, I judged, would not be for another three quarters of an hour.

Soundlessly I crept along the passageway, giving praise at every silent step for the invention of carpets. The soles of my bare feet could feel the grit left behind by yesterday's parade of mourners, and I made a mental note to get out the carpet sweeper before breakfast and give the rug a jolly good cleaning. It was the least I could do.

At the entrance to Harriet's boudoir, I put my ear to the door and turned up the sensitivity.

Not a sound.

I put my hand on the knob and—nothing.

It didn't budge.

The door was locked, and the keys were inside.

For a brief, crazy moment I thought of fetching a ladder and scaling the outer wall, but I remembered that every one of the boudoir's windows was firmly shut and locked.

The only other way into the room was through Father's bedroom. I would need to slip in without knocking, tiptoe to the door which connected to Harriet's boudoir, then enter and leave without a sound.

I retraced my steps in perfect silence. At Father's door, I inhaled as much air as my lungs would hold.

I turned the knob and the door opened.

I stepped inside and began my long trek across the room.

As my eyes became accustomed to the lesser darkness, a lighter patch in the corner showed that Father's pillows were untouched—his bed was empty.

I froze in my tracks and let my eyes move slowly round the room.

He was nowhere to be seen.

Had he gone to his study?

This was, after all, the morning of Harriet's funeral. Perhaps he hadn't slept and had gone downstairs to console himself among his collection of postage stamps, which to him, I suppose, seemed all that he had left.

His wife was gone, his house and estate as good as gone.

None of us were so simpleminded as to think that the moment the funeral was over, the anonymous buyer who had made the sole humiliating offer for our estate would not be pounding at the door.

We would be homeless.

For the first time in its long history, Buckshaw would not be in the hands of a de Luce. It simply didn't bear thinking about.

I was now at the connecting door to Harriet's boudoir. I put my hand against the green baize and pushed softly.

The door swung open without a whisper.

Inside, a single candle flickered at the head of the catafalque.

Father was kneeling on the prie-dieu, his face buried in his hands.

Dare I?

Putting each foot down as if I were treading on broken glass, I began making my way across the room.

As one always does in dangerous circumstances, I counted my steps:

One . . . two . . . three . . . four—

I stopped. If Father lowered his hands and opened his eyes I would be plainly visible. The flickering light made my shadow dance faintly on the velvet hangings, black on black.

Five . . . six . . .

I reached out and touched the pall, squatted.

My knees gave off an alarming crack.

Father's fingers dropped and his eyes shot open. He was looking to the right of where I was now crouching. He cocked an ear, turned his head towards the door, then evidently decided that the noise had come from the candlewick. Or perhaps cracking wood.

He gave a heartrending sigh and lowered his face again into his cupped hands.

He began whispering something, but I could not make out his words.

Was it the Lord's Prayer?

I didn't wait to find out. His own whispered words would be masking whatever small sounds I might make.

I stuck my hand under the hem of the pall, moved it ever so slowly from side to side, feeling with my fingers for the coal scuttle.

A slight *click* from my nails told me that I had found it.

I made my fingers walk like spider legs, up the side of the scuttle, over the lip, and down into its depths.

I stifled a sigh of relief as my fingers touched the oilcloth packet.

It was still there! The men from the Home Office had obviously been so preoccupied with their task that they hadn't wanted—or hadn't thought—to search the room.

Slowly—ever so slowly—I lifted the wallet clear of the metal coal scuttle, taking great care to not make the slightest scraping. I pulled it out from under the velvet drape and, concealing it with my body, began creeping like a slow crab towards the door.

But wait! The alarm clock!

I could hardly leave the thing behind in the coal scuttle! One coal scuttle was as anonymous as another, but the brass alarm clock was uniquely mine.

Back I crawled, delving again in the near-darkness into the scuttle's depths. If I touched the wrong thing and the alarm went off, I was done for.

It was like defusing an unexploded bomb. I had to rely on my sense of touch alone.

Slowly . . . painfully . . . carefully I raised the clock from its tin tomb.

The silence was so excruciating I wanted to scream.

But a few moments later, I was on my way to the door again.

If Father discovered me now, I decided, I would pretend I had just come in to keep him company. He could hardly object to that.

But he didn't move a muscle. When I looked back from the doorway, he was still on his knees, his back ramrod straight, his head bowed, and his face pressed into his hands.

It was a picture of my father that I would never forget.

I closed the door gently, passed quickly through his bedroom, and slipped into the hall.

Moments later I was back in my bedroom.

The clock showed 4:18.

It had taken me just sixteen minutes.

Sixteen minutes? It had felt like sixteen hours.

Somewhere a WC flushed and the ancient water pipes gurgled and clanked like chains in a distant dungeon. Buckshaw was coming awake.

In precisely ten hours, I would be arriving at St. Tancred's with my family for my mother's funeral.

It seemed incredible.

For as long as I could remember, I had lived in a world in which a missing mother was a somewhat exotic fact of life. But all of that was now about to change.

From this day forward, I would be a girl—and presumably someday a woman—whose mother, like everyone else's who has ever been bereaved, lay in the village churchyard.

Nothing romantic about that.

I would be just another quite ordinary person.

And there was nothing I could do about it.

·TWENTY·

THE BEDROOMS AT BUCKSHAW, as I have said before, were like vast, damp zeppelin barns, especially those in the east wing where the loosened, water-stained wallpaper bulged from the walls in the form of wind-filled sails. Some of the rooms possessed papered ceilings that drooped overhead in musty, sagging bags like lowering thunderclouds, except that they were green.

No one ever came here, and even I had only once or twice peeked into the moldering bedchamber at the northeast corner of the house, which, for some long forgotten reason, had always been known as "Angels."

There was nothing angelic about it: "Mushrooms" would have been a far more appropriate name. I knew for a fact that parts of the room glowed in the dark due to the bioluminescence of the various fungi that were happily eating away at the rotting wooden paneling which lay beneath.

The lighted candle I had brought from the laboratory guttered and spat in the drafty corridor.

The rusty doorknob gave a fiendish squeak, which was closely followed by a wooden groan as the door swung slowly inwards.

The pong of the place struck my nose like a blow from a boxing glove. I would have to work quickly.

I reached for a Louis-the-something chair, but it crumbled at the touch of my hand, as did a Victorian chaise longue, which, when I accidentally kicked it, collapsed in a shower of dust and woodworms. I knew that I had no choice but to return to my laboratory for something sturdy enough to stand on.

Esmeralda shifted impatiently from foot to foot as I threw into a petri dish a handful of feed, which she fell upon with the ferocity of a famished *Tyrannosaurus rex*, one of her early ancestors.

"Manners," I reminded her, as I seized a tall laboratory stool and left her to her breakfast.

Back in the room called Angels, I placed the stool near the fireplace, directly in front of an angled and jutting section of the wall that had something to do with the chimney, which lay hidden beneath. The spot was more damp than I should have liked, but it was the only part of the upper wallpaper that was within my reach. The oilcloth wallet, though, would be more than protection enough for the short time I planned on leaving it there.

I won't pretend I wasn't tempted to read Harriet's will, but I also knew instinctively that it would be wrong: an unforgivable invasion of Harriet's and Father's privacy that could never, ever be explained away. And besides, there wasn't time.

When I had slid it into an ancient rip in the wallpaper, it was no more than just another bulge in a room full of bulges: safe from the Home Office, safe from the police, safe even from my own family.

As I climbed down from the stool, I noticed the marks its legs had left in the dust on the floor—to say nothing of my own footprints.

Even Inspector Hewitt's men, Detective Sergeants Graves and Woolmer, would have been able to tell at a glance that someone in Flavia-sized shoes had stood on a four-legged stool in that very spot, and could probably even have made a fair guess as to how far up the wall I had been able to reach.

I hadn't the time to find and scatter fresh dust to cover my tracks, which left only one option: I would make even more of them.

So round the room I went, stamping four-legged impressions with the stool's legs everywhere, and making sure to leave as many footprints as I could manage.

When I had finished, Angels looked like a ballroom in which the Dance of the Chimney Sweeps had been held.

I was proud of myself.

I had made it halfway back along the hall, stool in hand, when a voice said, "What are you doing, Flavia?"

It was Undine. She was standing in a little nook where breakfast tea trays had once been prepared, and I hadn't seen her until she'd already spotted me.

"How long have you been there?" I demanded. "Does your mother know you're prowling round in the middle of the night?"

"It isn't the middle of the night," she corrected me. "It's morning, and Ibu has already been up for hours. Besides, that's two questions, and Ibu always says:

"Riddle me no more than once

"Unless *you* wish to be the dunce."

I could cheerfully have strangled Ibu—and her daughter—with the nearest pair of nutcrackers, but I controlled myself.

"Ibu says today is your mother's funeral and that we mustn't mention it because it might cause you deep distress."

"Ibu's very considerate"—I smiled—"and you may tell her I said so."

I had hopeful visions of Undine parroting my words to Lena and receiving a sound thrashing for her troubles.

"What are you doing with the stool?" Undine asked.

"Watering plants," I replied, almost without thinking about it. I had become a deft liar when required—and sometimes not.

"Ha!" Undine said, planting her hands on her hips. But she left it at that.

"Run along now," I told her, surprised at the great pleasure I took in doing so. "I've got work to do."

Which was no more than the truth. I had gone to the library to ferret out the meaning of the stranger's message, only to be distracted by Daffy's news about the unexpected arrival of Adam Sowerby.

"He and Father are old friends," Daffy had reminded me.

It was true, but why was Adam suddenly here? And why now? Had he come as a friend of the family to pay his respects to Harriet, or was he here in his role of inquiry agent?

These were things I needed to know.

But first—a return to the library.

As I had hoped it might be, the library was now in darkness. Daffy must have gone to bed soon after I left her, because *Paradise Lost* was still lying open, facedown, in the same position I had last seen it—which was a sure indication of my sister's state of mind.

If *I* had left a book lying open on its face like that, she'd have flung it into my face, along with a fiery lecture on what she always referred to as "respect for the printed word."

I knew well enough what a gamekeeper was, since there had once been one at Buckshaw, although that was long before my time, of course. Much more recently, Daffy had read to us selected passages from *Lady Chatterley's Lover*, which was interesting if you were keen on country houses but far too full of gush and mush if you were not.

I switched on a small table lamp and went directly to the *Oxford English Dictionary*, "The Holy of Holies," as Daffy called it: twelve volumes plus supplement. The *N*s were in the seventh volume. I lifted it down, opened it in my lap, and ran my finger down the page:

Nictation . . . Niddering . . . Niddicock—

Aha! So *that* was where Daffy had dredged up the word.

"Flavia, you dim-witted niddicock," she was fond of saying.

Daffy is the only person I know who mines the *Oxford English Dictionary* for insults in the same way others dig for diamonds.

Ah, here it was:

> **Nide** (nəid), sb. [ad. F. *nid* or L. *nīd-us*: the older F. *ni* is represented by Nye. Cf. Nid.] A brood or nest of pheasants.

My blood was instantly ice water.

Pheasants! A nest of pheasants!

"Pheasant sandwiches!" Harriet's words on the ciné film.

"And have you, also, acquired a taste for pheasant sandwiches, young lady?" Mr. Churchill's words at Buckshaw Halt.

But what did they mean?

My brain was crawling with words, with images, and with half-formed ideas.

I knew suddenly that I needed to get away from this house of perpetual gloom, get away to somewhere I could think new thoughts—my own thoughts, rather than the worn-out thoughts of others.

I would pack a breakfast-lunch.

Where would I go? I didn't know.

The dovecote at Culverhouse Farm, perhaps. The dusty tower, silent save for the cooing of the doves, was a tempting hideout. Even a couple of hours away would give me time to think without having to worry about bargers.

I'd be back in plenty of time to get dressed for the funeral.

·TWENTY-ONE·

MRS. MULLET JERKED AWAKE as I opened the kitchen door. I could tell by her eyes that she had been crying.

"Mrs. M. What are *you* doing here?"

Her head was still half raised from where it had been cradled in her arms on the kitchen table. She looked as if she didn't know where she was.

"No, don't get up," I told her. "I'll put the kettle on and make you a nice cup of tea."

Less than five seconds in the room and I was already taking charge of a woman in distress. How very, very odd.

I patted her shoulder like mad, and surprisingly, she let me.

"You've been here all night, haven't you?"

Mrs. M nodded and pressed her lips tightly together until they were white.

"It's too much for you," I told her. "You've been working

too hard. Daffy told me Adam Sowerby arrived last night. I'll knock him up and have him run you home."

" 'E's gone already, love. Hours ago."

Adam gone already? It didn't make sense. Why, he'd only just arrived.

I dawdled over the sink, taking my time with the kettle, waiting for the water to run cold to allow Mrs. Mullet time to wipe her eyes and poke in the ends of her hair.

"You've been overdoing it, Mrs. M," I said. "You must be exhausted. Why don't you go up to my room and have a nap? No one will disturb you there."

"Workin' too 'ard?" Her voice was suddenly battleship steel. "That's where you're wrong, Miss Flavia. I 'aven't been workin' 'ard *enough. That's* the trouble."

I put the kettle on the stove and waited for her to subside, but she didn't.

"There's work to be done and it's my place to do it."

"But—"

"Don't but me, miss. 'Tisn't every day Miss 'Arriet comes 'ome, an' 'tisn't every day I gets to welcome 'er. No one shall take that away from me—

"Not even you, Miss Flavia."

I went to her and put my arms around her from behind, resting my cheek on top of her head.

I didn't say a word because I didn't need to.

Outside, seen from the kitchen garden, one of the larger planets—Jupiter, I think—was well up above the pink ribbon of the eastern horizon.

It was the dark of the moon, and overhead, the stars sparkled in the inky blue-black vault of the heavens.

I was wiping the dew from Gladys's cold seat when something rustled near the greenhouse.

"Dogger?" I called quietly.

There was no reply.

"Adam?

"All right," I said. "I know you're there. Come out before I call the police."

Someone stepped out of the shadows.

It was Tristram Tallis.

"Sorry," he said. "I didn't mean to frighten you. I was trying not to wake the household."

"You didn't frighten me," I told him. "I thought you were a prowler. You're lucky I didn't shoot you."

This was a bit of a stretch, even for me, and I think he knew it. Although Buckshaw did have a firearms museum—or "muniment room," as Father called it—most of the weapons in its glass cases had likely not been fired since the Roundheads and the Cavaliers had squeezed their triggers in the days of "Jolly Ollie" Cromwell.

"Good job you didn't," Tallis said. "I should have been hurt if you'd potted me."

Was the man twitting me?

I decided to let it pass and find out what he was up to.

"You're up early." I tried to put a pinch of accusation in my voice.

"I couldn't sleep. I thought I'd come down and check on *Typhon*. Sorry, *Blithe Spirit*, I mean. Oil and so forth."

It seemed an unlikely excuse for a moment until I remembered that I felt the same way about Gladys.

"Since it might be our last day together, I thought I'd get an early start."

Our last day together? Was he referring to me? Or to Blithe Spirit?

"Yes, that's right," he said, seeing the look of puzzlement on my face. "I'm selling up. Cashing in my chips. As the old song says, I'm off to Tipperary in the morning. I've been offered a post shuffling papers in South America."

"That's not exactly Tipperary," I said. I didn't know where Tipperary was, actually, except that it sounded as if it might be somewhere in Ireland.

"No, not exactly." He grinned. "I hadn't thought of that. Do you think I should wire them and tell them I've changed my mind?"

Now I knew he was teasing me.

"No," I said. "You should go. But leave *Blithe Spirit* here at Buckshaw, so that when I'm old enough, I can learn to fly her."

"I would if I could. But the old girl—See? You've got me calling her an old girl!—needs hangaring. Plus the gentle hand of a good mechanic."

"Dogger could look after her," I said.

Dogger, after all, could do anything.

He shook his head sadly. "I'm afraid I've sold her," he said.

I felt my heart sink within me.

Blithe Spirit sold? I don't know why, but it didn't seem right. She had, after all, been sold before.

"Look here," Tristram Tallis said. "How would it be if I took you for a flip?"

At first I didn't understand him—didn't know what he was suggesting.

"A flip?"

"A flight."

Could this be true? Could it actually be happening to me? I had once asked Father what Buckshaw looked like from the air. "Ask your aunt Felicity," he'd said. "She's flown."

I never had, of course. Now the opportunity was staring me straight in the face.

"That's very kind of you, Mr. Tallis, but I couldn't possibly accept without permission."

I knew already what Father's reply would be, even if I was willing to intrude upon him, which I wasn't.

What a disappointment, though: having to refuse my only chance to take to the air in Harriet's *Blithe Spirit*.

My spirits were already sinking when a second figure stepped from the shadows.

It was Dogger.

He handed me a red woolly jumper I had mislaid a week ago in the greenhouse.

"Put this on, Miss Flavia," he said, without so much as a smile. "The air can be remarkably cold in the mornings."

Then I, with a silly grin splitting my face from side to side in the damp dawn, was sprinting across the Visto towards *Blithe Spirit*.

Tristram Tallis strapped me into the front seat and left me sitting there alone as he made a tour of inspection round the aircraft, touching here, wiggling there, peering at one thing and another.

I took the opportunity to have a quick look round the cockpit in which I was sitting. I think I had been expecting something quite wonderful in a machine which was capable of flying up among the gods, but this one seemed horribly underequipped for such a journey: a simple stick that jutted up out of the floor and a couple of dials and gauges on a wooden panel.

And that was all. Surely this thing was too frail to fly.

I was beginning to think I had made a mistake. Perhaps I should beg off. But it was too late.

After a couple of halfhearted swings at the propeller, Tristram returned to the cockpit, threw a switch, and gave it another try. There was an alarming mechanical clanking from the engine, a burst of smoke, and with a roar the propeller disappeared in a blur.

The wings teetered alarmingly as he clambered aboard.

"All set?" he shouted as he fastened himself in the back seat, and I, clutching the edges of the cockpit, managed a grim nod.

The roar became a tornado and we began to move, slowly at first, but with ever-increasing speed until we were rattling along cross-country like the Hinley Hunt in full cry.

Faster and faster still we went until I thought *Blithe Spirit* was about to tear herself to pieces.

And then a sudden smoothness.

We were flying!

Rather than us rising up into the air as I had expected

we would, the earth fell away beneath us like a carpet being jerked out from under one's feet by some unseen practical joker.

I had no more than a fleeting impression of the roofs of Buckshaw before the ornamental lake was floating quickly past below us.

The sun was an enormous red fire balloon on the horizon as we rose up out of the shadows and into the sudden daylight.

It was breathtaking!

If Feely and Daffy had dashed to their windows at the noise of our takeoff, I would be no more to them now than a flyspeck in the distance.

Just as I always was, I couldn't help thinking.

But beneath our wings, the marvelous toy world slid slowly by: hills, fields, woods and valleys, dales, dells, ponds and groves. Far below us, miniature sheep grazed in handkerchief pastures.

It made me want to write a hymn. Hadn't even Johann Sebastian Bach composed something about sheep?

Away to the east, the rising sun struck a sharp glint off the river, and for a few moments, as we turned away from it, the Efon was a shimmering snake of rubies crawling off towards a distant sea.

How Harriet must have loved this, I thought: the freedom of it all—the sense of having left one's body, but not one's mind, behind. Unless you happened to be a bird, the body was of little use up here: You could not run or jump as you did on the ground, but only observe.

In a strange way, being an aviator was like being a departed soul: You could look down upon the Earth without actually being present, see all without being seen.

It was easy enough to see why God, having called the dry land "Earth" and the gathering together of the waters "the Seas," saw that it was good.

I could picture the Old Fellow lifting up the horizon like the lid of a stewing pot and peeking in with one red eye to admire His Creation: to see how it was coming along.

It *was* good!

Tristram was waving a hand, pointing downwards. *Blithe Spirit* tilted precipitously to one side, and I found myself looking down the wing at an oddly familiar collection of buildings.

Bishop's Lacey's High Street!

There was the Thirteen Drakes, inside which all those official people from the railway station—those bullies from the Home Office, presumably billeted in every nook and cranny, even unto the broom cupboards, if Daffy was to be believed—were dreaming their dreadful dreams of power.

And down there, in Cow Lane, was the Bishop's Lacey Free Library—and Tilda Mountjoy's Willow Villa, even more gaudily orange than usual in the light of the early morning.

We had now flown through half of a vast clockwise circle and were turning south again. Ahead I could see the Palings, that curious bend in the river at the edge of our estate, and I wondered what the Hobblers, that peculiar cult who had once baptized their babies at that spot, might have made of our flying machine appearing suddenly in the sky.

A little to the east, the Gulley ran along the river to Goodger Hill, down which Gladys and I had so often raced and fallen breathless at the bottom.

And there was the Jack O'Lantern, the skull-like outcropping which loomed over the Palings. I had promised to meet Lena there for a picnic after the funeral.

Almost directly to the east, at the very bottom of Pooker's Lane, was Rook's End, and I smiled at the thought of Dr. Kissing. The old gentleman would already be up and puffing at his first cigarette of the day.

Perhaps we could give him a bit of a show: Buzz the aerodrome, as the pilots at Leathcote would have said. It would be good to let Father's old headmaster know that someone was thinking of him. I grinned at the thought of his speculating for hours about whom it might have been.

Flavia de Luce was the last person on earth he'd ever think of!

I waved frantically with both hands to get Tristram's attention and pointed down at Rook's End.

He must have done this sort of thing before because the stick in front of me lunged suddenly forward and to one side, and we were hurtling down towards the earth at a terrific speed, the wings whistling and the wind howling in the wires like banshees.

"Yaroo!" I wanted to shout, but I kept it to myself. I didn't want Tristram to think I was immature.

Just when it seemed we must become a permanent blot on the landscape, we pulled up out of the dive, and I watched as our winged shadow raced across the stony face of the Jack O'Lantern. We had cheated death.

Now we were floating lazily along just above the treetops of the park at Rook's End. As the house came into view, I noticed several motorcars parked in the forecourt. It would have been difficult to miss them.

One was an apple green Rolls-Royce with the rear part of its roof peeled away to form a makeshift greenhouse. There couldn't possibly be another like it in the entire world.

It was Nancy, Adam Sowerby's old Roller.

And parked beside it was an angular mint green Land Rover.

Lena de Luce!

What the dickens was *she* doing here?

Why would she and Adam be meeting at Rook's End at such an ungodly hour of the morning? What could the two of them possibly want with Dr. Kissing?—for surely it was him they had come to see.

Who else could possibly bring them to this remote and frankly uninviting home for decayed gentlefolk?

My thoughts were interrupted by a sudden silence. Tristram had throttled back *Blithe Spirit*'s engine and we had entered into a gentle glide. Buckshaw was dead ahead.

We're going to crash! I was sure of it as the ground rushed up to meet us.

But we slipped through the quiet air above the Mulford Gates, skimmed the treetops of the avenue of chestnuts, and alighted on the Visto as gently as a mayfly on a rose petal.

"Well?" Tristram demanded. We had come to rest and he was already climbing out of the back cockpit. "What did you think?"

"Most instructive," I said.

·TWENTY-TWO·

"DOGGER," I ASKED, "WHAT possible reason could Adam Sowerby and Lena de Luce have for driving to Rook's End before sunrise?"

"I'm sure I can't say, Miss Flavia."

"Can't say—or won't say?"

My conversations with Dogger were often like that: a gentle game between two chess masters.

"Can't say. I don't know."

"What *do* you know?"

Dogger gave the ghost of a smile, and I knew that he was enjoying this as much as I was.

"I know that each left in his or her own vehicle at approximately twelve minutes past five this morning."

"Anything else?"

"And that the elder Miss de Luce—your aunt Felicity—accompanied them."

"What?!"

It was unheard of that Aunt Felicity, who loved nothing better than to barricade herself in her bedroom armed with no more than toaster, tea, and the latest thriller, should go gallivanting round the countryside in the dark of the moon.

Simply unheard of.

"Where were they going?"

"At a guess, Rook's End," Dogger said. "An assumption confirmed perhaps, at least in part, by your own aerial reconnaissance."

His placid, utterly impassive face told me there was more.

"And?" I demanded. "What else?"

"Colonel de Luce accompanied them."

My whole world tilted, as if I was still in the air, making a steep turn in *Blithe Spirit*.

If it was unheard of for Aunt Felicity to venture out beyond the bounds of Buckshaw, the fact that Father would—

No! I simply refused to believe it.

"Are you sure?" I asked. Perhaps Dogger was having a gentle joke, although it seemed unlikely.

"Quite sure," he said.

"Did he say where he was going?"

"He did not. And I did not inquire."

Was there a message in Dogger's words? Was he warning me to mind my own business?

Dogger's loyalty, I sometimes had to remind myself, was first of all to Father, and I must never, for any reason, impose upon that devotion.

"Thank you, Dogger," I said. "You've been very helpful."

"Not at all, Miss Flavia," he said, with that look on his face. "I am always pleased to be of service."

Alone in my laboratory, I tried desperately to keep my mind occupied in the hours remaining before the funeral by resuming an experiment I had been considering when news had come of Harriet's discovery in the Himalayas.

It is a fact of nature that, given sufficient quantities, poison can be obtained from even the most harmless organic substances. Tapioca and rhubarb, for instance, contain exquisite death if the wrong parts of the plant are used in their preparation, and even our dear old friend water, H_2O, is capable of poisoning if too much of the stuff is drunk in too short a span of time.

I made a couple of notes but my heart just wasn't in it. I threw down my pencil.

Although I loathed the very idea, it was likely time to begin dressing for the day. Mrs. Mullet had fetched out and cleaned one of the mothballed school uniforms that Harriet, when she was my age, had been made to wear at Miss Bodycote's Female Academy in Toronto, Canada: a black-belted horror worn with long black stockings and a white blouse that made me look like one of those grotesque but amusing creatures from Ronald Searle's St Trinian's cartoons. Like Father and Dogger, Mr. Searle had been a prisoner of the Japanese in Singapore, and his work was much admired by some of us at Buckshaw.

I scrubbed my face and teeth, cleaned the remnants of

my nails, sighed deeply, and turned to the task I most truly despised: the braiding of my hair into pigtails.

I had tried everything I could think of to make it an adventure. I had pretended that I was a pirate, lashed to the mainmast in a howling hurricane, splicing the only rope that could secure the last remaining sail.

Right over left . . . and up . . . and under. Left over right . . .

"Ha, ha, me hearties. Simple as sin. Break out the grog!"

But it was no use. Transforming a haystack of mousy brown hair into a length of romantic rigging was too much to hope for.

The worst thing about dressing one's own hair was the fact that it needed to be done backwards. It was like playing a game of "In a Glass Darkly" in Girl Guides, in which one must try to write one's full name with pencil on a scrap of paper while looking in a mirror:

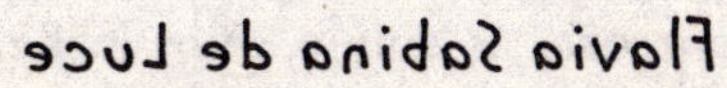

—a game during which I always wished I had been born plain old AVA OXO, or at least someone with a more symmetrical name.

The losers and the clumsy players were always hooted heartily, and it was at those times I most often found my thoughts turning to the subject of poisons.

I secured the ends of the pigtails with a couple of blue ribbons tied into neat bows. Yellow was too cheerful for the occasion, red too gaudy, and orange out of the question.

I stared at myself in the looking glass. Who was this girl

with her mother's face? It was as if I were wearing a Harriet mask for Carnival and had not noticed it until now.

And, to tell the truth, it frightened me.

Breakfast at Buckshaw was always a glum affair, and this morning was no exception. Tristram and Adam were seated at the foot of the table, as if to keep a respectful distance from the grieving family.

Father, all in black, sat at the head, his palms flat on the table. He had touched not a crumb of his breakfast and it seemed unlikely that he would do so.

Beside him, Feely was a pale ghost, nibbling absently at a piece of dry toast. She needed to keep her strength up if she was to be at the organ for Harriet's funeral.

Everyone from family to the vicar and his wife had tried to dissuade her, but all in vain. Feely was as steely cold in her stubborn resolve as only a wispy-looking musician can be.

Daffy, cocooned in some kind of comic, musty Victorian mourning outfit, was helping herself to another kipper. Her acid glance defied me to say anything.

When she was like this, even Father knew better than to risk a single word.

Aunt Felicity sat at the middle of the table, well apart from both groups, humming mindlessly to herself like a hive of distant bees.

Adam gave me the tiniest of nods before resuming his quiet conversation with Tristram, who did not give me so much as a glance. It was as if our early morning flight had been merely a dream—and perhaps it had. Perhaps it had never happened.

A time traveler, materializing at our breakfast table from some far future, would have supposed that Mrs. Mullet was the only one of us who was flesh and blood with the deceased.

Mrs. M, to be perfectly honest, looked a wreck. Her face was flushed, her eyes brimming with unshed tears, and her hair sticking out like jackstraws.

She fished a kipper and a couple of bangers from their serving dishes and placed them on my plate. Her lips were even more tightly pressed together than they had been before—as if they were now additionally secured by C-clamps.

She said not a word, and I realized in that instant how deep was her despair.

I reached out to touch her hand but she was already gone.

Breakfast broke up with no more than a few hushed words exchanged between the two guests at the foot of the table.

I excused myself and left the room. I would go to my laboratory and try to set down in my notes the confusion that was in my mind.

I was no more than halfway across the foyer when the doorbell rang. Dogger appeared from nowhere, as he often does so uncannily, and swung the heavy door back on its hinges.

Two delivery men in overalls, their arms filled with flowers, stood waiting. Behind them, on the gravel sweep, their van, open at the back, overflowed with bouquets, wreaths, and carpeted arrangements of carnations, cornflowers, arum lilies, and forget-me-nots all nestled in beds of Queen Anne's lace. There were gladioli, peonies, and roses; marigolds, chrysanthemums, and irises.

It was as if the gardens of Heaven had been raided and the plunder delivered to our door with more than enough flowers to overflow the foyer.

In spite of the early hour, a fresh queue of mourners had already formed, snaking round the van and making a straggling half circle in the forecourt.

As the men spat on their hands and began the long job of moving the flowers into the house, Dogger produced a small notebook from his vest pocket and began carefully cataloging the names of the senders, which he read from the pasteboard cards attached to each arrangement.

It was as if all the world had known Harriet, and all the world in mourning had sent their floral tributes.

"Sorry about your mother," a voice said at my ear. "Rotten bad luck. I should have hoped it would turn out better than this."

I spun round, knowing already that it was Adam Sowerby, or, to give him the whole McGillicuddy—as it was so prominently printed on his card, which I still had tucked away in the pages of a recent notebook:

Adam Tradescant Sowerby, MA., FRHortS, etc.
Flora-archaeologist
Seeds of Antiquity—Cuttings—Inquiries
Tower Bridge, London E.1 ***TN Royal 1066***

He was, of course, something of a fraud. While working in the guise of an archaeological botanist, retrieving and coaxing back into germination the seeds of plants and flowers thought to be long extinct, the man was actually an inquiry agent, or—to put it more plainly—a private detective.

When he learned of my recent successes, he had tried to recruit me as his partner in criminal investigation, but I had quickly discovered that the man took more than he gave. Worse than that, he had point-blank refused to tell me whom he was working for.

Since Adam was an old friend of Father's, there wasn't much that I could do to keep him off my pitch, but there was no law that said I had to cooperate.

"It must have been a very great shock," he said, still talking, even though I hadn't been listening.

I nodded and headed for the staircase.

"As must have been that poor bloke at the station."

I stopped in my tracks. How did Adam know about that? Had he been there?

I thought he had only arrived last night. Had he already been in consultation with the police?

I could hardly believe that Inspector Hewitt would confide in a private inquiry agent—and a private inquiry agent from London, at that!

Of course, by now, the circumstances of the stranger's death must be the talk of the village. Perhaps that was why some of the mourners had looked at me so oddly. Adam might well have stopped and been given the goods at Bert Archer's petrol station or at the Thirteen Drakes. Or might he have heard the grisly details from someone here at Buckshaw?

If that was the case, the burning question was—from whom?

Who else in the house had seen what happened on the railway platform? If Inspector Hewitt, out of sympathy for the family, had delayed his questioning of the household's inhabitants, who else had witnessed the murder?

Who else was keeping silent?

"All right," I said, turning round reluctantly. "Tell me what you know."

There are people who are able to deflect direct questions as easily as a duck sheds water, and Adam, I knew, was one of them.

"Terence Alfriston Tardiman, bachelor, of 3A Campden Gardens, Notting Hill Gate, London, W8, aged thirty-seven."

Adam's frankness surprised me.

"How do you know that?"

"No magic involved," he said. "I'd been following him for five days. This time."

"What do you mean 'this time'? Have you followed him before?"

Adam nodded. "Off again, on again, gone again, Finnegan. It's been going on for years."

I hadn't the faintest idea what he was referring to, but I pretended I did.

"Who was he?" I asked. "Other than his name."

"That's what I've been trying to discover," Adam said. "As Mr. Churchill once so aptly put it, Tardiman was a riddle inside a mystery wrapped in an enigma. And now that he's dead, more so than ever."

"Mr. Churchill was at the station," I found myself saying. "He spoke to me."

Oh, fluff! I had blurted it out without thinking.

"Winnie quite often likes to insert himself at the heart of the action," Adam told me. "Rather like Alfred Hitchcock's cameo appearances in his own films, but somewhat more risky.

"What did he have to say?" he added casually.

"Just that he was sorry," I said.

I was certainly not going to tell him that Mr. Churchill had asked: "*And have you, also, acquired a taste for pheasant sandwiches, young lady?*"

With Inspector Hewitt and his men of the Hinley Constabulary and Adam Tradescant Sowerby (Inquiries) on the case, I knew instinctively to keep certain information to myself.

That I had let slip the fact that Mr. Churchill had spoken to me was troubling. I would need to be far more discreet in future.

I was trying to think of a way to remove myself from this dangerous conversation when someone laid a large hand on my shoulder.

It was the vicar, Denwyn Richardson, and behind him stood his wife, Cynthia.

"Dearest Flavia," he said. "We've been looking for you everywhere. I've spoken to your father, of course, but—I told him we were sorry not to have traveled with you to Buckshaw from the station yesterday, but what with poor

Mrs. Dainty being taken so suddenly, and everything being consequently at sixes and sevens, to say nothing of the fact that our telephone at the rectory chose that moment to—well, how very, very sorry we are that things have come to such a—"

Cynthia brushed past him and wrapped me in such a tight and quaking hug that I thought my bones would surely shatter.

We had had our battles, Cynthia and I, and it was only recently that I had learned of the tragic death, seven years ago Christmas, of their daughter, Hannah.

Hannah had been four years old, my exact age at the time, when she fell beneath the wheels of a train at Doddingsley station. She had been laid to rest in a so-far unmarked grave in the churchyard of St. Tancred's, and the villagers had begun a conspiracy of silence to shield the Richardsons from grief and guilt. The little girl had darted away from her father on that tragic long-ago Christmas, and he had blamed himself.

The trembling of Cynthia's embrace became a chill as I realized what a harsh reminder the death of Terence Tardiman must be to them: that whole ghastly nightmare on the railway platform brought back to life and shoved in their faces, as it were.

I felt my tears coming, and before I could stop them, they were dribbling down Cynthia's neck. Rather than pulling away, though, she was now hugging me all the harder.

How sorry I suddenly felt for this poor little woman: this poor unfortunate little creature upon whom I had wasted so much hatred over the years. What kind of life did she have, when you stop to think about it? All of her days and nights were given over to visiting the sick, arranging flowers for the church, chairing meetings of this committee and that, booking the parish hall, cooking three meals a day for her husband, typing up and printing handbills and posters on a hectograph or churning out church bulletins on a Banda machine, to say nothing of managing her husband's timetable, mending his clothes, starching his surplices, running the church library, and listening to the troubles of everyone in Bishop's Lacey.

Being married to a man who dressed himself in vestments was no holiday camp.

She didn't seem to want to let me go. The hug went on until I thought to say, "Oh! I'm sorry, I must be hurting you."

At that point we both gave a little laugh and released our life-and-death grip on each other.

Adam, meanwhile, had wandered away and was critically inspecting the funeral flowers. I was dying to ask him what he thought, but I didn't dare.

Dogger had now admitted those from the head of the queue, and the long trudge up the stairs to Harriet's boudoir had resumed. It would go on until just after noon, when preparations for departure would begin.

I could only hope and pray that those officious creatures from the Home Office had thought to stop the dripping.

I took my leave of the Richardsons and climbed the stairs to the east wing. In the top corridor, I knew instantly that I was not alone.

There is a vibration in the air that is not a sound and not a smell but more a *feeling* in the atmosphere that signals without fail the presence of another.

I flung open the door of my bedroom and marched inside, but no one was there. Then the laboratory. Except for Esmeralda, it, too, was empty.

Down the hall I crept on tiptoe, taking great care to avoid the squeaky floorboard in front of the nook. I put my hand on the knob of Angels—and threw open the door.

Undine was standing on the laboratory stool, the oilcloth wallet in her hand. She had fished it out of its hiding place behind the baggy wallpaper.

"You lied to me," she said, wide-eyed with indignation. "You told me you were watering plants."

I have to give the girl credit. Not only had she found the hidden wallet, but she had manufactured a remarkably good response when I caught her red-handed. It was exactly the kind of thing I might have thought of myself. Someday I might even tell her that—but not now.

I marched smartly across the room and snatched the packet from her hands. "You little beast!" I said. "Is this how you repay kindness?"

"You crept up on me," Undine pouted. "Ibu *said* you were devious."

"Ibu did, did she? Did she say anything else?"

"Yes. She told me to keep an eye on you."

Keep an eye on me! That was the last straw.

"Tell me something, Undine," I said. "Do you know how to say 'buzz off' in Malay?"

"*Berambus*."

"Excellent! *Berambus!*"

"Are you dismissing me?" she asked.

"You're a very perceptive child," I said, shoving her out the door. "Now tallyho, and don't come back."

"Brute!" Undine said, getting in the last word, as I somehow knew she would. "Ibu was right."

I gave her the response she deserved: I crossed my eyes horribly and stuck out my tongue at her.

"Ain't you beautiful!" She giggled, and then she was gone.

Beautiful? It was the first time anyone had called me that—even as an insult.

I examined my image in one of the dusty, peeling mirrors that hung in the dim hall.

If I were a painting, I thought, *it would be called* Girl in Black *and would probably be by one of those artists such as the American Whistler.*

I was little more than a white face staring out at myself from a gloomy background, the only spot of color my eyes.

It made me feel so old, so sad, so much a part of the house, so much a de Luce.

The face was, of course, Harriet's face. Father had told me recently that I wasn't just *like* Harriet, but that I *was* Harriet.

I didn't even have a face to call my own.

It was in that moment, looking at myself staring back at myself, that something somewhere deep inside went *click*—as if the universe, and I with it, had, like a grandfather clock, moved on to the next cog of a clunking wooden gear.

I can't explain it any more clearly than that. One instant I was plain old Flavia de Luce, and the next instant—*click*—I was plain old Flavia de Luce, but with a difference. For all the tea in China, I couldn't say what the difference was, but only that a distinct change had taken place.

And I knew in that instant what I must do.

With my heart in my mouth—this wasn't going to be easy; in fact, it was going to be the most difficult moment of my entire life—I made my way to the west wing. The long line of mourners was still shuffling slowly across the foyer and up the stairs. Most of them averted their eyes as I pardoned my way through the queue and made for Father's study.

There could be no half truths, no excuses, no evasion. No appeals to sympathy, no claims of ignorance, no sweeping of inconvenient facts under the carpet.

It was that breathtakingly simple. Really, it was.

I did not knock. I opened the door and walked in.

Father was standing silhouetted at the window, and how old he looked: how very, very old.

He had heard me come in, of course, but he did not turn. He might have been a carving in ebony of a dark shadow looking out over the lawn.

I went to his side and, without a word, handed him Harriet's will.

And without a word he took it.

For a moment we stared at each other. It was the first time, I think, that I had ever looked my father in the eye.

And then I did what I needed to do.

I turned and walked out of the room.

* * *

Of course I had wanted to tell Father exactly how Harriet's will had come to be in my possession. I had wanted to make a clean breast of it—the whole scheme: my plans for Harriet's resurrection and my surprise presentation of her, newly restored to life, to her grieving husband, to my grieving father.

What a scene it would have been!

But my well-meaning plan, alas, through no fault of my own, had been thwarted by those interfering killers from the Home Office.

Because of them, Harriet would now remain dead forever.

Father would realize from the document what I had done. I wouldn't need to say a word.

I had no right, of course, to read my mother's will, and I was glad I had not done so. I had realized that while staring at my own reflection in the looking glass. Her will was not mine to read.

I had removed it from its rather unpleasant wallet and put it into Father's hands.

For better or for worse, I had done what I had done, and now there was no going back.

I had done the right thing and I would jolly well have to live with it.

·TWENTY-THREE·

HARRIET'S FUNERAL WAS NOW just hours away. There wasn't a moment to lose.

I sauntered off across the Visto as if I was going for an aimless walk.

At the far corner of the ancient, overgrown lawn, Tristram Tallis, in blue coveralls and almost invisible in a cloud of blue smoke, was tinkering with the idling engine of *Blithe Spirit*. He waved a spanner in the air.

"If you've come for another hop, I'm afraid you're out of luck," he said as I reached his side.

" '*And he opened the bottomless pit*,' " announced a loud, dramatic, and rather familiar voice, " '*and there arose a smoke out of the pit, as the smoke of a great furnace*.' "

Adam Sowerby popped round from the other side of the aircraft. I hadn't noticed he was there.

" '*And the sun and the air were darkened by reason of the*

smoke of the pit.' The author of the Book of Revelation, whoever he might have been, was doubtless thinking of recalcitrant aero carburetors when he wrote those words."

Adam was always spouting poetry. It oozed out of him like jam from a squeezed bun.

"Spare the child," Tristram said, as if I wasn't there.

The whole scene had an air of dreamlike unreality: the three of us standing on a ruined lawn in the blowing smoke of a ticking aero engine, and Adam all the while spewing poetic nonsense that would have made even the author of the Book of Revelation, whoever he might have been, fall gasping to the ground in helpless laughter.

Only Tristram seemed remotely real, even though, in his baggy coveralls and with the spanner in his hand, he reminded me of a court jester with a bladder on a stick.

Who was he, anyway? Beyond the fact that he had once come to Buckshaw to buy *Blithe Spirit* from Harriet, that he claimed to have fought in the Battle of Britain, and that Mrs. Mullet doted upon him, I knew nothing whatsoever about the man.

Was he really who he pretended to be? It had been my experience that strangers were not always truthful about their identity. Some seemed able to shrug it off as easily as a wet raincoat.

I was simply dying to ask Adam about his visit in the early hours to Rook's End, but to risk doing so in front of Tristram could well turn out to be a bad mistake.

As if he were reading my mind, Adam gave me a sly wink behind the pilot's back. I ignored it.

Tristram reached into the cockpit, and the propeller

clattered to a standstill. "Fouled plug," he announced. "Nothing to do with the carburetor. So much for Revelation, Sowerby."

Adam shrugged. "I'm afraid the Apocalypse of John is rather slender on the subject of sparking plugs, unless of course, his 'lightnings and thunderings' and 'seven lamps of fire burning before the throne' foresaw the rotary aero engine, although that won't quite do, will it? This old girl has four cylinders, not seven, and besides—"

I gave him *such* a look! Foolishness in a grown man, no matter how lighthearted, is disgusting.

There was more here than met the eye. I was sure of it. Why, on the morning of a funeral, would two houseguests be fiddling with an aeroplane on an out-of-the-way lawn and burbling bits of Revelation? It didn't make any sense.

Was Tristram Tallis the tall man I had glimpsed at the window of my laboratory in the ciné film? Or could that man have been the one who was pushed under the train?

It might have been neither, and I could hardly ask. One of them was dead, and the other—well, the other, if he was who I suspected he might be, would hardly blurt out the truth to a mere girl, even if she *was* almost twelve years old.

And Adam Sowerby. It all came down to this: What was he doing in Bishop's Lacey and for whom was he working? Was he here as a private investigator? Or as a friend of the family?

Until I knew the answers to these questions, I could trust neither of these two men.

As usual, I was on my own.

"If you'll excuse me," I said, "I have things to do."

* * *

South I walked, towards the ornamental lake, until my direction was hidden by the brick wall of the kitchen garden. Then, slowly, I made my way back towards the east, working round the ornamental lake until I was safely hidden by the trees of the Palings. Then, across the little bridge to the Gully, and it wasn't long before I was climbing Goodger Hill.

If it hadn't been for the steepness of Goodger Hill and the Jack O'Lantern, I'd have brought Gladys. I thought of her sitting alone at home, wondering why I had forsaken her. Although Gladys loved nothing better than whizzing hell-for-leather down hills, she loathed being shoved up them. It made both of us cranky.

With a sigh, I trudged on towards my destination.

Set among acres of moldy grass and ancient beech trees, Rook's End was a damp, subsiding monstrosity consisting on the outside of countless gables and on the inside of stale endless corridors.

A *mushroom farm for humans*, I thought.

It was not the first time I had visited the place. I had, on several occasions in the past, found it necessary to consult with Dr. Kissing, and I must admit I was quite looking forward to seeing the old gentleman again.

I crunched across the gravel of the now empty forecourt and opened the front door. I thought it quite unlikely that anyone would be at the desk, and I was right.

The same silver bell sat beside the same smudged sign that read "Ring Plse."

I didn't bother.

From somewhere in the distance came the sound of many human voices and the clink of crockery. The air was sour with the smell of food prepared by the bucketful, the chiefest of which was cabbage and its derivative gases.

I knew that I would find Dr. Kissing where I always found him: at the far end of the narrow solarium.

The bubbling brown linoleum hissed and popped disgustingly beneath my shoes as I made my way across the vast, empty space.

From behind the high back of the familiar wicker bath chair, a silvery cord of cigarette smoke spiraled its way up towards a dark and distant ceiling.

"Hello, Flavia," he said without turning round. He put down his *Times* with a faint rustle of paper.

I walked quickly into his field of view and gave him a polite peck on each cheek. His skin was as crisp and dry as must be one of those scrolls which have been found in a cave on the shore of the Dead Sea.

"You've come about your mother," he said.

I remained silent.

"As I knew you would," he added.

Dr. Kissing was not a person to beat about the bush.

Nor should I be, I decided.

"My father was here this morning," I said. "Before sunrise."

Dr. Kissing gazed at me coolly from amidst the rising cigarette smoke. In his mouse-colored dressing gown and tasseled velvet smoking cap, he might have been one of those impossibly old Oriental idols sitting placidly in a cloud of incense that I had seen on the jackets of the thrillers at Foyle's.

If I was going to enter into the game, I might as well show the full strength of my hand.

"So were Aunt Felicity and Adam Sowerby," I added.

"Yes," he said at last, but pleasantly. "So they were."

"I saw their cars in the forecourt."

"Did you indeed?"

"From *Blithe Spirit*. Harriet's aeroplane. Her owner took me up for a ride."

Dr. Kissing nodded knowingly as he stubbed out his cigarette and reached for another.

"You heard us?"

"The sound of a Gipsy Moth engine clattering away like a contented sewing machine in the skies above this scepter'd isle is one of the few remaining assurances in our changed world. The time, I believe, was five minutes before six and approximately a quarter hour after sunrise."

Did nothing escape this aged hive of information?

"I am very sorry about your mother," he said suddenly grave, and then, after a moment's thought: "You must be especially brave today."

He looked at me with his old, faded eyes, and I knew that this was the moment: the moment when I would have my only chance to do what I was planning to do, to say what I had come to say.

Dr. Kissing had ordered me to be brave, and so brave I must be.

I took a deep breath. "You're the Gamekeeper, aren't you?"

Maddeningly, even though it was barely lighted, he stubbed his cigarette in the overflowing ashtray and selected another meticulously from the flat tin—not because he was nervous, but because he was in control, totally in control.

"Fetch that chair," he said, pointing to an overstuffed horror in a corner.

I pushed the thing—which grated unnervingly on the rippled linoleum—into a position between Dr. Kissing and the window.

I seated myself demurely and waited.

"Let me tell you a story," he began. "Let us pretend that, once upon a time, there was, somewhere in England, an ancient and ramshackle old rectory in which were brought together, in utmost secrecy, some of the greatest Brains that could be found in all the land."

I grinned at the thought of all the rows and rows of brains, each in its own glass jar, lined up neatly on a shelf in some dim pantry.

"Is this a fairy tale?" I asked. "Or a true story?"

"The Official Secrets Act, even after all these years, still possesses a remarkably long and powerful arm. And so this must remain a fairy tale."

"My sister Daffy says that, in one way or another, all fairy tales and myths are based on truth."

"Your sister exhibits the hallmarks of a lady and a scholar," he said. "And I predict that she will prosper. Now then—

"These Brains, as I shall call them—Brains with a capital *B*, for they deserve nothing less—were charged with breaking the codes of a faraway Emperor."

"Was the Emperor wicked?" I asked.

"Of course he was—as all Emperors in all fairy tales must be. Otherwise there would be no point, would there? The evil Emperor, you see, is crucial to democracy."

I didn't see, but I tried to look as if I did.

"Let us suppose also that for many years, our far-flung monitoring stations had been gathering and recording all the coded radio transmissions from all the Emperor's ships in all the oceans of the world, and all his ships of the air—and that there had been some little success in cracking one or two of his codes, but not all of them, of which there were many."

"You're talking about Japan, aren't you?" We had listened to a remarkably similar discussion on the BBC Home Service during one of the compulsory "Wireless Nights" Father had laid on. Besides, everyone knew that of all the enemies with whom we had recently been at war, Japan was the only one with an Emperor.

Dr. Kissing ignored me and went on: "The problem was this: No sooner would we break a code than the Emperor would change it."

"How did the Emperor know it had been broken?"

"Ah, Flavia! I am delighted to see that my hope in you has not been misplaced. How *did* he know, indeed!"

"Someone was informing him. A spy!"

I was proud of myself.

"A spy," Dr. Kissing echoed. "A short, nasty word with

long, nasty consequences." He blew a small puff of smoke followed by an elongated gray-blue trumpet to illustrate his words. "And what if," he asked, "what if this spy were to be one of our own—one of the highest among us—one who had even, so to speak, the ear of our King?"

"Treason!" I said, probably too loudly.

"Treason indeed. But what are we to do about it?"

"Stop him!"

"How?"

Dr. Kissing had pounced upon me like a cat. The answer to his question seemed obvious, but I found myself not wanting to put it into words.

"Well?"

"Well—kill him, I suppose."

"Kill him." Dr. Kissing repeated my words in a flat, matter-of-fact voice. "Just so. But 'kill,' as you will have observed, like 'spy' and 'stop,' is really just one more of those short but exceedingly troublesome words."

"Well, capture him, anyway."

"Precisely. Let us pretend, however, that this traitor, in this fairy tale of ours, is firmly entrenched in one of the far-off branches of our own Foreign Office. Let us further imagine that he also possesses impeccable credentials. What then?"

I thought long and hard before replying. "Bring him home to justice," I said at last.

Father had lectured us on the subject of justice during one of his Wednesday lectures on the various aspects of British Government, and I thought I had quite a good grasp of the topic.

I was not sure I was happy with my solution, though, but I could not think of a better one. To be perfectly honest, I was becoming a little tired of Dr. Kissing's imaginary story. No—not tired—I was becoming uneasy.

"How does it end, this fairy tale?"

Dr. Kissing took an eternity to answer. He removed his spectacles, produced a spotlessly white handkerchief from a pocket of his dressing gown, polished both lenses with fanatic intensity, put them on again, and with infuriating deliberation, chose another cigarette from the tin box.

"That . . . shall be up to you, Flavia," he said at last.

There was a silence between us, which began comfortably enough, but all too quickly became unbearable.

I found myself getting up and walking to the window. I couldn't believe it—I was behaving like Father!

This whole fairy-tale business needed thinking about. From my own chemical experiments, I was used to working with hypotheses, but this one seemed beyond me. There were simply too many variables; too many assumptions; too many meanings veiled in mystery.

Outside, beyond the windowpane, the ancient beeches squatted in green splendor. The madwomen who had danced among them on my previous visits were nowhere in sight.

There were no convenient distractions. I had to face up to reality. "You didn't answer my question, Dr. Kissing. You're the Gamekeeper, aren't you?"

"No," he said, suddenly and sadly—perhaps even a little reluctantly. "No, no . . . I am not."

"Then who is?"

Much as I loved the old gentleman, I was becoming impatient with his diversions.

Dr. Kissing, almost unaware he was doing so, covered his lips with his right forefinger—and then his left.

His voice, when it came, was suddenly old, suddenly tired, and for the first time since I had met him, I feared for his life.

"That you must find out for yourself, Flavia," he said, his voice as faint and far away as if it were no more than an echo of the wind.

"*That*, too, you must find out for yourself."

·TWENTY-FOUR·

DIETER MET ME JUST to the east of the ornamental lake. He was wearing what looked like a borrowed black suit, which was very slightly too small for him.

"Everybody has been looking for you," he informed me.

"Sorry," I told him. "I needed to go for a long walk. Who's everybody?"

"Your father, your aunt Felicity, Ophelia, and Daphne—" Dieter always insisted on calling my sisters by their proper names. "Mrs. Mullet, also."

I have to admit that that *was* pretty well everybody, although I was secretly pleased that Dogger hadn't been asking my whereabouts.

"How did you know which direction to come looking for me?"

"Mr. Tallis and Mr. Sowerby told me they had seen you walking off towards the Palings."

"Mr. Tallis and Mr. Sowerby are a pair of bloody village gossips!"

Dieter laughed. With Dieter, I could be myself without fear of being corrected, punished, or ratted upon.

"What did you think of *Blithe Spirit*? Tristram took me up for a ride this morning. Aren't you jealous?"

A pilot in the Luftwaffe, Dieter had been brought down during the War not far from Bishop's Lacey and, as a prisoner of war, had been put to work on Ingleby's farm. When the War ended, he had chosen to stay in England, and now, six years later, was engaged to be married to my sister Feely. It's a funny old world when you stop to think about it.

"She's a beautiful craft," he admitted. "But no, I am not jealous. I have had my time in the air."

"How's Feely bearing up?" I asked. I had scarcely given her a moment's thought.

"She doesn't eat, she doesn't sleep. She thinks only of the music at your mother's funeral."

"Poor you," I said, meaning it as a joke.

"I wish you would have a word with her, Flavia. I should take it as a great favor."

Me? Have a word with Feely? What a preposterous idea!

"She respects you. She is forever talking about 'my brilliant little sister.'"

"Ha!" I said. I was not at my most articulate when I was stupefied.

Respect *me*? I couldn't believe it. Feely would rather eat frogs in clotted cream than listen to anything I might have to say.

Still, I didn't want to miss an opportunity.

"I'll see what I can do," I said. "I should have thought you'd want to comfort her on your own."

"It is not comforting she needs," Dieter said, "but a female shoulder. Do you know what I mean?"

Well, a female shoulder was a female shoulder. There was no great mystery about that.

I nodded. "But it won't be easy," I couldn't resist adding.

"No," Dieter agreed. "I think she feels the loss of your mother more keenly than—"

"Than Daffy and I do?" I cut in.

Dieter did not deny it. "She has more memories than you and Daphne," he said. "She has more of your mother to mourn."

Dieter had hit the nail on the head. It was one of the things I resented most about my sister—although when you stopped to analyze it, the jealousy was entirely on my part, not hers.

"Poor Feely," I said, and left it at that.

"She'll be better after we're married," Dieter said. "When she is able to get away from Buckshaw. There are so many ghosts here."

Ghosts? I'd never thought of it in that way. Any truly self-respecting ghost would rather die than haunt the halls of Buckshaw.

Which set me to wondering: *When the dead die, do they come back to life? Is that what resurrection is all about—the death of the dead?*

Although I had failed in my attempt to restore Harriet to the arms of her family, I could hardly be blamed. The men from the Home Office had interrupted my experiment, and I knew that I would never have another chance. Harriet would now be laid to rest and that would be that.

How sad it was that we should never get to know each other.

It was more than sad—it was a damned shame.

We paused at the corner of the redbrick wall which marked the corner of the kitchen garden.

"Cheer up," I said, realizing even as I spoke the words, that I had said a similar thing to Daffy. "How are the teaching plans coming along?"

More than anything in life, other than perhaps the hand of my sister, Dieter wanted to teach English literature to the English. He was a lifelong devotee of the Brontë sisters and was positively champing at the bit to be able to share his enthusiasm in a proper classroom.

He brightened at once. "Can you keep a secret?" he asked.

I nearly laughed in his face. Of all the billions of people who have ever trod the face of planet Earth, none of them—not a single blessed one!—has ever been as much a master of the zipped lip as Flavia de Luce.

I crossed my heart and my lips and showed him the two-fingered bunny-ear sign.

"In blood," I vowed. It was an oath known to very few.

"Your father has put in a word for me at Greyminster. I am to begin my teaching duties there in the autumn."

I threw my arms around him. I couldn't help myself. I had known that Dieter had been away on some mysterious interview during the Easter holidays but had heard no more about it.

"Yaroo!" I shouted. "That's spiffing! Congratulations, Dieter!"

"Keep it under your hat—is that how you say it? We didn't want to announce it until we've got through the funeral."

I didn't fail to notice the word "we."

I gave him another hug. "Hullo, Mr. Chips," I said. "Fear not. Your secret's safe with me."

Dieter shot me one of his gorgeous grins and offered me his arm. "Shall we go in?" he asked. "I shall inform them that you have been found."

In spite of the lovely weather, there was a coldness inside the house which I could not easily explain. It was as if the world had suddenly entered a new ice age: a change that had caught everybody by surprise and left them, every single one, in a kind of chilly lethargy.

In the foyer, the last straggling mourners stared at one another in a kind of antishock, as if they had abruptly lost the ability to recognize their neighbors.

There was an uneasy hush, broken only by the scuffling of shoes on the black-and-white marble and the suppressed sobs and sniffling of a woman I had never seen before in my life.

I think we all of us were realizing that the time of Harriet's funeral was drawing near.

It was going to be a bloody awful afternoon.

* * *

I found Feely in the drawing room, seated at the piano, her face white and her eyes the red of raw meat. Her fingers were moving over the keys but no sound was coming from the instrument. It was as if she hadn't the strength to summon music from the thing. I stood for a moment or two at the door, trying to guess by watching her fingers what silent melody she might be playing.

The very least I could do was to begin the conversation on a civil note.

"I'm sorry, Feely," I said at last. "I know how difficult this must be for you."

Her head came slowly round and her swollen eyes settled unsteadily on me.

"Do you?" she asked. And then after an immensely long time she added, "I'm glad."

She certainly didn't look glad.

In ordinary circumstances, although I never tell her so, my sister Feely is strikingly beautiful. Her hair shines with a golden glow and her blue eyes sparkle vividly. Her complexion—at least since its volcanic activity settled down—was turning out to be what the cinema magazines called "English peaches-and-cream."

But now, with Feely hunched miserably before me at the keyboard, I had a brief glimpse of what she was going to look like when she was an old woman, and it was not a pleasant picture. In fact, it was frightening.

Worse, I felt an overwhelming wave of pity.

I longed to tell her how desperately I had tried to bring

Harriet back from the dead so that we all of us, she and Father and Daffy and I, and not forgetting Dogger and Mrs. Mullet, of course, should live happily ever after.

It was, in a way, like Dr. Kissing's story: half truth, half fairy tale. But which half was which?

I no longer knew.

Was this nightmare pulling me towards reality or fantasy?

"Is there anything I can do?" I asked, fighting the undertow of my tired mind.

I realized how little sleep I'd had and how powerfully it was affecting me.

"Yes," Feely said. "There is. Don't do anything this afternoon to embarrass us."

As if I were a tramp at the kitchen door.

I think it was the "us" that hurt the most. Just one more of those little words with long shadows: two plain little letters, *u* and *s*, that transformed me from a sister into an outsider.

"Has Aunt Felicity had her talk with you yet?" Her voice suddenly as cold and stiff as whipped egg whites.

"Talk? What talk?"

Feely turned back to the keyboard and her hands crashed down in the most harsh, the most grinding, the most tortured series of chords imaginable.

I clapped my hands to my ears and fled the room.

I raced along the hall and across the echoing foyer—hang the gaping mourners!—up the staircase and into the east wing.

I flung open the door of my laboratory, dashed inside,

slammed the door behind me, and pressed my back against it.

A tall man turned round, and in his raised hand was the test tube which he had been examining.

It was Sir Peregrine Darwin.

·TWENTY-FIVE·

"I BELIEVE THIS IS cyanide," he said, and not at all pleasantly.

I nodded. I could hardly deny it—particularly to a man whose specialty it was to professionally identify cyanide.

"The laboratory belonged to my great-uncle, Tarquin de Luce. Perhaps you've heard of him?"

I was taking a risk, I knew, but it was at the moment the best I could come up with. Perhaps Sir Peregrine, I thought, had been at Oxford with Uncle Tarquin—but no, he wasn't old enough. But surely he must have heard of my uncle's work—perhaps he'd even idolized him as a boy.

Blood among chemists runs thick—at least I hoped it did.

But it was no use. Sir Peregrine didn't rise to the bait. He replaced the cyanide in its rack with a careful precision that I had to admire.

This man knew what he was doing.

"Your mother's inner coffin was cut open with a pair of ten-inch tinman's snips," he said accusingly.

I tried to look incredulous.

"Yes, you left the tools of your trade behind. We've sent them up to London for analysis and have just received back the report that your fingerprints—and your fingerprints alone—are all over them. Explain."

Well! Had my fingerprints on file, did they? I must admit I was flattered. The Hinley Constabulary must have handed them over from one of my earlier investigations.

Still, I had to give the man credit. He certainly didn't believe in letting the grass grow under his feet. If he had the ability to whisk a piece of evidence up to London, and have it analyzed and brought back to Bishop's Lacey within hours, the man was clearly no slouch. Inspector Hewitt would be chartreuse with envy. I could hardly wait to tell him.

"Well?"

He was waiting, and the look on his face could only be described as grim. "In case you are not aware of it, Miss de Luce, interference with the burial of a dead body is not—"

"I didn't interfere with her," I interrupted, the blood rushing to my face. "I didn't touch her!"

"Then what, pray, may I ask, were you doing?"

"She was my mother," I said. "I'd never seen her face. I wanted to—before she was buried."

I tried to stare him down but my lower lip was trembling.

Sir Peregrine did not look away.

Slowly he began to walk towards me, seeming to grow

taller with every step until he was hovering over me like a bird of prey.

I found myself shrinking away from him—cringing.

"Peregrine!" The voice cut through the air like a thrown knife.

I spun round. "Aunt Felicity!"

"Felicity!" said Sir Peregrine.

"What are you doing to that child?"

I could have cheered—even if she *had* committed the unforgivable sin.

"Well, Peregrine? Explain yourself."

"I was merely doing that which I am required to do by His Majesty's Government."

"Poppycock. You were trying to intimidate the girl. You ought to be ashamed of yourself."

"Felicity—"

Sir Peregrine was gaping as if he had been set upon by the Furies, those avenging goddesses of the underworld with their black robes, bloodshot eyes, and snaky hair, whose happy job it is to punish evildoers.

"Come along, Flavia," Aunt Felicity said, almost dislocating my arm as she seized me by the elbow and marched me out of the room. "It's time we had a talk."

We were halfway down the staircase before she let go of me.

"Quickly," she said, hustling me through the kitchen, holding open the door, and urging me through.

"Where are we going?"

"You'll see," she said.

I hate people who say that.

Halfway across the Visto, I was still trying to catch up. For an elderly lady, I realized, Aunt Felicity was remarkably fit.

Blithe Spirit was still parked as I had last seen her, but Tristram Tallis was nowhere in sight. Nor, for that matter, was Adam Sowerby.

"Get in," Aunt Felicity ordered, pointing.

I clambered up onto the wing and dropped into the front cockpit. Aunt Felicity, without further ado, went round the nose of the craft and gave the propeller a couple of remarkably powerful pulls.

"Switch on!" she shouted.

I looked at the instrument panel and could see only one switch. It was marked "Magneto" and I twisted it to the right.

"Switch on!" I called back.

I had seen this done in the cinema but had never actually had the opportunity to do it myself.

Aunt Felicity gave the prop another sharp spin, and as it had done this morning, it vanished with a roar.

Whatever Tristram had done with the faulty sparking plug must have cured the problem. The engine was running with a silky, self-satisfied rumble, popping a bit with joy as if it could hardly wait to get off the ground and into the air.

Now Aunt Felicity was lowering herself into the rear cockpit and the stick and pedals in front of me began to wigwag of their own accord.

The throttle shot forward in its metal quadrant, and we began to move.

The Visto became a blur. Buckshaw rotated slowly in the near distance as if it were on a turntable and we were standing still.

And then the ground dropped, and for the second time in my life I was flying.

Blithe Spirit pitched and bucked as the stick in front of me shook in its socket.

Aunt Felicity was trying to get my attention.

I twisted my head round and was just able to catch a glimpse of her. She was jabbing a bony finger to indicate the flying helmet, which she must have dredged from the depths of the cockpit, and she was obviously signaling me to do the same.

I reached under the seat and, sure enough, there was an identical helmet. I strapped it on.

Now the stick was waggling again, and I turned to see Aunt Felicity waving the end of a ribbed rubber tube. She put it to her ear, then to her mouth, and then her ear again.

At first I thought she was merely trying to entertain me: that she was miming some lurid magazine cover such as *Thrilling Tales* in which a pilot is wrestling at 5,000 feet with a boa constrictor which some nefarious villain has concealed in the cockpit, until I was made to realize by the violent and impatient shaking of the stick, that there was a similar tube beside me in the front cockpit and that Aunt Felicity wanted me to use the thing for speaking and listening.

I nodded and held the yellow tube to the ear-socket of my helmet.

Again the stick shook like a cornstalk in a hurricane.

Aunt Felicity was pointing to her ear and I saw at once what she wanted me to do. There was a socket in the side of my helmet into which the tube was meant to be inserted. I plugged it in, gave it a twist, and Aunt Felicity's voice was suddenly in my ear.

"Can you hear me?" she asked. I gave her a thumbs-up, which seemed the right thing to do in the circumstances.

"Good," she said. "Now listen to me. We've precious little time and what I have to say to you is of the utmost importance. Do you understand?"

I gave her three more thumbs for emphasis as she banked *Blithe Spirit* round towards the west.

Beneath our wings, Buckshaw lay spread out in the sun, a dreamy mirage of green lands, a fairy-tale kingdom in miniature. From this altitude, you could not see the black line painted in the foyer that divided the house into two camps, nor could you detect the frost that had recently descended upon the house.

Or had it been there all along, and I had only recently learned to notice?

"Take a good look, Flavia," Aunt Felicity's metallic voice was saying. "You may never see the likes of it again."

We were suspended in the air, the two of us, perhaps a mile above that special part of England which was ours. Tomorrow, after the funeral, it would probably belong to someone else.

Even if Harriet's will untied Father's legal entanglements, there was no money left to go on. Buckshaw had become a crushing burden that could no longer be borne.

Like Atlas, forced to put down the world from his shoulders in order to fetch apples from his daughters, the Hesperides, Father would not likely have the heart to take it up again.

In the old legends, anyone who willingly took up the Earth upon their shoulders was doomed to carry it forever: a curse, it seemed, with no way out.

"All of this belonged to your mother," Aunt Felicity said through the speaking tube, shouting to be heard above the roar of the engine, her voice coming through the tube in machine-gun bursts. "She loved it here. Nothing was more precious to her . . . than her home and her family. Harriet went away only because she had no other choice. It was a matter . . . of life and death. Not your life and death or mine . . . but that of *England*. . . . Do you understand?"

I nodded and looked out at the England that was beneath our wings.

"Your father had already been taken prisoner by the Japanese . . . but your mother was unaware of that . . . when she volunteered to go on a mission . . . which only she could accomplish successfully. She was . . . devastated at having to leave her three children in the care of others."

Aunt Felicity's words brought back barely recalled memories of being dressed and fed by strangers—a failed succession of nannies and governesses, none of whom, I later learned, had been Mary Poppins.

"But your mother knew her duty," Aunt Felicity went on. "She was a de Luce . . . and the life of England was at stake."

Behind and below us to the southwest, Buckshaw Halt was vanishing in the slight haze that had appeared, and I remembered the words that Mr. Churchill had spoken to my father.

"*She was England, damn it,*" he had said.

"*She was more than that, Prime Minister,*" Father had replied.

Only now was I beginning to realize how *much* more.

Harriet had volunteered for the mission Dr. Kissing had spoken of in his so-called fairy tale: a mission to bring home to justice a traitor who had sold himself out, and England with him, to the Emperor of Japan.

"Under diplomatic immunity, she had made her way to Singapore," Aunt Felicity continued, breaking into my thoughts, "where, unknown to her . . . your father was already attached to the Far East Combined Bureau. But before she could discover that . . . he was captured by the Japanese—on Christmas Day!—and thrown, with a handful of his staff, into Changi prison."

Aunt Felicity's voice came strangely to my ears, constricted to an insect buzz by the speaking tube. But her words were clear enough. Father had been imprisoned and Harriet was likely to be.

"At this crucial instant . . . the Japanese were still playing a double game. On the one hand, they had captured your father . . . . while at the same time, they were trying to demonstrate that they were . . . masters of the world. They even took your mother on a guided tour of the prison . . . at Changi . . . to show off to her the British officers they had in custody. She was to carry the word back to London . . . and the War Office would capitulate at once. Such was their thinking. Sheer madness!"

My mind was as blurred as the spinning propeller. How could this whole chapter of my family's history have taken place without my suspecting? It seemed impossible. Perhaps Dr. Kissing had been right: Perhaps it *was* a fairy tale.

"It was there . . . in that dreadful compound at Changi . . . that your parents were thrust suddenly and unexpectedly face-to-face—your mother being shown the prisoners who had been trotted out for her inspection . . . your father being taunted with the sight of an English visitor. Neither of them knew the other was in Singapore . . . but neither batted an eye."

Oh, how it must have torn their hearts, I thought. *How killing it must have been to show not a flicker of recognition: to have to pretend that they had never been in love, had never married, and that their three children—the youngest no more than a baby, left behind in England to be brought up by strangers—had never existed.*

I twisted round in the seat so that I could see Aunt Felicity. Her eyes were enormous—like an owl's behind her goggles—as she gave a nod as if to say, "Yes! It's true—every word of it."

My own eyes stung with tears. I didn't want to hear any more. I threw my hands up to cover my ears, but they could not block out Aunt Felicity's words, which came seeping again through the rubber tube.

"Flavia, listen. There's more—you must listen to me!"

I could not ignore the sound of crackling command that had suddenly come into her voice.

"The traitor your mother had come to deal with had apparently vanished. The political situation had become far too dangerous to remain in Singapore. She was making her way home . . . by way of India and Tibet. But . . . she was followed. Someone had betrayed her."

My mind went numb. Black thoughts tossed in my mind like the billows of some dark sea.

Had Harriet been murdered? I had wondered that before but set it aside as incredible beyond belief. But was that now the suspicion of the Home Office? Was that why Sir Peregrine Darwin had shown up so unexpectedly on our doorstep? Was the killer still at large?

I wanted to curl up like a salted slug and die.

Aunt Felicity's voice broke into my agony. "You've heard no doubt of MI5 and MI6?"

I managed a nod. Because she could see only the back of my head, she could not possibly know I was crying.

"Well, you need to know that there are MI numbers beyond 19. Indeed, there exists a section with so high a number that not even the Prime Minister is aware of it."

Now the tube fell silent. What was she telling me?

Far below, the green world circled.

On the ground, you were like a bug in a carpet, believing every crumb to be a castle. But from up here, you had a whole new view of things. You could see far more.

More, perhaps, than you ever wanted to.

I gave a feeble wave to show Aunt Felicity that I was listening and that I had understood her words.

Seeing my hand, she went on: "We de Luces have been entrusted . . . for more than three hundred years . . . with some of the greatest secrets of the realm. Some of us have been on the side of good . . . while others have not."

What was the old woman saying? Was she mad? Was I alone in the air with a person who should be locked away in Colney Hatch?

And yet—she was flying *Blithe Spirit*, wasn't she?

Again I remembered asking Father what Buckshaw looked like from the air, remembered his reply: "*Ask your aunt Felicity. She's flown.*"

I had assumed, I suppose, that she had flown with someone else as a passenger. But Father's words had been literally true.

"Did you hear what I said, Flavia?"

Aunt Felicity reduced the throttle, and the sound of *Blithe Spirit*'s engine died away to a whisper. Now there was only the howl of the wind around us as her voice, containing a new urgency, came crackling through the rubber tube.

"We must go down now. There's no more time. But before we begin our descent, you must understand: From this day forward, much will be expected of you. Much has already been given to you. In many ways, your training has already begun."

Realization crept slowly into my mind.

My laboratory . . . the almost magical way in which the gases and glassware had never been exhausted . . .

Someone had seen to it.

"You must never speak of this to anyone but me—and then only when we are out of doors and absolutely alone."

That day last summer on the island of the ornamental lake!

"You must never be deflected by unpleasantness," Aunt Felicity had told me. *"I want you to remember that. Although it*

may not be apparent to others, your duty will become as clear to you as if it were a white line painted down the middle of the road. You must follow it, Flavia."

"Even when it leads to murder?" I had asked.

"Even when it leads to murder."

The full impact of her words came crashing upon me now like a breaking wave. My father's sister had been guiding my life for ages—maybe forever.

It was only with the greatest effort that I managed to grip the sides of the cockpit and twist round in my seat so I was looking Aunt Felicity directly in the eye—or, at least, in the goggles.

Her face was utterly impassive as she stared directly into mine.

Borne up by no more than the rush of the wind, it was as if we were riding the hurricane.

Slowly—but with great deliberation—I raised my right hand and gave her a thumbs-up that might have made Winston Churchill proud.

And Aunt Felicity returned it.

An instant later, she poured on full power and we were diving towards the ground.

As we glided in over Bishop's Lacey, I could tell by the shadows that it was well past noon, and cars were already being parked on the road on both sides of St. Tancred's.

Even before our wheels touched like thistledown on the Visto, Tristram Tallis was striding in the distance towards us.

Aunt Felicity cut the ignition and we both scrambled out onto the wing. I had already torn off my helmet and waited until she had removed her own.

For one brief moment we were out of doors and we were alone.

"Pheasant sandwiches," I blurted suddenly, risking all.

My aunt's face was as impassive as if it were cut from cold marble. A stone sphinx, perhaps, transported by magic from Egypt.

Tristram Tallis was now halfway to the aircraft. There were just seconds left before he was upon us.

"You're the Gamekeeper, aren't you?" I asked.

Aunt Felicity stared at me, her face a mask. I had never been so bold in my life. Had I said too much? Had I gone too far?

And then my aged aunt's mouth opened just wide enough to allow one small word to escape.

"Yes," she said.

·TWENTY-SIX·

Aunt Felicity and I spoke not another word as we entered the house from the kitchen garden. To an observer, it might have appeared as if we were a couple of casual acquaintances returning from an afternoon stroll on the lawns of Buckshaw.

Things were beginning to make sense; pieces were falling into place. Aunt Felicity, I knew, had rather a peculiar and unlikely circle of acquaintances. As far as I could deduce, she seemed to have been some kind of Queen Bee at the BBC during the War but had always refused to discuss it.

Had the MI department—the one with a number so high that not even the Prime Minister was aware of its existence—been quartered at Broadcasting House? It was a distinct possibility.

By "the Prime Minister," she had obviously meant the *present* Prime Minister. Winston Churchill, the former

PM, as everybody knew, still had certain secrets which he kept even from God.

And Tristram Tallis had seemed not at all surprised at our sudden departure in *Blithe Spirit.* He must have had some prior understanding with my aunt, since, when we landed, he had done no more than inquire pleasantly if "the old girl," as he put it, had behaved herself.

As Aunt Felicity went silently to her room, I walked slowly through the narrow passage to the front of the house.

The foyer was empty. The last mourners had gone, and the place was now steeped in utter silence. It was the dramatic pause in the moment before the curtain goes up on a different and as yet unknown world.

The scent of flowers hung heavily in the air. What was the word Daffy had once used to describe it? Cloying. Yes, that was it: cloying.

It felt as if your sinuses, your nostrils, and your adenoids, all at the same time, were about to vomit.

Perhaps I was coming down with a cold.

In spite of the fine weather, my laboratory, too, seemed unusually cold. Had I caught a chill during one of my flights in *Blithe Spirit*? I shrugged into an old brown bathrobe I kept hanging on the back of the door for just such emergencies and bundled myself as tightly as if I were setting out for the Pole.

I must have looked like a medieval monk or an alchemist fussing over his flasks as I prepared my experiment.

From the bottom drawer of Uncle Tar's desk, I brought

out the oilskin wallet which had contained Harriet's will, placed it on one of the benches, and lit a Bunsen burner.

I have to admit that I wasn't yet quite sure what I hoped to discover, but most objects, analyzed both visually and chemically, will eventually give up whatever secrets they hold, however incidental they may at first have seemed.

I began with the outside surface. The wallet was made from a kind of yellowish oilcloth: cotton or linen, perhaps, which had been varnished with several coats of linseed oil and pipe clay.

Aside from a few mottled stains—which I would leave for later analysis—the packet presented no remarkable features. I brought it to my nose and sniffed gently: a brackish odor of oily fungus, as if the wallet had been brought not long ago from the underworld, which I suppose, in a way, it had.

I pried it gently open and looked inside, turned it upside down and tapped it. A few particles of debris fell out onto the bench.

Lint? Dust? Soil? It was difficult to know. I brushed them carefully onto a piece of filter paper for later examination under the microscope.

Next was the taste test. I stuck out my tongue and, touching its tip to the packet, inhaled gently, waiting for the warmth of my body to release whatever essential oils might remain after all these years to be sensed by my taste buds and my olfactory system.

Linseed oil, definitely—as I had supposed.

For an advanced analysis of the material, I would snip off a sample and subject it to steam distillation, which would reveal any of the less obvious ingredients that might have been used in the wallet's manufacture, or to which it had later been exposed.

Body fluids, such as sweat, were a distinct possibility, and I couldn't say I was much looking forward to their discovery. On the other hand, the packet had been preserved for ten years by freezing and might well be a treasury of hidden chemical clues.

But first I would carry out the simplest and least destructive test: a gentle warming over the flame of the Bunsen burner while watching intently for any physical change. The volatile oils heated and combusted at varying degrees of temperature depending upon their chemical structure, and the first changes, however slight, were often visual.

By starving it slightly for air, I adjusted the burner for its coolest flame and began by holding the oilskin packet several inches off to one side. It wouldn't do to have the oily wallet catching fire.

Keeping it in constant motion and waving gently back and forth, I gradually brought the wallet closer to the flame.

After a minute or so, there had been no perceptible change.

I increased the flow of air and watched as the flame changed instantly from orange to blue.

Again I began waving the wallet: to and fro . . . to and fro.

Still nothing.

I was about to give it up when something caught my eye. It was as if parts of the oilcloth were darkening ever so slightly.

I held my breath. Was it—could it be—?

Yes!

A pattern was becoming visible on the oilcloth: at first no more than a mottled appearance—tiny rivers of black similar to thin, dark veins on marble.

But even as I watched, they began to blur. The heat was causing these stains—whatever they might be—to spread and absorb into the fabric of the oilcloth.

There wasn't a moment to waste! I needed to outline this twisting shape before it could blur beyond all recognition.

I shut off the burner, pulled a pencil from a drawer, and sketched quickly on the warm surface, trying to trace each part of the pattern before it could disappear.

Some far corner of my brain recognized the shape even before I became consciously aware of it.

Look, Flavia! Look! Think!

It was handwriting.

Letters. A word.

Invisible writing! A black word brought to light by heat—brought to light by the flame of the burner in the same way that the invisible images on the ciné film had been made visible by the chemicals of the developer.

A word resurrected. A word presumably written by Harriet, trapped in a glacial crevasse, knowing that she would never escape alive.

Why would she leave a message in invisible ink? Why wouldn't she have written it on the paper, and in pencil, as she had done with her will?

The answer seemed obvious: She wanted the will to be legible to anyone who found it—found *her*—but the two words scribbled on the oilskin wallet to remain invisible to everyone but a person who was looking for them.

But how on earth could a woman trapped in a glacier contrive to leave a message in invisible ink? It could easily be done in a country manor house with access to even a few common household chemicals. But in the Himalayan ice?

Any acid could be used to produce invisible writing. It was only necessary to take care that its strength was not so great as to burn the paper.

But invisible inks? They were everywhere: lemon juice, vinegar, milk—even spit could be used in a pinch.

Spit? Saliva?

Of course!

Like all great simple solutions, the answer had been there all along.

Urine! How clever of her.

One's urine was a rich stew of chemical constituents: urea, sulfates of potash and of soda, phosphate and muriate of soda, ammonia, lactic acid, and uric acid, to name just a few. A better invisible ink could hardly be concocted if it had been prepared by an apothecary and bottled in the back room at Boots!

Besides that, the stuff was readily available and free.

In ordinary circumstances, I would have begun my analysis by examining the wallet under ultraviolet light, but the bulb in my UV lab lamp had recently snuffed it, and I hadn't had an opportunity to manage a replacement. Bathed in ultraviolet light, the urine would have fluoresced at once, saving me the trouble of using the Bunsen burner.

I stared at the squiggly lines, straining to make sense of their twistings and turnings. It is a fact that any unfamiliar pattern takes a certain amount of time for the brain to recognize. One moment it is garbled nonsense, and the next—

And then I saw it.

"LENS PALACE" it said.

Lens palace? Whatever could that mean?

If I remembered correctly, there was a place in France called Lens. Our neighbor Maximilian Brock, the retired concert pianist, told me he had once been pelted there with lumps of coal by miners in the audience when he absentmindedly began his performance with a patriotic piece by Percy Grainger rather than the Debussy which had been listed on the program.

Was there a palace in Lens? I hadn't the foggiest notion. If Max was at the funeral, I could ask him.

Or had I misread the word? Because the letters had blurred so quickly as they were heated, it might originally have read "Linz," which was a city in Austria. I was quite sure of that because Feely had mentioned that Mozart wrote one of his best symphonies there at white heat—in just four days—for some old count or another. Was there a palace at Linz? It seemed more likely than Lens, but I would have to ask Daffy, who was more or less our household *Inquire Within Upon Everything*.

But what connection had Linz or Lens with Harriet? What possible message could those words contain?

It was evident—at least to me—that Harriet, having fallen into a glacial crevasse and knowing that all hope of rescue was gone, scrawled her last words in urine on the oilskin wallet in which she had placed her penciled will.

The treated surface would keep her writing crisp and sharp, at least until such time as some future investigator—I shivered at the thought that it was me—should warm the wallet and retrieve her message to the world.

But Lens palace?

It didn't make sense.

Could it be a reference to a cinema? And if so, which one?

The Gaumont in London? The shabby little cinema off the High Street in Hinley could hardly be described as a picture palace, and besides, when you came to think of it, every cinema in the world had lenses in its projection machines.

It wasn't likely that Harriet would leave so vague a clue as that, and although it was cryptic, it must have been meant to be decoded by somebody—somewhere.

The message must have been important to be worth going to so much trouble.

If you had only a couple of words left to you before you died, what would they be?

One thing was for certain: They would not be frivolous.

Perhaps it was an anagram—a simple rearrangement of letters: l-e-n-s-p-a-l-a-c-e.

I jotted down a few of the more obvious ones with my pencil: "claps an eel," "canal sleep," "lance leaps," "sea nap cell," and so on. It was easy to see that there were hundreds of possibilities, but none seemed promising. "Acne lapels," for instance, was outright ridiculous.

I thought for a moment that it might be a simple substitution cipher, one of those parlor games in which A equals *B* and *B* equals C that our governess Miss Gurdy used to force us to play on rainy afternoons before the Troubles. But if Harriet's message was worth writing in code, it would not be one so easily broken.

The obvious solution, of course, would be to show it to Aunt Felicity—the Gamekeeper herself. She would know how best to handle it.

And yet something was keeping me from doing so. I had handed over Harriet's will to Father because it was the right thing to do. But this message from my mother was a different thing entirely.

Why?

It's hard to put your finger on it. For one thing, the will was personal. It was meant to convey Harriet's wishes—whatever they might have been—to her family. But an invisible message on the outside of a packet was aimed at someone else entirely.

That, at least, was my thinking.

And then, of course, there was the undeniable fact that I wanted to keep something for myself. I could easily give the packet to Inspector Hewitt and let him bask in the glory of cracking the code—if he was able to.

But wouldn't that be, in a sense, giving away what little remained of my mother?

Quite honestly, I didn't want to share Harriet's last two words: not with Father, not with Aunt Felicity, not with the police—not with anyone. I felt that, in some weird way, the words, as they had taken form from nothingness in the heat of the Bunsen burner, were meant for me, that they were mine alone.

It may sound idiotic, but there it was.

I would tell no one.

I turned off the gas to the Bunsen burner and watched as the flame went out, leaving the room colder and somehow sadder than ever.

I pulled the bathrobe tightly round my neck and sat with my heels hooked on one of the stool's rungs, thinking about what Aunt Felicity had told me.

Harriet had been making her way home by way of India and Tibet. Someone had betrayed her. She was followed.

On the glacier, she had fallen.

Or had she been pushed?

It was uncomfortably like what had happened to the man on the railway platform at Buckshaw Halt. Could it be a coincidence?

Or was it more than that?

Was Harriet to go to her grave a murder victim?

There was a polite knock on the door. I knew who it was even before I said "Come in."

Dogger came slowly into the room.

"It's time, Miss Flavia," he said quietly.

I took a deep breath.

This was it.

The moment I had been dreading all my life.

·TWENTY-SEVEN·

FATHER WAS NOT A person who wore his heart on his sleeve. In fact, I sometimes used to wonder if he kept it anywhere about his person at all. Perhaps, I thought, his heart was preserved in some icy cave: in some frozen glacier of his mind.

But now, as I perched on the jump seat of Harriet's Rolls-Royce, I could tell by Father's face the agony he was in.

The more pain he felt on the inside, the less he showed on the outside.

Why hadn't I realized that years ago?

His face was like a photographic negative of his soul: White was black and black was white—exactly like the ciné film I had developed. He had been trained to be utterly impassive, and how very, very good at it he had become!

He was staring blankly out the window at the passing hedgerows as if he was no more than someone in the city, going up to London for another day of boredom at a varnished desk in some ghastly office. Seated between Feely and Daffy, he did not notice that I was studying him.

How gray he was, and how pale.

Sometime within the next hour, I thought, *this man is going to watch his beloved put into the earth.*

Harriet, at this very moment, was ahead of us in the hearse, in a box, which had been draped once more with the Union Jack.

She would be brought briefly into the church, a few words would be said, and that would be that.

I had attended enough funerals to know by now that all the comforting words of the vicar could never be enough, that the vivid imaginations of the mourners would more than cancel them out. All the sober words of John and Job and Timothy could not put Harriet de Luce together again, and I could only hope that our Lord Jesus Christ would have better luck resurrecting my mother than I had had.

I know it sounds bitter, but that is what I was thinking.

Daffy was clutching the *Book of Common Prayer* from which stuck out at every angle a messy sandwich of papers. She had been asked by the vicar to speak briefly about our mother, and although she had at first protested, she had finally come round and grudgingly agreed. I could tell by the smudges that her penciled writing had been erased again and again in an attempt to bring it up to the standards of Dickens, say, or Shakespeare.

I pitied her.

Feely had a folio of organ music on her lap. She, at least, would have the distraction of remembering to hit the right keys and pedals and would not be left, as the rest of us were, with nothing to look at but the coffin. That's the beauty of being an organist, I suppose: Business first, no matter what.

Adam and Tristram were following us with Lena and Undine in Lena's Land Rover. Adam had offered to drive, and Lena had accepted. Adam's old Rolls with its roof stripped away and overflowing with potted seedlings was not fit to be seen parked outside the church during a funeral, and so it had been left behind at Buckshaw.

Mrs. Mullet and her husband, Alf, were following in Clarence Mundy's taxicab. Mrs. M had draped her face with a black veil before setting out and would not remove it "until," she said, "Miss 'Arriet is laid to rest proper like."

"Bishop's Lacey 'as never seen Margaret Mullet cry," she had whispered to me fiercely, "nor will they."

Alf, wearing full medals, had put his hand on her arm and said, "Steady on, old girl," and it was only then I realized that beneath her black pall, his wife was already quaking with tears.

The churchyard and the road in front of it were simply crawling with people, so Dogger was forced to slow the Rolls to a snail's pace. We were fish in a tank with faces staring in at us through the glass.

Puffy white clouds floated solemnly overhead, dappling the landscape with shadows of sadness.

It was dreadful. Simply dreadful, and the tolling of the great bell in the tower somehow made it even worse.

All eyes were upon us as we stepped down from the Rolls, and a murmur swept like a wave through the crowd, although I couldn't make out what they were saying.

"That's Dame Agatha Dundurn," Daffy whispered, swiveling her eyes repeatedly in the direction she wanted me to look.

"The Air Vice-Marshal?" I asked from the corner of my mouth.

"Something like that," Daffy replied. "She parachuted into Arnhem."

"Good lord!" I said, although it didn't take much imagination to see her doing it. The woman was a cannonball with stripes on its sleeves.

We both of us jumped as our elbows were pinched.

"Please shut up," Feely said in a low voice. "This is a funeral—not a mop fair."

She shot us a villainous look and moved off alone in the direction of the porch, her music clutched far too tightly in her fist. Nobody tried to stop her.

The vicar met us at the lych-gate, and we stood in awkward silence as Harriet's coffin was removed gently from the hearse by the six pallbearers, all of them men, and all of them strangers, except for Dieter, upon whose broad shoulder Harriet's head was now resting. Tongues would soon be wagging in Bishop's Lacey, I knew.

"Father insisted," Daffy whispered.

I tried to give Dieter a grateful smile but could not catch his eye.

Now the vicar was leading us towards the church. Worn with a purple stole over a black cassock, his surplice was blindingly white in the April sunshine.

In the porch, Mr. Haskins, who served as both sexton and verger, his chin tucked tightly in as a sign of office, indicated by hand signals that we were to follow him.

The pews were already packed with people, and the dozens left standing at the back and in the side aisles fell suddenly silent as the organ began to play a haunting melody. I recognized it at once as G. Thalben-Ball's *Elegy*, which Feely thought she had been practicing in secrecy for days.

Here, on the left, was Jocelyn Ridley-Smith with a new attendant whom I didn't recognize. Poor Jocelyn: He believed that I was Harriet, and I couldn't help wondering whose funeral he thought he was attending. I gave him a reassuring smile which he returned with as much of a courtly bow as he could manage from a sitting position.

Over there, looking strained, was Cynthia Richardson. She and Harriet had been particular friends and I realized with a start that this funeral could well be even harder on her than it was on me.

At the end of a row of pews, in his wicker wheelchair, was Dr. Kissing. Although I managed to catch his eye, he gave not a flicker of recognition. Our acquaintance, I realized—at least publicly—was not one he wished to advertise. He was Father's old headmaster and no more.

Our small procession made its way up the center aisle behind the pallbearers, and as Harriet's coffin was placed with military precision on wooden trestles outside the chancel gates, Mr. Haskins wigwagged us with broad ceremonial gestures to our private seats in the transept.

Dogger, Dieter, and the Mullets were seated directly behind us. It was comforting just to know that they were there. Dieter had obviously changed his mind—or had it changed for him—about remaining on the sidelines.

By leaning forward, I could see almost to the back of the church. Most of the village of Bishop's Lacey had already crowded themselves inside and were busily looking up the Burial of the Dead in the *Book of Common Prayer*.

My heart gave a little leap. There on the aisle sat Inspector Hewitt and his wife, Antigone. He leaned slightly towards her, speaking quietly, and she nodded gravely.

I wanted to wave but because it wouldn't have pleased certain people, I didn't.

Antigone Hewitt had once invited me to tea and I had made a hash of it. I'd been waiting for a chance to beg her forgiveness in person but so far had not had the opportunity.

I had last seen her a little more than a week ago when she had driven us home after the Easter service. She had promised to take me—just the two of us!—on a shopping trip to Hinley. "A girls' day out," she had called it.

Of course the tragic news of Harriet had come at that time, and it now seemed doubtful that such a giddy outing was likely to take place in the foreseeable future.

At the end of our pew, Lena and Undine edged crabwise into their places beside me. Lena was wearing a black tailored suit, and Undine, in a red velvet dress, had a black bow tied in her hair.

"I hadn't realized it would be such a cavalcade," Lena muttered to no one in particular—perhaps to me. "Push over."

Somewhere in one of the twisty mazes at the back of my brain, a single shred of silver confetti fell. But it was no more than a single flake in a blizzard of images.

Undine raised a copy of *Hymns Ancient and Modern* to her face, as if she was shortsighted, and under cover of the book, stuck out her tongue and crossed her eyes grotesquely.

I mouthed an improper word at her which I'm sure she understood, since she now widened her eyes, sucked in a noisy and greatly exaggerated breath, and let her mouth fall open as if in shock.

She whispered something into Lena's ear, but I didn't care.

The organ swelled into a song of triumph, the glorious music causing me to feel suddenly as if caterpillars were crawling up my spine.

All eyes were upon my mother's coffin, and every last one of us gasped as a sudden beam of sunshine broke through the stained-glass windows to illuminate the Union Jack.

Daffy and I stared at each other in astonishment. It was as if Harriet's funeral were being stage-managed in Heaven.

Now the vicar was coming forward. He paused for a moment until Feely had brought the elegy to a hushed conclusion and then spoke those words I was afraid he was going to speak, the words I had been dreading: "I am the resurrection and the life, saith the Lord: he that believeth in me, though he were dead, yet shall he live: and whosoever liveth and believeth in me shall never die."

This is real! This is actually happening!

Part of me had believed, somehow, that until these words were actually pronounced over her body, there was still hope, however vague it may be, that Harriet was still alive. Yet now—and this was difficult to understand—the vicar's assurance that Harriet should live and never die were the very words that made her death official: a death which had become all too real and was being all too visibly celebrated before our very eyes.

I shuddered.

Beside me in the pew, Lena, under cover of pretending to wipe away a tear, had produced a small silver compact and was now secretly examining herself in close-up.

Now the vicar had passed on to "I know that my redeemer liveth, and that He shall stand at the latter day upon the earth. And though after my skin worms destroy this body; yet in my flesh shall I see God: whom I shall see for myself and mine eyes shall behold."

As he spoke, a wonderful idea popped into my mind!

Why don't they embed the dead in blocks of plate glass and bury them in crypts beneath transparent floors? In that way, the deceased would easily be able to see God for themselves, and He to see them, to say nothing of the fact that the descendants would be able to keep an eye on their ancestors' return to dust during a quiet Sunday stroll.

It seemed like a perfect solution, and I wondered why no one had ever thought of it before. I would make a note to mention it to the vicar at a more appropriate time.

"I said, I will take heed to my ways: that I offend not in my tongue. I will keep my mouth as it were with a bridle: while the ungodly is in my sight."

He was already into the Thirty-ninth Psalm and we had barely begun.

I knew that the Thirty-ninth was not the longest of the psalms—not by a long chalk—but it would be followed by the Ninetieth: "Lord, thou hast been our dwelling place in all generations," and so forth. After that would come the Lesson: part of one of Saint Paul's rather lengthy letters to the Corinthians, the one which ended with "O death, where is thy sting? O grave, where is thy victory?"

I let my attention wander.

Across the church in the opposite semitransept, the stained-glass windows gave off a glorious glow. I remembered with pleasure the catalog of chemicals that had been used in their manufacture hundreds of years ago: manganese dioxide for the purples, iron or gold for the reds, salts of ferric iron for the brown skins, and silver chloride for the yellows.

In one of the panels, a brawny man dressed in lion skins like a circus strongman lay sleeping with his head in the lap of a woman in a red dress who was cutting his hair with what appeared to be sheep shears. From behind a hanging drape in the corner of the room, half a dozen men were craning their necks for a view of the operation.

When I was smaller, I had believed—because Daffy had told me so—that the woman, whose name was Brenda, was a barber apprentice and that the men hiding behind the curtain were the examiners who either would or would not grant her a barber's license.

The characters were, of course, Samson and Delilah,

and the onlookers were the lords of the Philistines at Gaza, who were paying her to betray him.

Below the scene was a beautifully lettered yellow scroll with the words in black:

Samson—Delilah

In the next panel, Samson was toppling the two pillars between which he had been chained, as the spectators, with comical looks of astonishment on their faces, tumbled headfirst from the roof like so many ninepins.

The sound of organ music dragged my mind back from Gaza. We were standing to sing a hymn. I had returned just in time to join in the first line.

"Who would true valor see,
Let him come hither;
One here will constant be,
Come wind, come weather
There's no discouragement
Shall make him once relent
His first avowed intent
To be a pilgrim. . . ."

It was that grand old hymn from *Pilgrim's Progress*, which John Bunyan had written while in prison. Rather than the watered-down version which had been allowed to creep in about fifty years ago, Feely had chosen to use the original words, which, in the book, Mr. Valiant-for-truth had spoken to Mr. Greatheart. The melody was called "Monks

Gate," she had told me, and it was a ripsnorter! I could hardly wait for the last verse.

"Whoso beset him round
With dismal stories
Do but themselves confound;
His strength the more is.
No lion can him fright,
He'll with a giant fight,
But he will have a right
To be a pilgrim."

Dame Agatha Dundurn, her old military face upturned to the light, was putting her whole heart into it, as if she had written this mighty battle song herself and had finished leading, just moments ago, the overthrow of all the forces of evil.

Daffy, too, was singing her heart out, and what a lovely voice she had! Why had I never noticed it before? How could I have missed it?

I suddenly realized that there's something about singing hymns with a large group of people that sharpens the senses remarkably. I stored this observation away for later use; it was a jolly good thing to know for anyone practicing the art of detection. Perhaps that was why Inspector Hewitt so often came to church.

I shot a glance in his direction just in time to see Antigone give his arm what she probably thought was a secret squeeze.

Now the organ and the congregation were taking a great

breath before launching into the final verse—and my favorite part:

"Hobgoblin nor foul fiend—"

Oh, how I adored the hobgoblin and the foul fiend! They were the making of this particular hymn, and if I had my way, more songs of praise would be required to include such interesting creatures.

"—Can daunt his spirit,
He knows he at the end
Shall life inherit.
Then fancies fly away,
He'll fear not what men say,
He'll labor night and day
To be a pilgrim. . . ."

As we sat down, the vicar gave Daffy an almost imperceptible nod. She picked up her bundle of papers and walked briskly to the lectern, where she shuffled them until I thought I'd go mad.

She produced her spectacles from somewhere and put them on, which gave her the appearance of a grieving owl.

"I barely remember my mother," she said at last, her voice quavering only a little but suddenly small in the vastness of the church. "I was not quite three years old when she went away, so that I have only memories of a bright shadow who fluttered on the peripheries of my little world. I don't remember what she looked like, nor can I recall the sound of her voice, but what I do remember is how she made me feel—which was that I was loved. Until she went away.

"After she was gone, I stopped feeling loved and began believing that my sisters and I must have done something horrid to drive her away, although I could not for the life of me think what that might have been. We have never been given, you see, any reason for her leaving. Even now—now that she has been returned to us—we still don't know the reason why she left.

"I hope you won't mind my speaking so frankly, but the vicar told me that I must say what I felt and be honest about it."

Could this possibly be true? Could it be that Feely and Daffy hadn't the faintest inkling of Harriet's activities? Was it possible that Aunt Felicity, who had been, and presumably remained, the Gamekeeper, intended to withhold the truth from them forever?

I looked over at Father, and he was just standing there—so cleanly shaven, so still, and so upright that I could have wept.

Daffy had paused and was looking from one member of the congregation to another. There was dead silence, and then a nervous shuffling of feet.

"By what we have observed yesterday and today," she went on, "one can only presume that my mother's body has been returned to us for burial by a grateful government, and for that, at least, I must express our thanks."

The church had again in an instant gone so quiet you could hear the breathing of the saints in the stained-glass windows.

"But it is not enough," Daffy continued, her voice now louder and accusing. "It is not enough for my father—nor is it enough for my sisters, Ophelia and Flavia. And it is not *nearly* enough for me."

Somewhere behind me Mrs. Mullet let out a sob.

Daffy went on. "I can only hope that one day we shall be entrusted with the truth. We the bereaved deserve nothing less.

"The word 'bereaved' comes down to us from the Old English word *beréafian*, meaning 'to be deprived of'—to be stripped, to be robbed, to be dispossessed—and it describes accurately what has happened to what is left of our family. We have been robbed of a wife and mother, stripped of our pride, and are soon to be dispossessed of our home.

"And therefore, I beg of you your prayers. As you pray today for the repose of the soul of our mother, Harriet de Luce, pray also for those of us who have been left behind, bereaved.

"We shall now join in singing another of my mother's favorite hymns."

I wanted to applaud, but I didn't dare. "Bravo!" I wanted to shout.

A vast and ominous silence hung in the church. The multitude were staring at the roof, at their shoes, at the windows, at the marble memorial tablets on the walls, and at their own fingernails. No one seemed to know where to look.

"*Play, Feely!*" I begged her mentally. But Feely let the silence lengthen until several people began coughing to break the tension.

And then the music came. Those six stunning notes sprang from the throats of the organ pipes!

Dah-dah-dah-DAH-dah-dah.

They were unmistakable.

People looked at one another as they recognized the tune, first in astonishment and disbelief, but then with growing smiles at the sheer audacity of it.

Daffy began to sing in her fine, loud voice: "Ta-ra-ra BOOM-de-ay, ta-ra-ra BOOM-de-ay . . ."

And then someone else—I think it was, incredibly, Cynthia, the vicar's wife—took up the words. Others joined in, somewhat uncertainly at first but growing in confidence with every beat: "Ta-ra-ra BOOM-de-ay, ta-ra-ra BOOM-de-ay . . ."

And now even more, until practically everyone in the church was singing: "Ta-ra-ra BOOM-de-ay, ta-ra-ra BOOM-de-ay . . ."

The booming bass of Mr. Haskins, the verger, came echoing from somewhere back behind the font.

The vicar was singing, Inspector Hewitt and Antigone were singing, Dame Agatha Dundurn was singing—even *I* was singing: "Ta-ra-ra BOOM-de-ay, ta-ra-ra BOOM-de-ay!"

Feely finished off with a flourish of trumpet stops, and then the organ fell silent, as if suddenly embarrassed at what it had done.

As the music faded and died up among the beams and king posts of the ancient roof, Daffy folded her papers and walked placidly back to her seat beside Father in the transept.

Father's eyes were closed. Tears were trickling down his face. I placed my hand on top of his on the rail but he seemed not to notice.

People were still smiling at their neighbors, shaking their heads, whispering to one another, and everywhere except in the de Luce pew, a lingering glow hung in the air.

I turned round and looked at Dogger, but his face was, as they say in the thrillers on the wireless, inscrutable.

Daffy and Feely cooked this up together, I thought. Behind closed doors they had plotted it note by note. I wished they'd let me in on their plan. I might have advised against it.

But now the vicar was coming forward.

"Now is Christ risen from the dead," he said, without batting an eye, "and become the first-fruits of them that slept."

As if butter wouldn't melt in his mouth; as if something wonderful hadn't just happened in his church—a miracle, perhaps; as if "Ta-ra-ra BOOM-de-ay" hadn't been the last words upon his lips, and upon everyone else's to boot.

"For since by man came death," he was now telling us, "by man came also the resurrection of the dead. For as in Adam all die, even so in Christ shall all be made alive," and on and on from there, wading through all those lovely words about the glories of the sun and the moon and the stars, until at last, as I knew he must, he came to that inevitable passage:

"O death, where is thy sting? O grave, where is thy victory?"

Just like that. We had been torn from a jolly good sing-song and plunged back into grief. I was struggling with my feelings, staring at the stained glass as if help could possibly come from there, as if hope could possibly spring from the colorful chemicals of the glass.

The yellow scrolls had most likely been achieved with sulfur and calcium, the black letters enameled with a paint compounded in the Middle Ages from a closely guarded formula containing precisely measured amounts of powdered iron or copper oxide, adhesive, and the glassmaker's own urine.

I read the words again.

Samson – Delilah

At first glance, it seemed as if the artist had made a stained-glass misprint. Sawson – Defifak, the letters appeared to spell out. The M looked like a *W*, the *H* like a *K*. It was only when your eye and brain locked in to the intricate curlicues of the Gothic lettering that you saw that "Sawson – Defifak" was actually "Samson – Delilah."

It was easy once you got the hang of it.

Like so many other things.

It was in that fraction of an instant—in that finest sliver of time—that the penny dropped.

In my mind, the words "Lens Palace" took form: those urgent words that Harriet had scribbled in her own urine.

Of course! How clear it all was, once you saw!

The *S* was an A. The *P* was a *D*, and by all that was holy, the As were *E*s.

Except for the second one, of course, which couldn't possibly be anything but a *U*!

When I had begun to thaw Harriet's oilcloth wallet, the letters of her message had immediately begun to diffuse into the old fabric, becoming more spidery and fantastic with every passing moment.

Her message had not been "Lens Palace." It had, rather, spelled out the name of the woman who was now sitting next to me buffing her fingernails on the hem of her skirt.

Lena de Luce.

It was Lena who had followed Harriet from Singapore to India, and from India to that final confrontation in Tibet. Who else could it have been? For what other reason would Harriet have scribbled Lena's name in invisible fluid on the outside of the packet containing her last will and testament?

My blood ran cold—then hot.

I was sitting next to a killer!

This creature beside me, preening herself like the cat that ate the canary, had murdered my mother. Her own flesh and blood!

Get a grip on yourself, Flavia. You mustn't let her know.

At this particular moment, I thought, *on the face of this vast globe which is spinning in its gravitationally appointed place among all the other planets, you are the only one of its two and a half billion inhabitants—other than Lena, of course—who knows the truth.*

What was it Aunt Felicity had shouted through the rubber tube during our flight in *Blithe Spirit*?

"We de Luces have been entrusted . . . for more than three hundred years . . . with some of the greatest secrets of the realm. Some of us have been on the side of good . . . while others have not."

It was as plain as the nose on your face: Lena was one of those who had not.

Why hadn't I listened to my instincts the first time I laid eyes on the woman? How could I have allowed her to sleep—she and her abominable daughter—under the roofs of Buckshaw? Even now, the very thought of it made my marrow itch.

The question was this: Why had Lena come to Bishop's Lacey?

The full horror came crashing down upon me like the stones of the house that Samson wrecked.

The man at the station—the man beneath the wheels of the train, the man in the long coat: "The one who was talking to Ibu," Undine had told me.

He had being trying to warn me—or at least to warn Father.

"The Gamekeeper is in jeopardy. The Nide is under—"

"Attack" was the word he was almost certainly going to say.

But Lena had been there on the station platform!

The man in the long coat had been talking to her. Undine had blurted that out during our playing of Kim's Game.

I had, in fact, confronted Lena with this fact in my laboratory, but we had been interrupted by the sudden arrival, outside the window, of Tristram Tallis in *Blithe Spirit*.

And then, as if that weren't enough, there had been that word: "pushed."

"Someone pushed him," a woman's voice had said on the platform.

"Push over," Lena had ordered, less than an hour ago as she wedged her way into the pew beside me. There had been something familiar about the voice, but I hadn't had time to think about it.

At the station she had cried out those words herself in order to distract attention.

Of course! How fiendishly clever of her—and how cold-blooded.

In the same calculating way, she had arranged to lure me to the Jack O'Lantern.

"After the funeral," she had said.

Within the hour!

But now, I realized, this much was certain: If Lena found out I was on to her, I was no better than a dead duck.

The next funeral at St. Tancred's would be mine.

·TWENTY-EIGHT·

WHAT HAPPENED NEXT IS no more than a blur—as if the world had become a mixture of paints, or of fluids, in a spinning centrifuge.

I realized that whatever the outcome, I could not confide in Inspector Hewitt. If the truth be told, I had been looking forward to patiently unknitting the knot of evidence for him and laying it out at his grateful feet.

And Antigone's, of course. I was beginning to suspect that Antigone Hewitt was pregnant. She had that same mysterious radiance about her which I had observed last autumn in Nialla Gilfoyle, the traveling puppeteer: a kind of warm luminescence that was so much more than just a healthy glow. I knew that the Hewitts had lost more than one baby in the making, and I could only pray that the next one would be a howling success.

Saint Tancred, please watch over her, I begged.

No, I could not possibly tell Inspector Hewitt. Aunt Felicity had made it quite clear that I was to discuss the Nide and its activities with no one but her. They were beyond Top Secret. The Gamekeeper had spoken.

Nor, then, could I tell the Inspector anything about the stranger at the station: *Terence Alfriston Tardiman, bachelor, of 3A Campden Gardens, Notting Hill Gate, London, W8, aged thirty-seven,* Adam had said.

I would have to remain no more than a witness—an important one, to be sure—but a witness nonetheless.

I don't mind admitting it was a bit of a bitter pill. I would have to fade into the wallpaper, so to speak, and let the Inspector take all the credit.

I could only hope that he and his henchmen had done their homework and were close to discovering on their own who had shoved Terence Tardiman under the train. Surely by now they must have discovered who at Buckshaw Halt had called out "Someone pushed him."

If they were still baffled, I would perhaps have to send them an anonymous letter, made up of cutout letters from various newspaper headlines, pasted up on a sheet of waxed butcher's paper, and posted from a pillar box in Fleet Street to avoid suspicion.

I should have to break my braces again to contrive a trip up to London, but it would be worth it. Perhaps Inspector Hewitt would suspect anyway, in his heart of hearts, the identity of the sender. He would recognize the fingerprints of my intelligence. Even so, he would never be able to prove it, or to admit openly that it was Flavia de Luce who had cracked the case.

We would smile at each other pleasantly over crumpets, the Inspector and I, and ask each other if we took cream or sugar with our tea, both of us knowing, but not speaking, the delicious truth.

I was dragged back into the present by the vicar's voice saying: "Man that is born of a woman hath but a short time to live, and is full of misery. He cometh up, and is cut down, like a flower; he fleeth as it were a shadow, and never continueth in one stay. In the midst of life we are in death—"

Due to the circumstances, it had been agreed—although it was unusual—to have the committal to the grave inside the church as part of the funeral service.

Harriet was to be laid to rest in the family vault in the crypt below. Her coffin would be moved there later, at such time as, the vicar told us, "the mourners have dispersed."

We were now nearing the end.

"Thou knowest, Lord," the vicar said, "the secrets of our hearts."

I glanced over at Lena. I couldn't help myself.

She turned her head suddenly and met my gaze and held it, and I found that, try as I might, I could not look away.

It is said that certain poisonous snakes are able to petrify small animals with their gaze: a fact which I had doubted until now, even though Mrs. Mullet had warned me against Gertie Mumfield who had the evil eye and whose ignorant stare was not to be returned at any cost.

Whatever the case, I was simply unable to break the gaze in which Lena had locked me. Something unknown was passing back—and surprisingly *forth*—from her eye to mine: a silent telegraphic conversation which I was too inexperienced to decode.

She knew that I knew. There could be no doubt about it. She was sucking the truth from my eyes and there was nothing I could do to stop it.

Only with the greatest effort was I able to lower my lids, although it was like trying to force down a paint-encrusted window sash.

I turned my head away and rolled my eyes down towards the floor before I dared open them again.

To my horror, the vicar had already arrived at that part of the service where we would be asked to step forward, each in turn—Father, Feely, Daffy, me—to sprinkle a small handful of dirt from the graveyard onto Harriet's coffin.

"—thou most worthy Judge eternal," he was now saying, "suffer us not, at our last hour, for any pains of death, to fall from thee."

He nodded at Father, who rose up and tottered forward like an automaton which had not been actuated for a century.

Daffy and I followed.

"Ashes to ashes, dust to dust; in sure and certain hope of the Resurrection to eternal life—"

How cruel those words were! I didn't want to hear them.

I clapped my hands to my ears and took a backwards step. In doing so, I must have caught my foot on the lower of the chancel steps. I reached out to steady myself from falling by grabbing the corner of Harriet's coffin.

As I regained my balance, I saw Inspector Hewitt coming quickly up the center aisle.

Could he be *that* worried about me?

Probably not, because Detective Sergeant Woolmer, moving like a heavy lorry, was already halfway up one of the side aisles—and Detective Sergeant Graves was blocking the other.

What was going on here? Had they been asked to participate in the committal?

Or had they—as I had desperately hoped—worked out the identity of the killer on the platform?

There was a loud bang behind me.

Lena had broken from her pew and was already at the top of the chancel steps. She reminded me for a moment of a panicked horse whose stable has been struck by lightning. Her nostrils flared, and as her head swung round, I could see the whites of her eyes.

Into the choir she galloped, not seeming to realize that there was no way out. All the while, Inspector Hewitt was approaching the front pews with slow but deliberate steps.

Sergeant Graves, smaller, lighter, and younger, had already reached the front of the side aisle. He was so close that I could have reached out and touched him. He stopped in his tracks as Inspector Hewitt raised a warning hand.

In the far aisle, Sergeant Woolmer had not yet reached the front.

Lena put a hand on the altar, as if she was planning to climb onto it, but she quickly found that it was too high. Spinning round, she saw that Inspector Hewitt and Sergeant Graves were on the move again, slowly closing in on her—trapping her in an invisible net.

She ripped at her waist and stepped—shockingly, defiantly—out of her tight black skirt. She could not be hobbled: She needed to be able to run. Her silk slip glistened obscenely in the sunlight.

Of the three policemen, Sergeant Woolmer was farthest from her, and she chose to make her break in that direction.

Except for the insistent shuffling of one pair of shoes and three pairs of police boots on marble, all of this took place in near silence. It was uncanny: a scene from a silent film in the earliest days of experimental sound.

At the last possible moment, just as she was about to run into the powerful arms of Sergeant Woolmer, Lena veered unexpectedly to the left and bolted into the chapel: the little chapel in which Samson lay with his head in the lap of his lady love, and in which he also crumbled the house of his tormentors.

It was a bad mistake, and Lena must have realized that at once.

She was cornered.

She froze in her tracks, turned round looking this way and that, and even though it was for only a fraction of a second, my brain took a mental snapshot of her. In fact, if I close my eyes, I can still see her as she was in that moment—her long red hair broken loose from its moorings, her eyes wide, the tip of her tongue licking her lips—but only once. Her chest was heaving visibly as she glanced back over her shoulder, her ragged, rasping breath now clearly audible in the shocked silence.

I wish I could say that there was a twisted look of hatred

on her face, but there was not. Rather, she had the look of a woman who has realized halfway to the car that she has left her purse on the kitchen table.

They stood like that for an endless moment, unmoving, Lena and the police, like actors frozen in a tiring *tableau vivant.*

And then someone in the church—could it have been me?—let out a little cry.

The spell was broken.

Lena was in motion again—a bolt of lightning in a black jacket. In no more than a few strides, she had crossed the chapel. She sprang onto the small altar and, summoning all her strength, hurled herself at the stained-glass window.

Samson and Delilah vanished in a shower of ancient glass. Shards and splinters of acid yellow and cobalt blue hung in the air, suspended in time before crashing down onto the marble in a wave that was somehow like the sea.

A sea of glass.

Lena had not gone fully through the window.

It would have been better for her if she had.

Those ancient craftsmen of the Middle Ages, working to the west of Buckshaw in Ovenhouse Wood, had mixed sand with the ashes of a reed called glasswort to make a window which would endure until the Last Trump: until that day when the door to Heaven would be opened, and the rainbow throne with its seven lamps of fire would be seen sitting in a sea of glass.

To be certain of this, they had suspended their handiwork in a matrix of tracery: thin metal filaments to form a spider's web of lead.

And it was this metallic net in which Lena had embedded herself, half in and half out of the window.

She must have severed an artery as she struggled, impaled on a thousand colored needles of glass, unable to move.

At first her blood oozed, then became trickles and rivulets, each finding a fresh pathway through the broken shards, their streams joining finally in a river of red which dripped horribly onto the cold marble floor.

It was all over in a remarkably short time.

There was pandemonium in the church. Someone was screaming and Dr. Darby was making haste from the back of the nave.

I found myself at the crossing, drawn as if in a dream past the pulpit and the lectern and into the little chapel. Inspector Hewitt tried to hold me back, but I shook him off—perhaps a little too roughly—and walked resolutely on until I was standing in front of the glass-littered altar, gazing up at the wreckage.

Lena had ceased to move.

Except for a few loose red hairs at the back of her neck, which stirred uneasily in the little breeze coming in round the broken glass, she hung impaled in perfect stillness.

And then—

I wish I didn't have to write this, but I must.

One of her eyes opened, turned slowly in its socket as if it didn't know where it was—and came finally to rest on me.

It widened.
That blue, unfathomable eye. Staring.
Before fading finally . . .
That blue de Luce eye.
So much like my own.

·TWENTY-NINE·

I HAVE SOMETIMES WONDERED what Lena was thinking as she died.

I wonder if she had time to suspect, as she saw me standing there staring up at her, that Harriet had come back from the dead for vengeance.

I hope in a way that she had, and in another way, I hope she hadn't. I'm trying hard to be a better person, but it doesn't always work.

I am finding, for instance, that I'm having a great deal of trouble forgiving Harriet for being dead. Even though it was not her fault, and even though she died for her country, I feel deprived, and deprived in a way that I never felt before her body was found. Daffy was right: We deserved better.

It makes no sense, I know, but there it is. The best I can do is to allow myself to hate her for a while. Well, perhaps not hate, precisely, but to be highly cheesed off with her, as Undine would put it.

And Lena, of course. I deserved better from both of them.

The drive back to Buckshaw was made in utter silence. There had been no lingering in the churchyard to receive condolences as there sometimes is. Because of Lena, and so forth, we had been quickly bundled into the Rolls by Cynthia and the vicar with gripped hands under cover of surplices and furtive pats on the shoulder.

Since most of the congregation were still jockeying for a better view of Lena's removal—some of them in the churchyard, even though one of the verger's tarpaulins had been hastily rigged to cover the window and its captive—we had no real difficulty in making our getaway unnoticed.

As Dogger pulled away from the lych-gate, we passed within a few feet of Inspector Hewitt, who was questioning Max Brock, his notebook at the ready. Max, since retiring from the concert stage, was rumored to have taken up writing "true confession" tales for some of the more lurid magazines, and I'll bet he had gathered plenty of usable detail from the front pew where he had been seated.

The Inspector didn't give me so much as a passing glance.

It was decided that Undine would ride back to Buckshaw with Adam and Tristram in her mother's Land Rover. Aunt Felicity had protested, but Father put his foot down. It was the first time he had spoken all day.

"Let the girl go, Felicity," he said.

I had no idea how much the child had witnessed, and because Dogger had whisked her off so quickly into the vestry at the very outset of the excitement, there'd been no opportunity for me to find out.

We arrived home to a silent house. Father had given Mrs. Mullet the rest of the day off, and she'd required no persuasion.

"I've left meats enough in the 'fridgerator," she whispered to Dogger. "Puddings and that in the pantry. Make sure they eat."

Dogger had nodded delicately.

Adam and Tristram pulled up at the front door just seconds behind us with Undine, all three of them engaged in a serious discussion, apparently about dragonflies.

"There are *far* more species in Singapore than in England," she was telling them, "well over a hundred—but of course I'm including the damselflies."

Did she know yet about her mother? Surely she must—Aunt Felicity must have told her.

It was going to be difficult for the little girl, growing up without her precious Ibu. Who knows? In time, she might even come to appreciate a few pointers.

Our party broke up in the foyer, each of us going our separate way. Father was the first to leave, climbing slowly up the stairs. I wanted to follow him—to console him—but to be perfectly honest, I didn't know how.

Perhaps in time I shall learn the antidote for grief. But for now, I would just have to make do with silent pity.

Since I had no interest in damselflies, nor was I hungry, I went directly to my laboratory to feed Esmeralda, who appeared not to have missed me. She fell upon her feed as if I didn't exist.

It seemed an eternity since I had last been alone with myself.

For the first time in my life, I didn't know what to do. I didn't want to read, I didn't feel like listening to music, and chemistry was out of the question.

I took a wooden match from a box and idly lit the flame of the Bunsen burner. With my elbows on the bench, I stared into the changing flame—yellow, orange, purple, blue—as if, from a great distance, from the outer edge of the universe, I was an onlooker to the birth of galaxies.

There was only me, and nothing more. Nothing else existed.

Light and heat: That was what it was all about.

The secret of the stars.

But when you came right down to it, light *was* energy, and so was heat.

So energy, when you stopped to think about it, was the Grand Panjandrum: the be-all and the end-all, the root of all things.

The flame flickered, as if taunting me. I warmed my hands for a moment and then switched off the gas.

Poof! The end of Creation.

Extinguished by an almost-twelve-year-old girl in pigtails.

Just like that.

It was not much consolation, but it was all that I was likely to get.

I had not heard the door open, nor had I heard Dogger come into the room. I can only suppose he didn't want to startle me.

"Oh! Dogger," I said. "I was just sitting here thinking."

"An uncommonly good pastime, Miss Flavia," Dogger said. "I often do it myself."

There was a time when I might have asked Dogger what it was that he thought about: if saving Father's life and being forced to work in Hellfire Pass on the Death Railway ever crossed his mind.

It wasn't that I didn't dare, but rather that I didn't want to inflict these shadows on his waking soul. Lord knows, he has enough of them already in his dreams.

Until now, I had never even stopped to consider what agonies might be visited upon him by even the sight of railway tracks.

It was a great mercy that, at the time of our family's greatest distress, Dogger had suffered not so much as a single one of his night terrors. He had been a rock. In future, I would try to keep our conversations interesting and steer clear of railways.

"Dogger," I asked, "how long does it take a person to bleed to death?"

Dogger cradled his chin between his thumb and forefinger. "On average, the human body contains about a gallon of blood. Slightly less in women than in men."

I nodded. That seemed about right. "And how long does it take—a woman, say—to bleed to death?"

"Complete exsanguination," Dogger said, "may take place in little more than a minute. It depends, of course, upon the size and health of the individual and upon which vessels were severed. Were you thinking of Miss Lena?"

I couldn't hide it.

"Yes," I told him.

"I can assure you that she died very quickly."

"Would she have been in pain?"

"Initially, yes," Dogger replied. "But that would have been followed quite quickly by unconsciousness and then death."

"Thank you, Dogger," I told him. "I needed to know."

"I understand," Dogger said. "I thought you might."

"How's Father getting on?" I asked. It had occurred to me suddenly that Father was due the same consideration that Dogger was.

"He's bearing up," Dogger replied.

"Is that all?"

"Yes. He has asked to see you at 1900 hours."

"All of us?"

"No, Miss Flavia. Only you."

A sense of dread seized me.

Father had waited until after the funeral to punish me for opening Harriet's coffin. I had foolishly expected that having her long-lost will dropped into his hands would somehow make him happy, but he had given not the slightest sign that his troubles had been eased.

In fact, now that I thought about it, he had seemed even more troubled, more silent today than he had ever been before, and it frightened me.

How could we possibly go on? With Harriet dead and buried, Father no longer had the slightest shred of hope. He appeared to have given up.

"What are we going to do, Dogger?"

It seemed a reasonable question. After all he had been through, surely Dogger knew something of hopeless situations.

"We shall wait upon tomorrow," he said.

"But—what if tomorrow is worse than today?"

"Then we shall wait upon the day *after* tomorrow."

"And so forth?" I asked.

"And so forth," Dogger said.

It was comforting to have an answer, even one I didn't understand. I must have looked skeptical.

It was still early; 1900 was hours in the future. It might as well have been nineteen hundred years.

What was I going to do until I was summoned?

The answer came to me in a flash, as it so often does when you're at your wit's end.

Ordinarily, I might have sat waiting, biting my nails, counting the hours, and working myself up into a lather. But not today—no, not today.

This time I would seize control before control had a chance to seize me. I would not wait until 1900 hours. Why should I? I was sick and tired of being a pawn.

Besides, there was a lot to be said for getting it over with. Since half of punishment is in the waiting, I could, simply by showing up early, reduce my sentence by half. I was not looking forward to confessing my sins to Father, but it had to be done, like it or not. Best get it over with.

I marched down the stairs, and if what was in my heart was not a species of happiness, it was not far off.

I tapped lightly on the door of Father's study. There was no answer.

I put my ear to the door panel, but the hollow roar of an

empty room told me that he was not inside. It was unlikely that he had gone upstairs; after all, hadn't Dogger just been talking to him?

A quick trip round the west wing showed that he was not in the drawing room, where Feely was at the piano, staring in silence at a piece of sheet music; nor was he in the library, where Daffy sat cross-legged on the floor leafing through a pulpit-sized Bible.

"Shut the door when you leave," she said without looking up.

I had just passed Father's study when I heard a sound that stopped me dead in my tracks.

It was a sound I had heard often enough on the weekly episodes of Philip Odell, the private detective on the wireless, and one that I recognized instantly: the sound of a revolver being cocked. It had come from the firearms museum.

My blood turned to ice.

Foolhardy as it may seem—I can hardly believe now that I did it—I threw open the door and stepped inside.

Father was standing in front of an open glass case, and in his hand lay as nasty-looking a weapon as you would ever care to see.

I had peeked at it often enough in its case to remember that the tag identified it as an 1898 Rast & Gasser service revolver, made in Vienna for the Austro-Hungarian Army. Although the thing held eight 8mm cartridges, you could easily tell by looking at it that one would be enough.

Malevolent is the word Daffy would have used to describe the gun.

My mind was seething. What could I possibly say?

"You wanted to see me?" I asked. It was the only thing I could think of.

Father looked up in surprise—almost guiltily, and yet, as if from a dream. "Oh, Flavia . . . yes . . . I . . . but not until later. Surely it can't be 1900 hours already?"

"No, sir," I said. "It isn't. But I thought I'd come early so as not to keep you waiting."

Father ignored my twisted logic. It clearly didn't make any sense, but Father didn't seem to notice. Slowly, as if it were made of cut glass, he returned the pistol to its case and ran an opened hand across his brow.

"Badgers," he said. "I was thinking of frightening off a few of the little blighters. They're making such a frightful shambles of the west lawn."

My heart broke a little for my father. Even *I* could have come up with a better excuse than that. Whatever was he thinking? What must be going through his mind?

"That's very thoughtful of you," he began, referring to the fact that I had come early, but before he could say another word, I broke in.

"I want to tell you how sorry I am about the will. I didn't mean any harm. I didn't intend to be disrespectful."

No need to tell him about my failed scheme for Harriet's resurrection. The less said about that, the better.

Yes, Father need never know.

"Sir Peregrine felt it his duty to inform me that your mother's coffin had been tampered with."

Blast the man! Had the Home Office no discretion? No heart?

"Yes, sir," I said, steeling myself.

I waited for the blow to fall. Whatever punishment Father had planned, this would clearly be the end of Flavia de Luce.

Here it comes, I thought: *They're going to either cast me into Wormwood Scrubs or throw me into the Isle of Dogs Home for Delinquent Girls*.

I watched as he raised a hand and pinched the bridge of his nose between a thumb and forefinger.

When his words came, they were words not of anger, but of infinite sadness.

"I am going to have to send you away," he said.

·THIRTY·

SEND ME AWAY? IT was unthinkable!

I can't even begin to describe what was ripping through my mind.

It was beyond shock.

I knew in that instant how a cow must feel when it steps into an abattoir and is poleaxed between the eyes by someone it thought was going to feed it.

Simply because I had tampered with my mother's coffin?

I stared at Father in disbelief. This couldn't possibly be happening. It was a dream—a nightmare.

"Mind you," he added, "I should have been greatly surprised if you hadn't."

Surprised if I hadn't?

What was the man saying?

What mad Alice in Wonderland world had I been plummeted into? Who was this stranger dressed in my father's clothing, and why was he talking such nonsense?

Had I died, perhaps, without realizing it, and been propelled into a Hell in which I was to be punished for evermore by this incomprehensible scarecrow who had taken on my Father's form?

Surprised if I hadn't?

"It was so very like you, Flavia. I must tell you I was expecting you to do something of the sort."

"Me, sir?" Eyes wide open—mouth hanging agape.

Father shook his head.

"I have told you several times how like your mother you are, and never more than now—at this very instant."

"I'm sorry," I said.

"Sorry? Whatever for?"

That old sadness came welling up, and my eyes were suddenly full of tears.

"I don't know."

"That's just it," Father said gently. "One often doesn't."

"No," I agreed.

As ludicrous as it sounds, Father and I had fallen into conversation. It was something I had experienced only a few times in my life, and it tended to leave me feeling as giddy as if I were walking a rope rigged between two trees in the orchard.

"I wanted to bring her back to life," I said. "I wanted to give her to you as a gift—so that you wouldn't be sad."

In spite of not wanting to, I had blurted it out.

Father removed his spectacles and cleaned them elaborately on his handkerchief.

"There is no need for that," he said at last, softly. "Your mother *has* been given back to me—in you."

Now the two of us were near to blubbering, restrained only by the slender thread of fact that we were both de Luces. I wanted to reach out and touch him, but I knew my place.

Love at Arm's Length: That should have been our family's motto, rather than the forced witticism of *Dare Lucem*.

"And now," Father was saying, "we must go on."

He spoke the words with such determination that they might have been coming from the mouth of Winston Churchill himself. I could imagine his bulldog voice issuing from the wireless speaker in the drawing room: "*We must go on*."

My brain supplied the sounds of cheering hordes in Trafalgar Square. I could almost see the flags waving.

"I have neglected your education," Father said. "You've dabbled in chemistry, of course, but chemistry is not enough."

Dabbled? Were my ears deceiving me?

Chemistry not enough? Chemistry was everything!

Energy! The universe. And me: Flavia Sabina de Luce.

Chemistry was the only thing with any real existence. Everything else was just bubbles on the broth.

Father had quenched our fledgling conversation with cold water before it ever had a chance to properly take fire.

Dabbled, indeed!

But he was not finished.

"Perhaps because they were older, your sisters have had an unfair advantage. The time has now come to set you straight."

Numbness was setting in. I could feel it in my face.

"I have discussed matters with your aunt Felicity and we are in complete agreement."

"Yes, sir?"

I was the prisoner at the bar, gripping the rail with white knuckles, waiting for the judge to drape his head with the black handkerchief and pronounce a sentence of death upon me.

"*And may God have mercy on your soul.*"

"Your mother's old school in Canada, Miss Bodycote's Female Academy, has agreed to enroll you in the autumn term."

There was a sickening silence, and then my stomach did what it does when the uniformed lift attendant in the Army and Navy Store gives you a furtive grin and shoves the lever full over to "Down."

"But Father—the expense!"

All right, I'll admit it: I was floundering—inventing excuses.

"Because your mother has left Buckshaw to you, I believe I am correct in saying that the expense should no longer be at issue. There will be many details to be sorted out, of course, but once put properly in order—"

What?

"Your aunt Felicity and I will, of course, act as trustees until such time as—"

I beg your pardon? Buckshaw mine? What kind of cruel joke is this?

I stuck my forefingers into my ears. I didn't want to hear it.

Father gently removed them and his hand was surprisingly warm. It was, I think, the first time he had ever voluntarily touched me, and I wanted to jam them back in so that he could pull them out again.

"Buckshaw?" I managed. "Mine? Do Feely and Daffy know?"

It was probably an uncharitable thought, but it was the first thing that came to mind and I had said it before I could stop myself.

"No," Father said. "And I suggest that you not tell them—at least for the time being."

"But why?"

In my heart of hearts, I was already swanking around my kingdom like Henry VIII.

"I banish thee, proud sister, and thee, oh bookish one,
To some far isle to rue e'ermore thy sauciness
T'ward sister piteous—"

Father's answer was a very long time in coming, as if his words needed to be fetched back, one by one, from the past.

"Let me put it to you this way," he said at last. "Why do you never add water to sulfuric acid?"

"Because of the exothermic reaction!" I cried. "The concentrated acid must always be added to the water, rather than the other way around. Otherwise it can play Old Hob with your surroundings!"

Just thinking about it made me boil over with excitement!

"Precisely," Father said.

Of course I saw instantly what he was driving at. O, how wise a man my father was!

But then, in a flash, the present intruded. The meaning of his words sank in.

I was to leave Buckshaw.

I wanted to fling myself down on the floor and kick and scream, but of course I couldn't.

It simply wasn't fair.

"I have done my best for you, Flavia," Father said. "In spite of the fierce opposition of others, I have tried so damnably hard to leave you alone, which seems to me the most precious gift one can bestow upon a child."

Realization came flooding in.

How clever I had always thought myself, and yet, without my suspecting it, Father had all along been my co-conspirator.

"We shall miss you, of course," he said, and then he had to stop, because by now, both of us were gulping like guppies.

Poor dear Father. And, come to think of it, poor dear Flavia.

How alike we were!

When you came right down to it.

It was the morning after the funeral, and Aunt Felicity and I were poling along in the sunshine on the ornamental lake in an ancient punt which Dogger had dug out and brought down from the attic of the coach house.

"Don't push too vigorously," Aunt Felicity cautioned, adjusting her ancient parasol. "Dogger warned me that it's only the paint that's holding this relic together."

I grinned. Even if we broke through the bottom of the

boat, we'd only find ourselves up to our knees in sun-warmed water.

"Life's like that, too," Aunt Felicity continued. "Too much push, and bang through the bottom one goes. Still, if one doesn't paddle, one doesn't get anywhere. Maddening, isn't it?"

I could hardly believe it: Here I was floating along on an eighteenth-century lake with the Gamekeeper herself, and yet to a spy lurking behind a ruined statue on the Visto, we would look to be no more than a pleasant painting by one of those French impressionists: Monet, perhaps, or Degas.

Light twinkled on the lake and under the hanging willows.

We were like an image on a ciné screen.

After breakfast, I had taken Aunt Felicity to my laboratory and shown her the film I had developed.

She had watched it in silence, and when the last frame had run through the projector, seized the spool of film and thrust it into her pocket.

"Pheasant sandwiches."

Her mouth formed the words, but not a sound came out.

"The phrase was chosen carefully for its combination of plosives and fricatives: consonants which could be formed in total silence. Innocuous to the casual observer, but a clear warning of danger to an initiate."

"But who was Harriet warning?"

"Me," Aunt Felicity said. "It was I who was shooting the film. I had a perfect view of your mother in the camera's viewfinder and recognized her warning instantly."

"Against who?" I was about to say, but caught myself just in time to correct it to "Against whom?"

"The late Lena," Aunt Felicity answered. "She had come down to Buckshaw unexpectedly, as she was wont to do, and had waded across to the Folly without our noticing, perhaps hoping to catch us off guard. Your mother—and it is to her eternal credit that she did so—had already begun, even then, to suspect Lena's leanings, if I may coin a rather tawdry phrase."

It took me a moment, but I nodded to show that I understood.

But why hadn't Harriet simply called out, "Hullo! Here's Lena!" or some such thing? Why had she chosen to mouth a coded warning to Aunt Felicity alone?

I recalled Lena's words: "We were quite chummy, your mother and I—at least when we ran into each other outside of a family setting."

Outside of a family setting, she had said. Perhaps *inside* of one they were at loggerheads. It was a situation I had no difficulty in understanding.

Families were deep waters indeed, and I still had much to learn about what luces lurked beneath the surface of my own.

Now, floating lazily on the lake with Aunt Felicity, surrounded by the reality, those black-and-white images from another time—filmed at this very location—seemed as distant as a half-forgotten dream.

"Who was the man in the window?" I asked.

It was one of the strands of the puzzle I had been unable to unwind to my satisfaction.

"Tristram Tallis," Aunt Felicity said.

"I thought as much. But why was he dressed in an American uniform?"

"A very perceptive observation," Aunt Felicity said, "since he was in view for mere fractions of a second."

"Well, actually it was Dogger who spotted that," I admitted.

"You showed Dogger the film?" She pounced upon my words like a leopard upon its prey.

"Yes," I admitted. "I didn't know it was important—I mean, I didn't know what it meant."

I still didn't, but I was hoping to find out.

"Was it wrong of me?"

Aunt Felicity did not answer my question. "It is essential," she said, "to know at all times who knows what. Keep Kipling in mind."

"Kipling was a goddamn Tory and a jingoist to boot," I said, hoping to seem wise beyond my years.

"Pfah!" Aunt Felicity said, surprising me by spitting over the side of the boat. "You picked up that nonsense from Lena, or at least from Undine."

I admitted I had.

"Kipling was no Tory, nor was he a jingoist. He was a spy in the service of Queen Victoria, and a damned good one at that. He as much as said so, but no one recognized it. They thought he was prattling on for children. Perfect camouflage that, you'll have to admit."

She sat up straight in the punt, and for a moment I had the uncanny feeling that I was in the presence of a queen.

She raised her voice an octave and in a royal accent began to recite:

"I keep six honest serving-men
They taught me all I knew;

Their names are What and Why and When
And How and Where and Who.

"As a member of the Nide, you will need to keep those words always in the forefront of your mind."

"Was Lena a member of the Nide?" I asked.

"Lena was the enemy!" Aunt Felicity hissed. "One of the dark de Luces. The Black Ones, we called them in my youth. We were told horror stories about them, and even made up a few of our own."

"She killed my mother, didn't she?"

It was the question whose answer I dreaded, but I needed to know.

"I have every reason to believe she did," Aunt Felicity said, "but we shall never be sure of it. When she died, the truth died with her. There was only one other person on that final trek in Tibet, and he unfortunately—"

"Terence Alfriston Tardiman, bachelor, of 3A Campden Gardens, Notting Hill Gate, London, W8, aged thirty-seven," I rattled off, my words tumbling over one another in the mad race to get out. "The man under the train!"

Aunt Felicity's eyes narrowed as if she were squinting at me through tobacco smoke, and I was reminded for an instant of Dr. Kissing.

"Sowerby has been indiscreet," she said. "I shall have to call him to account."

"Please don't be hard on Adam," I said. "He's more or less my partner—ever since that business with the Heart of Lucifer."

"I am aware of that," Aunt Felicity said, "but he must be

corrected notwithstanding. The Nide must not be jeopardized by loose lips. Lives may be lost—and one of them may be yours. Do you understand, Flavia?"

"Yes, Aunt Felicity. Adam had been following Tardiman for five days, and not for the first time, either."

I let my usual silence fall, hoping to open Aunt Felicity's floodgates, but it did not work. She was even foxier than I was.

"Was Tardiman one of the Nide?" I asked. "One of us?"

How proud I was to be able to say that!

"There are certain questions you must learn not to put to me," Aunt Felicity said. "Not, at least, so far as they concern the living."

"But Tardiman is dead," I protested.

"So he is," she said reflectively, and then after a time she added, "He may have been a double agent."

"He came to Bishop's Lacey to warn us of grave danger and that the Nide was under attack. Lena probably guessed that he would be here. She saw it as perhaps her last opportunity to silence him. Once he was dead, no one would know the truth about Harriet but Lena herself."

"Very likely," Aunt Felicity said.

"But why only now?" I asked. "Why did it take her ten years to find him?"

"Because he has been living all the while under an assumed name."

"Tardiman!" I said. "Tardiman was not his real name. Who was he, Aunt Felicity?"

"I have told you, Flavia, that there are certain questions you must not put to me insofar as they concern the living.

I must tell you also that certain questions must not be asked about the dead."

"I'm sorry," I said, realizing that I might never know the name of the man I had watched die under the train at Buckshaw Halt. Nor might I ever know why Tristram Tallis had stayed at Buckshaw in an American serviceman's uniform. Perhaps it had something to do with the Japanese naval codes and the fact that America had, at that time, not yet entered the War.

What had become of the traitor that Harriet had been sent to bring to justice? Had she found him before she was betrayed?

Had she perhaps killed him?

Had Harriet been an assassin?

My blood thrilled. These were deep waters indeed!

I made a mental note to pay a visit to the Bishop's Lacey Free Library at the earliest opportunity. The newspaper archives for 1939 might well be worth rooting through. I could always tell Miss Pickery, the librarian, that Daffy was encouraging me to take up knitting and had referred me to a photo of a not-too-difficult jumper that had appeared in one of the back issues, the name and date of which she had unfortunately forgotten.

In manufacturing a lie, it is important to get the amount of detail just so: Too much or too little is a dead giveaway.

Then, too, there was Mrs. Mullet. Hadn't she asked Tristram if she should now be addressing him as "Squadron Leader"? Did the U.S. Air Force have Squadron Leaders? I'd never heard one mentioned. Perhaps she had slipped up.

And then I had this thought: What if Mrs. Mullet was a member of the Nide!

Surely there was no one in the entire universe more privy to loose talk in a village so near to the military airfield at Leathcote.

I almost dropped the pole in my excitement.

Could Mrs. M be a spook? It would make perfect sense, wouldn't it?

And her husband, Alf, who was admittedly such a great authority on all things military.

It was, of course, one of those questions which Aunt Felicity had said must never be asked about the living, and perhaps not even about the dead.

Harriet, for instance.

There were so many things I would have to find out for myself.

"May I ask you one question?" I said to Aunt Felicity.

"You may," she said. "But you mustn't think I am obliged to answer."

"What about Father?"

"Well, what about him?"

"Is he a member of the Nide?"

Terence Tardiman had obviously thought he was, since it was Father he had told me to warn at the station—yet in the ciné film, Harriet had mouthed the words "pheasant sandwiches" to Aunt Felicity alone. But hadn't Father accompanied the others in their early-morning trip to consult with Dr. Kissing?

And Dr. Kissing himself—what role did he play in all this?

I think I realized then, simply by the look Aunt Felicity gave me, how deep these waters were: how deep, how murky, and how unfathomable. I'd simply have to learn to answer my own questions. That, perhaps, was the intended lesson.

"I believe we may be in for a rain shower," Aunt Felicity said, holding her hand out beyond the edge of her parasol.

Without my noticing, the sky had clouded over in the west.

"This school," I said. Surely I would be allowed to ask a question about myself! Father had already told me he'd discussed it with Aunt Felicity.

"Miss Bodycote's Female Academy."

"I should hate it. I'm not going."

"I wish you would reconsider," Aunt Felicity said. "For two reasons: the first being that you will change your mind when you have been there for a while, and the second being that you have no choice."

I stuck out my lower lip. I wasn't going to argue with the woman.

"One thing you don't know about your mother is this, Flavia. She, like you, protested being sent out to Canada. But, like you also, she had no choice. She always said later that it was the making of her."

"I don't care!"

All right, I'll admit it: "I don't care" is the last bit of baggage to be tossed overboard in a losing argument, but it was all I had left. Aunt Felicity would surely take pity on a poor girl who was hardly twelve.

"Don't be petulant," she said. "It is a tradition in the de

Luce family to hand down certain privileges—as well as obligations—to the youngest daughter, as was sometimes done in ancient Greece and Italy. Don't tell me you've never noticed how much your sisters resent you."

This was plain talk from a plain-talking old woman. Had she been aware of my torment all along?

"They know about the Nide?" I gasped.

"They don't know, but they have always suspected that in some *unknown* way, they are being excluded from some mystery which you are not—and believe me, they will feel so even more keenly when they hear that Buckshaw has been left to you as part of your inheritance."

"Has Father still not told them?" I asked. "I should have thought he—"

"They'll find it out soon enough when the solicitors read out your mother's will.

"You might not want to be around," she added, and I thought I spotted a twinkle in her eye.

Did she see that I was wavering? I shall never know. Aunt Felicity is *such* a deuced clever old trout.

"Besides," she said, "I am told that Miss Bodycote's Female Academy boasts a first-rate chemistry laboratory. Rumor has it that they are about to install an electron microscope. The Academy is exceptionally well endowed."

I could feel myself shifting, like a fish caught in the current.

"All the latest innovations," Aunt Felicity went on. "Spectrophotometers and so forth—"

Spectrophotometers! Ever since reading about the hydrogen spectrophotometer in *Chemical Abstracts & Trans-*

actions, I had been itching to get my hands on one of those beauties. Armed with the knowledge that each chemical has its own unique fingerprint, one was able to crack open the secrets of the universe, all the way from cyanide to the stars.

And although I was fighting to keep it down, the corner of my mouth was beginning to rise of its own accord.

"And the chemistry mistress," Aunt Felicity said, far too casually, "a certain Mrs. Bannerman, was acquitted several years ago of poisoning her wayward husband. Perhaps you've heard of her?"

Of course I'd heard of Mildred Bannerman. And who hadn't? Her trial had been covered in delicious detail by the *News of the World*. Mildred had done away with her husband by applying the poison to the blade of the knife he was using to carve the Christmas turkey. An old trick, to be sure: known to the ancient Persians but presumably not to a modern-day jury in Canada.

I could scarcely wait to meet her.

EPILOGUE

AND SO I AM to leave Buckshaw.

What a pity it is that Inspector Hewitt will no longer have me here to set him straight. I can only hope that Bishop's Lacey experiences no more murders, and that if it does, they are less baffling to him than those of the past year.

It is true, of course, that I was not entirely successful in identifying Lena de Luce as the killer of Terence Tardiman. But hadn't Inspector Hewitt, perhaps through sheer luck or trick of Fate, by his own methods, managed to run her down in the nick of time even without my assistance? It crossed my mind that I should send him a card of congratulations, until I thought better of it. He might take it as an insult.

Feely and Daffy will have no one to torture, although Feely will soon enough be gone, and Daffy left to subside into *Bleak House* forever and ever, amen, or at least until her reading is interrupted by the Apocalypse.

Today I made one final attempt to beg off being sent to Miss Bodycote for "finishing," as Father put it.

"But what about you?" I had pleaded. "You'll have only Daffy when Feely is gone."

"I shall have Daphne," he said. "And I shall also have Undine. I've already taken the necessary steps to have her stay with us at Buckshaw. After all, damn it, it's the only decent thing to do."

He was right, of course. And because Daffy would soon come to dote on the little girl—I was sure of it; they were birds of a feather—she would be coddled with books and buns. I could already imagine the pair of them hurling polysyllabic words at each other *ad nauseam*, or whatever that phrase is.

While I, as I have already remarked, am to be banished to the colonies.

My trunks are packed and Dogger is at the door.

But before I go, I must make note of the fact that all of this has been brought about by my aunt Felicity: the Gamekeeper.

She has already taught me this: Never underestimate either an old woman—or old blood.

ACKNOWLEDGMENTS

IT IS THE SECRET desire of every mystery novelist to be invited to speak at Oxford, the very cradle of the English golden-age detective novel, and I am no exception. Time spent among those dreaming spires in the pleasant company of such modern day practitioners as Simon Brett, Kate Charles, Ann Cleeves, Natasha Cooper, Ruth Dudley Edwards, Kate Ellis, Chris Ewan, Barry Forshaw, P. D. James, Gillian Linscott, Peter Lovesey, Val McDermid, Michelle Spring, Marcia Talley, Andrew Taylor, and L. C. Tyler is, in retrospect, like living a tale from the Arabian Nights.

To dine with idols is a privilege granted to few, and I thank them for their friendship.

Special gratitude is due to Eileen Roberts and the faculty and staff of St Hilda's College, Oxford, not just for making me feel at home, but for making me *be* at home.

David Appleton, of Appleton Studios, for his invaluable expert assistance in blazoning the de Luce coat of arms. The trails and footpaths of heraldry are littered with traps and pitfalls for the unwary, and it was comforting to have David along to illuminate so happily some of the darker corners.

Roger K. Bunting, Professor Emeritus, Inorganic Chemistry, Illinois State University. His book *The Chemistry of Photography*, which he so kindly put at my disposal, is what every good textbook should be: both fascinating and accessible.

Shelagh Rogers, of CBC Radio, whose words brought much-needed warmth to a bitterly cold winter's day, and Marc Tyley, of Manx Radio, who so kindly made it possible.

I am especially grateful to Fiona Clarke (www.bonezdesignz.com) for allowing us to use her gorgeous original font A Gothique Time to illustrate the Samson and Delilah panels of the stained-glass windows at St. Tancred's.

Shena Dyer, for planting the seed of a crucial idea over a lovely Manx dinner.

Chris Ewan (again) for his much-needed assistance. I would like to be in his debt, but he won't let me.

Robert Bruce Thompson, YouTube's *Home Scientist*, who has not only been a generous and helpful correspondent, but has done so much to encourage the development of home chemistry labs for teaching.

As always, to my patient editors on both sides of the Atlantic: Bill Massey, of Orion Books; Kate Miciak, of Delacorte Books; and Kristin Cochrane, of Doubleday

Canada; and to my agent, Denise Bukowski, of the Bukowski Agency, who has been with me every step of the way.

To Loren Noveck, senior production editor, and her terrific team at Random House in New York who go to such remarkable lengths to make it look easy. Any remaining egg on my face is strictly my own.

To John and Janet Harland, best of friends and co-conspirators.

And finally, my wife, Shirley, who, with love, has endured all things.

Alan Bradley

Isle of Man, Midsummer's Eve 2013

If you enjoyed

The **Dead** *in*
Their Vaulted Arches

read on for a special preview of
the next brilliant Flavia de Luce adventure

As **Chimney Sweepers**
Come *to* **Dust**

PROLOGUE

IF YOU'RE ANYTHING LIKE me, you adore rot. It is pleasant to reflect on the fact that decay and decomposition are what make the world go round.

For instance, when an ancient oak falls somewhere in the forest, it begins almost at once to be consumed by invisible predators. These highly specialized hordes of bacteria lay siege to their target as methodically as an army of barbarians attacking an enemy fortress. The mission of the first wave is to break down the protein forms of the stricken timber into ammonia, which can then be easily handled by the second team, which converts the smelly ammonia to nitrites. The third, and final, invaders, by oxidation, convert the nitrites into the nitrates that are required to fertilize the soil, and thus to grow new seedling oaks.

Through the miracle of chemistry, a colossus has been reduced to its essentials by microscopic life forms. Forests are born and die, come and go, like a spinning penny flipped into the air: heads . . . tails . . . life . . . death . . . life . . . death . . . and so on from Creation to the furthest ends of time.

It's bloody marvelous, if you ask me.

Left to the mercies of the soil, dead human bodies undergo the same basic 1—2—3 process: meat—ammonia—nitrates.

But when a charred corpse is swaddled tightly in a soiled flag, stuffed up a brick chimney, and left there for a donkey's age to mummify in the heat and the smoke—well, that's an entirely different story.

·ONE·

"Banished!" THE WILD WIND shrieked as it tore at my face.

"Banished!" the savage waves roared as they drenched me with freezing water.

"Banished!" they howled. *"Banished!"*

There is no sadder word in the English language. The very sound of it—like echoing iron gates crashing closed behind you, like steel bolts being shot shut—makes your hair stand on end, doesn't it?

"Banished!"

I shouted the word into the tearing wind and the wind spat it back into my face.

"Banished!"

I was standing at the heaving prow of the R.M.S. *Scythia*, my mouth wide open to the gale, hoping that the salt spray would wash the bad taste out of my mouth: the taste that was my life so far.

Somewhere, a thousand miles behind us over the eastern horizon, lay the village of Bishop's Lacey and Buckshaw, my former home, where my father, Colonel Haviland de Luce, and my sisters, Ophelia and Daphne, were most likely, at this very moment, getting on nicely with their lives as if I had never existed.

They had already forgotten me. I was sure of it. Only the faithful family retainers, Dogger and Mrs. Mullet, would have shed a furtive tear at my departure, but even so, they, too, in time, would have only foggy memories of Flavia.

Out here on the wild Atlantic, the *Scythia*'s bow was hauling itself up . . . and up . . . and up out of the sea, climbing sickeningly towards the sky, then crashing down with a horrendous hollow booming, throwing out great white wings of water to port and starboard. It was like riding bareback on an enormous steel angel doing the breaststroke.

Although we were still in early September, the sea was madness. We had encountered the remnants of a tropical hurricane, and for two days now had been tossed about like a cast-off cork.

Everyone except the captain and me—or so it seemed—had dragged themselves off to their bunks, so that the only sounds to be heard as one reeled along the pitching, rolling corridors to dinner were the groan of stressed steel and, on either side, the evacuation of many stomachs. With nearly 900 passengers on board, that was a sobering sound.

As for me, I seem to be blessed with a natural immunity to the tossing seas: the result, I supposed, of seafaring ancestors such as Thaddeus de Luce, who, although only a lad at the Battle of Trafalgar, was said to have brought lemonade to the dying Admiral Nelson, and to have held his cold and clammy hand.

Nelson's last words, actually, were not the widely reported "Kiss me, Hardy," addressed to Captain Thomas Hardy of the *Victory*, but rather, "Drink, drink . . . fan, fan . . . rub, rub," whispered feverishly to the wide-eyed young Thaddeus, who, although reduced to tears at the sight of his mortally wounded hero, was doing his best to keep the great man's circulation from crystallizing.

The wind ripped at my hair and tore at my thin autumn coat. I inhaled the salt air as deeply as I dared, the sea spray running in torrents down my face.

A hand seized my arm roughly.

"What the devil do you think you're doing?"

I spun round, startled, trying to wriggle free.

It was, of course, Ryerson Rainsmith.

"What the devil do you think you're doing?" he repeated. He was one of those people who thought that the secret of gaining the upper hand was to ask every question twice.

The best way of dealing with them is not to answer.

"I've been looking everywhere for you. Dorsey is *beside* herself with worry."

Does that mean there are now two of her to put up with? I wanted to ask, but I didn't.

With a name like Dorsey it was no wonder he called her "Dodo"—or at least he did whenever he thought they were alone.

"We were afraid you'd fallen overboard. Now come

below at once. Go to your cabin and put on some dry clothing. You look like a drowned rat."

That did it. It was the last straw.

Ryerson Rainsmith, I thought, *your days—your very hours—are numbered.*

I would go to the young and handsome ship's doctor, whom I had met at supper the night before last. On the pretext of an upset tummy, I would beg a bottle of sodium bicarbonate. A healthy dose of the stuff—I smiled at the word "healthy"—slipped into Rainsmith's invariable bottle of champagne would do the trick.

Taken on a full stomach—no worries about that where Ryerson Rainsmith was concerned!—sodium bicarbonate taken with effervescent alcohol could be deadly: first, the headache, which seemed to grow by the minute, followed by mental confusion and severe stomach pain; the muscle weakness, thin stools like coffee grounds, the tremors, the twitching: all the classic symptoms of alkalosis. I would insist on taking him out on deck for a healthy walk. Forcing him to hyperventilate in all this fresh, invigorating air would speed up the process—like sloshing petrol onto a fire.

If I could manage to raise the pH of his arterial blood to 7.65, he wouldn't stand the chance of a snowman in Hades. He would die in agony.

"I'm coming," I said sullenly, and followed him at the speed of a sleepy snail, aft across the rolling, pitching foredeck.

Hard to imagine, I thought, that I had actually been handed over to this rancid piece of humanity. Hard to forget, though, how it had come about.

* * *

It had all begun with that awful business about my mother, Harriet. After ten years of being missing in the mountains of Tibet, Harriet had returned to Buckshaw in circumstances so painful that my brain was still forbidding me to think about them for more than a couple of seconds at a time; any longer than that, and my internal censor snipped my thread of memory as easily as Atropos, that dreaded third sister of the Fates, is said to snip the thread of life with her scissors when our time has come to die.

The upshot of it all was that I was to be sent away to Miss Bodycote's Female Academy, Harriet's old school in Canada, where I was to be trained to assume some ancient and hereditary role of which I was still kept mostly in ignorance.

"You shall simply have to learn your way into it," Aunt Felicity had told me. "But in time you shall come to realize that Duty is the best and wisest of all teachers."

I wasn't quite sure what she meant by that, but since my aunt was rather high up in this mysterious whatever-it-was, she was not to be argued with.

"It's something like 'The Firm,' isn't it?" I asked. "The nickname that the Royal Family call themselves."

"Somewhat," Aunt Felicity, said, "but with this difference: royalty is permitted to abdicate. We are not."

It had been at Aunt Felicity's insistence that I was packed up like a bundle of old rags and put on a ship to Canada.

There had been protests, of course, at my going alone, notably from the vicar and his wife. There had been some talk, then, about having Feely and her fiancé, Dieter

Schrantz, accompany me on my trans-Atlantic journey, but that idea was scotched on the grounds not only that would it be improper, but also that Feely's position as organist at St. Tancred's was classified as an essential service.

At that point Cynthia Davidson, the vicar's wife, threw her own name into the hat. Although Cynthia and I had had our ups and downs, we had recently become great pals: an unexpected twist in my life I was still finding hard to believe. Away from her husband, Cynthia was brimming with fun: a girl again, in spite of herself. The vicar would have been horrified at the amount of tea the two of us sprayed out in hysterical laughter upon the floor of the vicarage kitchen.

But then, alas, Cynthia's name, too, was taken out of the running. Like Feely, she was too important to be released. Without her, there would be no church calendar, no church bulletins, no flowers for the altar, no home visits, no Girl Guides, no clean cassocks and surplices, no meals for the vicar . . . the list went on and on.

I knew that she was disappointed: she told me so.

"I should have liked to see Canada," she told me. "My father, as a young man, worked as a log driver—a river pig—on the Ottawa River. Instead of fairy tales at bedtime, he used to tell me horrific stories of the *loup garou*—the werewolf of the Canadian woods—and of how he once gave a good dunking to Big Jacques Laroque and Ole Bull in the log-rolling contest at the Rapides des Allumettes, both on the same morning.

"I had always hoped that I would one day be able to lace on a pair of spiked logger's boots and have a go at it myself," she added wistfully. "Now I suppose I shan't have a chance."

I could have wept at the sight of her sitting there at the vicarage kitchen table, her eyes looking damply into her past.

"The Altar Guild is likely just as dangerous," I said brightly, hoping to cheer her up, but I don't think she heard me.

That same afternoon, Aunt Felicity announced that the problem was solved: she had heard from Miss Bodycote's Female Academy that the chairman of the Academy's board of guardians, who had been summering in England, would be setting sail for home in mid-September.

He had been shooting for a few days with one of our neighbors, Lord Crowsborough, and it would be no trouble at all, he said, to drop by and pick me up—as if I were an empty milk bottle.

I shall never forget the day that he arrived at Buckshaw—an hour and a half late, I might add—in his borrowed Bentley. He had leapt from the car, dashed round to the offside to open the door for Dorsey, the queen of Sheba, who hauled herself out of the machine and stood blinking in the September sunshine like someone who had just been startled awake from a hypnotic trance. She was wrapped in a dress of turquoise silk, with a matching scarf on her head and far too much magenta lipstick on her mouth. Need I say more?

"Oh, Ryerson," she cooed, gazing at our ancestral home. "It's all so quaint—so tumble-de-dump. Just as you said it would be."

Ryerson Rainsmith, in a summer suit the color of cold coffee with curdled cream, stood looking round in a self-satisfied manner with his thumbs tucked into his yellow vest, drumming his fingers on his ample stomach. I was reminded of a partridge.

Father, who had gone to the front door to greet him, stepped out onto the gravel sweep and shook hands.

"Colonel de Luce, I presume," Rainsmith said, as if he had just solved some great mystery. "I'd like you to say hello to my wife, Dorsey. Come and shake hands with the squire, my dear. It's not every day you get such an opportunity.

"Ha ha ha," he added mirthlessly.

"And this must be little Flavia!"

On paper, the man was already dead.

"Mister Rainsmith," he said, shoving a damp hand into my face.

Dogger had once warned me to be wary of any man who introduced himself as "Mister." It was an honorific, he said, a mark of respect to be bestowed by others, but never, ever, under any circumstances upon oneself.

I ignored the extended hand.

"Howdy," I said.

Father stiffened. His eyes narrowed. I knew what was going on in his head.

Father was from an era when gentlemen were taught that politeness was everything: that the only sure way to lose out to the Philistines was to lose your temper and admit that they had wounded you. His years in a Japanese prisoner-of-war camp had perfected his ability to remain, in the face of insult, as silent as a stone.

"Please come in," he said, gesturing with his hand to the open door. I wanted to give him a swift kick in the trousers and at the same time I wanted to hug him. Pride in a parent often takes strange forms.

"What a quaint old hall!" Dorsey Rainsmith said. Her voice was as sharp as elderly cheese and her words echoed back unpleasantly from the dark paneling of the foyer. "We have the same trouble with cracking varnish in our *salon* back home in Toronto, don't we, Ryerson? Smithers, our handyman, says it's either from excessive heat or excessive cold."

"Or age," I suggested.

Father pierced me with a transparent look, but I knew what he meant.

In the drawing room, without being asked, the Rainsmiths subsided into the coziest chairs, while Father and I perched on the edge of the remaining seats.

After an interval timed to perfection, Dogger appeared and offered tea. I could see that the Rainsmiths were impressed.

"Thank you, Dogger," I said. "And please convey our thanks to Mrs. Mullet."

It was a game Dogger and I played: a game whose rules were so subtle that no one outside our immediate family could ever hope to grasp them.

"Not at all, Miss Flavia," Dogger said. "It is our very great pleasure to be of service."

"Yes, thank you, Dogger," Ryerson Rainsmith said, out of his depth but paddling madly to keep his head above water.

"And also your Mrs. Mullet," his wife added.

Dogger gave them a three-percent smile and vanished in the way he does.

After a while, Daffy and Feely came into the room, pretended to be bereft at the thought of losing me, chatted in a maddeningly polite fashion with the Rainsmiths, then drifted off to their respective books and looking glass.

But there's no sense in raking through the ashes of that dismal afternoon.

It was decreed that the Rainsmiths would be my chaperones on the voyage to Canada, where they would deliver me up safely to the doorstep of Miss Bodycote's Female Academy.

"Chaperones?" Daffy said when they were gone. "*Cicerones*, you mean. That's the proper word for it. Flavia on the Grand Tour—just think! I hope you appreciate it, you lucky chump. I'd give anything to be in your plimsolls."

I threw a handy tennis racket at her, but I missed.